Promised Valley Rebellion

RON FRITSCH

For Lee Ann, David, and my family

ISBN: 0615464513
ISBN-13: 978-0615464510

Front cover photograph © iStockphoto.com/Brett Charlton

Back cover photograph © John Moll

For information address:

Asymmetric Worlds
1657 West Winona Street
Chicago, IL 60640-2707

www.promisedvalley.com

Character List

A character list appears at the end of this novel, beginning on page 227.

Chapter 1

Soon after Blue Sky, his sister Rose Leaf, and the prince, Morning Sun, came of age, they incited their people to rise up against their king and the people he'd chosen to help him rule their kingdom. The three of them were as certain as the coming and going of the seasons that they had good cause to do what they did. Where it would take them, though, they couldn't foresee.

As for Blue Sky's part in it, he believed he was only doing what any person—having stumbled upon the truth of certain matters, as he had—would've done for his sister and the prince.

It was their rebellion before it was his. And he loved them both.

*****

When they were still children, Rose Leaf decided they should stage a play. They performed it during one of the king, queen, and prince's frequent visits with Rose Leaf and Blue Sky's family after the morning's full-moon ceremony in their people's town. The king and queen rode in the royal cart to what their people referred to as the "home village," which was where Rose Leaf and Blue Sky's family lived. Morning Sun always walked, leading the oxen.

The drama in the village orchard included a wedding in which Rose Leaf played the bride. She'd talked her and Blue Sky's best friend, the prince, into playing the groom.

Blue Sky couldn't help but notice the looks on the faces of all four of their parents when they realized where Rose Leaf's tale was taking them. It was easy to see they were far less amused than the neighbors in the audience. And the amount of wine and beer the villagers had consumed that day couldn't adequately account for the difference.

One of Blue Sky's roles was as the official who blessed Rose Leaf and Morning Sun's marital union. Their people called those officials "tellers" because they not only remembered and retold the stories handed down to them by their ancestors and the gods, they also told the people, often without being asked, what the gods wanted them to do to retain their benevolence—as well as the valley the gods had promised them they could keep during their good behavior.

The drama closed with Rose Leaf and the prince in one another's arms.

Blue Sky, in his role as the chorus, explained that they'd reached the end of their lives, after having spent so many happy years together and producing so many descendants that only the tellers with the best memories and mathematical skills could be certain of either number.

When the play was over and the neighbors, having laughed and wept, went home, the parents of the cast members were quick to praise Rose Leaf for her dramatic skill.

Tall Oak, the king, told them he was always glad to see the people entertained and their minds relieved, at least for a while, from having to dwell on more serious matters.

Then Blue Sky and Rose Leaf's father, who was known as Green Field, took Rose Leaf's hand and made a remark the likes of which none of the three children had heard before.

Green Field often frowned, as if he suffered some secret pain. He spoke deliberately, though, as older people who'd retained the respect of their neighbors did.

"I want you to always remember this," Green Field said to his daughter. "There's nothing wrong with your becoming the wife of the prince in your play. But you've also got to realize you can never actually marry the prince in this kingdom."

Rose Leaf and Blue Sky's mother, who was called Gentle Brook, and the queen, who was known as Rainbow Evening, nodded their heads in agreement.

They were first cousins who'd grown up, as first cousins usually did, in the same village. Neither having a sister near their age who'd survived her infancy, they'd become best friends.

Blue Sky was aware that many men found both of them as desirable as women coming of age who hadn't yet gone with a man and carried children in their bodies.

"And you," Tall Oak said, his hand on Morning Sun's shoulder. "You can never have Rose Leaf for your wife. I could never approve it."

Blue Sky, who was named after what his people took to be a heavenly sign that the gods were pleased with them, turned to the prince and laughed. "Well, of course, they'll never marry."

Morning Sun laughed, too. "Of course not," he agreed.

Rose Leaf laughed as well. "No," she said, looking Morning Sun up and down. "I'm certain my husband will be more pleasing to the eye than he'll ever be. I'd much rather have beautiful children than be married to a prince."

*****

Peaks rose on either side of the promised valley like jaws held open in death. A river wound back and forth down the middle of it like a spilled gut.

The flat land on either side of the river was fertile. The top layer of black soil went deep. Rains almost always came timely in the growing season. The "valley people," as they called themselves, found it impossible not to believe the gods favored them.

They grew wheat, barley, lentils, grapes, apples, and other crops on the valley floor. On the low mountain slopes where their ancestors had cut down the trees, they pastured their cattle, sheep, goats, and, for the few who had them, horses. From the forest on the higher slopes, they took wood for heating and cooking, as well as for building their clay-daubed houses, granaries, and barns.

The river left the valley through a narrow gorge at its southern end. Another upstream chasm actually divided the kingdom into two valleys. But because there was a passageway for people, livestock, and carts on one side of the river in the northern gorge, the two valleys together were taken to be the one the gods had promised them. The tellers, who kept track of such things, said the upper valley had about half as much land usable for fields and pastures as the lower.

A person could go out of or come into the kingdom only by riding a raft through the lower gorge or climbing over a mountain pass. Individuals foolish enough to leave the valley, though, gave up any claim to the protection of the kingdom—and sooner or later, they met their deaths at the hands of the people who lived in the hills beyond the mountains.

The "hill people," as they were known, would kill a valley person upon sight. The valley people learned that as children, as soon as they were capable of learning anything, even before they began working in the fields and caring for the livestock. If their people ever let down their guard, hill people would come into their valley and slaughter them all—old people, women, and children included. The tellers made certain every valley child understood that.

The hill people neither kept animals nor planted crops. They lived at the mercy of land untended and beasts untamed. When they spoke, the valley people couldn't understand what they said. Nor did they honor the valley people's gods. They instead worshiped strange, unreasoning deities—perhaps the hell gods themselves. The hill people's ceremonies supposedly made no sense, seeming more on the order of what children would think appropriate to do and say.

To keep the hill people out of the kingdom, the valley people maintained encampments and guard posts high in the mountains all around the valley. Their warriors, looking down on the other side like hawks in the sky, had one purpose: to kill any hill people who attempted to pass.

In the end-of-summer ceremony in their people's town, all the males in the kingdom who were coming of age presented themselves to the king. For the following year they'd be the guards, living in the encampments and protecting the kingdom from the hill people.

Even the prince had to do guard duty. It was how boys becoming men also became warriors. After the year of guard duty was over, the valley people's laws required every able-bodied man to continue practicing the arts of war with the other able-bodied men in his village. Green Field still practiced with his neighbors.

The village boys watched and attempted to do among themselves what the men were doing. During the year before their encampment, they practiced with the men as if they were already men, using spears, bows, arrows, and shields they'd either inherited from their fathers, uncles, and grandfathers or made themselves.

That was the valley people's army: all their able-bodied males of age, prepared to fight whenever war came again. And the gods in their stories, at least in the versions the tellers repeated, had left them with no reason to doubt it always would.

*****

Morning Sun and Blue Sky were still infants when the hill people, apparently believing they were numerous and skillful enough to drive the farmers out of their valley, started the last war. Rose Leaf came into Green Field and Gentle Brook's family during the fighting.

Tall Oak, then the eldest of three princes and heir to the kingship, and Green Field fought side by side. Their comrades said they both killed far more than their share of enemy warriors.

The hill people began their invasion at sunrise pass in the eastern mountains, as they invariably did in the tellers' stories. The pass was a three-day journey, most of it through mountainside forest, from the valley people's town, which was on a steep bluff above the river a short distance north of the lower gorge.

Green Field and Tall Oak were in the front rank of the warriors defending sunrise pass.

Although the army successfully held off the hill people in the first day of fighting, that evening, the king, Tall Oak's father, ordered his warriors to begin falling back to the town.

Tall Oak, Green Field, and a number of their comrades fighting in the foremost ranks begged the king to rescind his order. After he denied their plea and dismissed them, they went among the warriors, insisting they disobey the king and keep fighting at the pass.

They believed the hill people could be stopped in the mountains, there was no need to retreat, and the king, listening to cowardly advisors, had grievously erred in giving his order.

The army stayed put that night. The warriors spent their time, though, endlessly discussing what they should do, rather than starting their retreat or getting as much sleep as they could before the battle resumed.

When the fighting began again the following morning, the front ranks once more held their ground. The rear ranks, though, belatedly decided to obey the king and retreat, soon causing the middle ranks and even many of the warriors in the front ranks to change their minds as well.

Tall Oak and Green Field, both of whom later almost always refused to discuss the matter, soon found themselves cut off from their comrades and surrounded by enemy warriors.

Ordinarily, hill warriors immediately killed valley warriors in their grip. But that time, for some reason, they didn't kill their captives but took them prisoner.

When Green Field once chose to speak of the matter with Blue Sky, he speculated that the invaders must've realized they had the farmers' prince. He said some of his and Tall Oak's comrades who'd witnessed the capture began shouting, "They've got the prince! They've got the prince!" Green Field thought their extreme agitation must've tipped off the hill people to the truth.

Another time, though, he told Blue Sky it was possible the hill warriors somehow knew what the valley people's word "prince" meant. He'd heard them apparently saying it themselves.

The hill warriors took Tall Oak and Green Field to their main encampment on their side of the mountains just below sunrise pass. They presented their captives to their king.

Green Field further guessed that the king, not knowing which of the two captives was the valley people's prince and having no way to find out, decided to have them both killed the next day. The delay would give more of their people a chance to observe the once-in-a-lifetime event. Green Field and Tall Oak could see the crowd at the camp was steadily growing larger.

That evening, though, the hill people began imbibing the plentiful stores of the farmers' wine they'd happened upon at the pass. Unaccustomed to the charm of the beverage, they were soon quite drunk. Even the warriors guarding Tall Oak and Green Field nodded off, intoxicated.

In the stories the valley people told afterward, Green Field reached out with his foot, toward one warrior's spear. Using his toes, he painstakingly worked the weapon back to himself. Getting his hand on the spear, he cut the leather straps binding him and Tall Oak to a tree—and slit the throats of the three guards, who were waking and opening their mouths to scream for help.

The two captives fled, returning over the mountains to the valley as heroes.

On those rare occasions when Green Field spoke of his and Tall Oak's capture, he'd only say they undid their bindings, killed their guards, and escaped together.

They reached the town on the bluff just before the hill people's warriors surrounded it.

Older persons, women, and children among the valley people had to hide with the livestock in the forest, spending much of their time keeping wolves away from the calves, lambs, and kids.

The hill people's army laid siege to the town. Most mornings, they'd send warriors up the slopes, one day on one side and the next day on another. The problem for them was that every time they mounted an attack, they lost many more warriors than the valley people did.

In spite of the disparity of the losses, the hill warriors stubbornly fought on. Their siege, which began in the spring, lasted through the summer and late into the autumn. During that time they went from one end of the valley people's kingdom to the other, burning and destroying villages and crops and killing any valley people or livestock they came upon.

Although many of the farmers' warriors were killed or wounded, their army held off the hill people's army until the first blizzard of late autumn began. After that, it became apparent the hill people no longer had enough warriors to mount another attack.

With the old king dead and Tall Oak in charge, the valley people took the offensive, driving the hill warriors down the slopes of the bluff, chasing them through the forest to sunrise pass, and killing any of those who still had the strength and desire to fight.

Despite the valley people's devastating loss of warriors, noncombatants, livestock, and crops, they won the war decisively, forcing all the surviving hill warriors back over the mountains and into the hills beyond.

There, the valley people's tellers said, they and their people lived out their wretched lives in pathetic ignorance, hunting scarce wild beasts and whatever edible plants grew on the rocky terrain they roamed, never settling down, often starving, often dying young.

*****

At war's end, not only was the old king dead, but so were the old queen and their third and youngest son, the one who'd just come of age and the one the people might've loved the most. The old king and queen's only daughter who'd survived childhood had died before the war.

Tall Oak begged Green Field to help him rule the kingdom. Green Field was to be the king's chief warrior, which was the highest position in the kingdom other than the kingship itself.

The chief warrior commanded the army and enforced the king's orders. He also carried out punishments for those who broke the laws of the kingdom. In some cases, he might have to confiscate the wrongdoer's property. In others, he'd be required to cage, beat, whip, or execute the offender. In every case, he and his deputies would have to impose the punishment in full view of the people, for their instruction as well as their entertainment.

Green Field, having saved the life of the prince, now the king, was more than a hero. The people made it clear they wanted him to be their chief warrior as much as Tall Oak did.

Green Field's father, mother, and only sibling, a younger brother, were also killed in the war. Green Field therefore inherited his family's fields, pastures, livestock, house, granaries, and barns. He refused to accept Tall Oak's appointment to become chief warrior.

He also left the people, who could see what was coming, in voiceless shock.

Tall Oak decided instead—most reluctantly, many of the older people would say—to follow custom and appoint his surviving brother, Sturdy Limb, to be his chief warrior.

That didn't stop the king, though, every time a matter of any importance arose, from asking Green Field what he'd do if he were the king. Nor did it keep Green Field, as well as Gentle Brook and Rainbow Evening and later their three children, from giving him their opinions, even if at times they told the king something he didn't wish to hear.

*****

As children, Rose Leaf and Blue Sky would laugh whenever they went to their people's town for a change-of-season or full-moon ceremony and saw Morning Sun sitting high on the dais with the king and queen, dressed in the linen Rainbow Evening and the court people made him wear.

Most of the farmers refused to wear linen, considering it fit for affectation only. The court people and tellers, though, had no such concerns and wore it, especially at ceremonies, whenever it was warm enough to do so.

The prince would see Blue Sky and Rose Leaf in the crowd and begin laughing himself. One of his favorite responses was to close his eyes and squirm on his seat as if he were struggling not to break wind, even as his uncle Sturdy Limb announced Tall Oak's latest decrees.

A disapproving glance from Rainbow Evening would often bring Morning Sun's antics to an abrupt halt. But as much as Rose Leaf and Blue Sky liked and even admired the queen, it never stopped them from doing everything they could to get the prince started again.

"You have all the fun," Morning Sun would complain to them. "I'm the prince in this kingdom and have to do what I'm told to do. But you farmers do anything you please, and you get away with it."

Blue Sky and Rose Leaf were quite certain Morning Sun was wrong about that. They could get away with it not because they were the children of farmers but because the farmer who was their father had saved the life of Morning Sun's father, now the king, in the war.

If other children had tried to openly do in court what Blue Sky and Rose Leaf did, Sturdy Limb's people would've promptly removed them, and not without giving them a good cuffing on their way out—even as their parents, astonished and humiliated, watched. And as their siblings and cousins looked at one another and smirked, pleased with themselves for so skillfully concealing their own participation in the misbehavior.

But Green Field and Gentle Brook's two children didn't have to worry about their being removed or, heaven forbid, slapped by the chief warrior's men in front of their mother and father.

*****

Morning Sun did have good reason, though, to regret he'd been born the prince. For one thing, he was the only person in the kingdom who needed his parents' approval before the tellers would conduct a ceremony officially blessing his marital union.

Long ago, the tellers said, all parents arranged the marriages of their children. More recently, they still did so, but only in the sense that they were the people who usually asked the tellers to bless the unions their sons and daughters had chosen to enter into. Nobody in the kingdom could imagine the tellers refusing to conduct a wedding ceremony for two adults simply because their parents had objections to it, well-founded or not.

In fact, many of the people refused to believe the gods ever said parents had to choose mates for their children. The gods had ordered them to honor their fathers and mothers, but they'd also said people could never truly be happy living together if they didn't love one another.

Down to Tall Oak's father's time, though, the kings said the old law still applied to their children. He'd refused to let the tellers bless the union of his daughter, Tall Oak and Sturdy Limb's older sister, to a son of farmers who was quite pleasing to the eye but was widely rumored to have wanted the marriage only for the purpose of living at the court with people waiting upon him.

Shortly after the king's refusal, the body of Morning Sun's aunt was found floating in the river. The royal family insisted she must've accidentally fallen into the water. Everybody else believed she'd walked into it, drowning herself because she couldn't have the man she loved.

Strangely enough, the farmer never married anybody else. He was sometimes seen at his lover's grave, alone. He died fighting in the last war, but not without killing a great number of hill warriors. He threw himself at them, his comrades said, as if he didn't care if he got killed.

Most of the valley people's new men came back from guard duty alive. There were a few years within recent memory, though, when some of them hadn't.

Morning Sun and Blue Sky had long since decided, if they were to die doing guard duty, they wished to spend their last moments at the other's side. That way, they believed, they'd always be brave, do what needed to be done, and not disgrace their families. So they'd planned to do guard duty together, the two of them sharing an encampment hut.

But one day during their coming-of-age summer, Blue Sky had to tell Morning Sun they couldn't do it the way they'd assumed they would.

They'd spent parts of that full-moon afternoon with the younger men and older boys in the home village, performing the chores expected of males their age in the preparations for the feast.

Morning Sun, being the prince, could've opted out of the chores, but he never did, saying he was pleased he could do in a village what the court people wouldn't let him do in the town.

He and Blue Sky had spent the other parts of the afternoon in wrestling, spear-throwing, and running competitions with the other younger men and older boys, who considered it a great privilege to be working with and competing against the prince.

Blue Sky had made it known he didn't share their opinion on that subject.

Now he and the prince were by themselves, bathing in the village creek.

Rose Leaf had made several pointed remarks about the way they smelled.

The creek was pleasantly warm. It began as a brook high in the eastern mountains, joined others as it came down through the forest, made its way among the treeless slopes where livestock grazed in their pastures, and wound past the home village in the summer as lazily as a snake at dawn. It emptied into the river just before the larger stream flowed beneath the bluff where the valley people's ancestors had built their court and town.

Morning Sun was lying on his back near the water's edge, holding on to a low-hanging limb of the tree behind him, the water rippling over his naked body as if it were stone. Blue Sky was sitting on a submerged boulder next to him. The sun had deepened the umber hue of their bodies even as it had lightened their dark brown hair.

They were two of the tallest and strongest youths coming of age that summer, having gained their advantages, as the farmers' livestock did, from their ancestors.

The court people had made Morning Sun shave for that morning's ceremony. Shaving was something else the prince liked to complain about. It was another instance of the farmers having it so much better in their kingdom than he did.

All the men and older boys shaved their beards, but farmers and their sons, especially if they didn't go to the town very often, shaved as seldom as the people they lived with let them. But not the king, court people, and tellers—and certainly not the prince. He didn't dare appear in public with hair showing on his face.

The valley people learned as children that hill men, backward in every way they could imagine, kept—indeed, flaunted—their beards. This was additional proof they took their commands from the gods who lived in hell. When gods of that ilk appeared in the valley people's stories, they were often stroking their beards, proud of themselves for some evil they'd cleverly accomplished.

"Why do you complain?" Blue Sky asked. "You don't enjoy looking at that face of yours in your mirror?"

"No," Morning Sun replied, "I don't."

Blue Sky laughed. "If you were a handsome prince," he said, "you would."

The court people had another rule. They wouldn't let the hair of a male member of the royal family cover any part of his face, ears, or neck. The males among the court people and tellers scrupulously followed the rule themselves.

The males among the farmers, on the other hand, felt themselves free to cut their dark brown curls to whatever length and in whatever shape they pleased, as all the valley females did.

Some of the farmers, usually those most likely to neglect their chores and drink, fight, and fornicate to excess, seldom cut their hair, letting their curls bounce up and down on their shoulders and swing to and fro at the sides of their faces as if they were hill people.

Many valley people thought the rule for the royal family favored Morning Sun. Despite Rose Leaf's dire prediction to the contrary, he was ending childhood with the high forehead, wide-set eyes, prominent nose, full lips, and broad, chiseled jaw they favored in a man. His closely trimmed curls hid none of that.

"You don't think women find me desirable?" the prince asked his best friend.

"No," Blue Sky replied. "I don't."

They could've claimed a frightening thunderstorm was raging, and they still wouldn't have trifled with the truth more than they both already had—and the sky was cloudless all day that day.

*****

The farmers liked to tell a story concerning the time when Morning Sun began growing facial hair, and Rainbow Evening decided he needed to start shaving.

He surprised the court people by insisting he'd make his own razor. He wouldn't listen to their arguments that a prince had better things to do than grinding and polishing flint.

He hotly told them they wouldn't need to teach him how to do it either. His farmer friends would do that. Green Field and Blue Sky did, too.

Morning Sun followed up on that decision by grinding and polishing his own spearheads and arrow points, the smoothness and hardness of which impressed even the most accomplished stone craftsmen in the kingdom.

*****

"You're talking nonsense. We've got to do encampment together. You and me."

The sun was nearing the high ridge of the western mountains as late in the afternoon and as far to the north as it ever went, and Morning Sun was emphatically refusing to accept what Blue Sky had told him when they were bathing in the creek.

"I'm sorry," Blue Sky said. "Think about it some more. It'll be best for both of us."

If Blue Sky hadn't openly wondered if the court-people's hair rule wasn't as pointless as a hard rain in winter and let his own curls cover most of his forehead, ears, and neck, he might've passed for the prince's brother.

They were driving Blue Sky's family's livestock home from their pastures. Walking behind the animals was all they had to do. The kids, lambs, calves, and foals were still too young to attempt to wander away from their mothers. When they got older, a tap with a stick now and then would be needed to teach them to stay on the path and out of the fields.

The farmers who had pastureland constructed fences of fallen branches, small trees, and shrubs to keep their livestock in their pastures and their neighbors' livestock out. The fences couldn't, though, keep the animals on overgrazed plots from making every attempt to join neighboring herds and flocks in their more abundant pastures. Intrusions often led to accusations and harsh replies, sometimes to fighting among the men and boys, sometimes to the intervention of the tellers and the chief warrior's deputies, sometimes to visits to the town to argue the matter before the king.

In order to keep wild animals where they belonged, the valley people maintained a wall of boulders and stones separating the highest pastures from the forest. The wall, which extended all around the valley, was held in place by horizontal tree limbs tied with vine and sinew to upright tree trunks dragged down from the forest and buried in the ground as if they'd grown there.

Because the work required the efforts of many people working together at the same time, each village was responsible for the maintenance of a section of the wall. If a village failed to keep its section in good repair, the tellers and court people would arrive and take a portion of each family's grain to compensate whoever was willing to do their work for them.

Blue Sky and Morning Sun ran into a group of children coming in the other direction from a neighboring village, on their way to fetch their livestock from their pastures. When they saw who Blue Sky was with, they let their siblings and cousins know with a well-placed elbow or a whisper.

"The prince," Blue Sky, reading their lips, could tell they were saying.

The boys among them wore their hair the way Blue Sky had chosen to wear his.

Morning Sun didn't let his anger toward Blue Sky stop him from greeting each of the children by name, finding all sorts of reasons to flatter them, even telling them to be certain to cheer for their village's coming-of-age athletes in the summer games ahead.

"But what if they compete against you?" one of the older boys asked.

"You ought to be ashamed of yourself," Blue Sky interjected. "You'd actually consider cheering for a farmer against the prince?"

Morning Sun and the village children looked at one another and laughed. It wasn't the first time they'd gotten a taste of Blue Sky's sarcasm.

The children had something to tell their siblings, parents, grandparents, cousins, aunts, and uncles when they got home. They'd spoken with the prince, the same coming-of-age prince who'd sat on the dais with the king and queen during the ceremony that morning dressed in linen.

He'd joked and laughed with them and remembered their names—as he always did.

It sometimes saddened Blue Sky to know many of his people thought Morning Sun was somehow better than they were simply because he was the prince. On the other hand, Blue Sky couldn't see how the desire of a prince to be loved by his people and their willingness to give him what he wanted could harm the kingdom.

*****

The only people living outside the valley who were allowed to come into it were traders from a kingdom that lay to the south, where the river supposedly flowed into a body of water so vast no mere human could see land on the other side of it. Plying the stream on rafts pulled by oxen, the river people brought pottery, salt, linen, and other goods—like the polished stones the valley people used for mirrors—to the riverbank below the town to exchange for the farmers' surplus grain, lentils, wine, meat, hides, and cheese.

At some point in the past, the river people had insisted the valley people preserve meat with salt if they wished to get full value for it. Drying the meat wouldn't do. Eventually, the farmers used salt to preserve all their meat, unless it was winter and they could keep it frozen with ice. This state of affairs pleased the river people since the valley people could only get the salt from them.

On the other hand, the farmers wouldn't consider closing a deal until they found out what their cousins and neighbors were getting for the same things, and then they'd have the nerve to ask for even more. Although the river people invariably complained about the unfairness of the deals the farmers were forcing them into, it never stopped them from coming back. Only the last war could do that, and even then their return quickly followed the valley people's victory.

The river people always came in groups sufficiently large to keep at bay the hill people they encountered between their kingdom and the southern gorge entrance to the valley. But they seldom reported trouble. The hill people were apparently indifferent to their comings and goings.

The men and older boys among the river people chose for themselves whether to shave or let their beards grow. All those who came to the promised valley, though, were newly shaved. They didn't want their hosts—with their surplus stores of grain and other products of their fertile soil and hard work—mistaking them for hill people.

The valley people had a law prohibiting the river people from proceeding north of the town. Because of the law, it was difficult for the river people to deal directly with the farmers, including all the upper-valley farmers, who lived more than two days from the town.

Instead, the river people had to trade to the court people most of the goods destined for the upper valley and the northernmost part of the lower valley. The court people then transported the goods to the north using their own rafts and carts. As a result, the northern farmers had to put more into a deal than what the river people would've asked for, or the farmers living in villages closer to the town would've agreed to.

Many years previously, Gentle Brook and Green Field had taken the position that the old law made no sense and was unjust, and they often urged Tall Oak to change it.

As Rose Leaf, Morning Sun, and Blue Sky grew older and more clearly saw the disadvantage it imposed upon their friends living in the upper valley and farther north in the lower, they made their adamant opposition to it known.

In their private conversations with Tall Oak, he freely conceded the law was irrational, but he also insisted there was no way he could change it. He claimed that the court people with whom he, Rainbow Evening, and Morning Sun were required to reside would make life miserable for them. They might even connive with the river people and tellers, as they could, to cheat the king and army out of their tribute share.

And if that happened, Tall Oak insisted, the kingdom would fall.

But the farmers, wherever they lived in the valley, disagreed. Even the lower-valley farmers living near the town on the bluff, who were unaffected by the law, sympathized with the farmers the law hurt.

The prince was on their side, too.

Chapter 2

The prince and Early Harvest were at the starting line, chatting, stretching, keeping themselves limber for the race to come. Having no benefit of shade under the late-summer sun, they were already wiping sweat from their eyes.

At one point, grinning and making comments, they both turned and looked up at Rose Leaf.

Sitting next to his sister, Blue Sky could tell she was aware they were talking about her.

Early Harvest was the only new man that year taller than the prince and Blue Sky.

It was the afternoon of the second day of the last full-moon holiday of the summer. The race would be the final contest in the annual games for the boys becoming men.

The people had taken a special interest in the games that summer. For one thing, it was a year when a prince was a competitor, and the current prince had spent a great amount of time and effort training for the games. Sometimes it was with Blue Sky. Other times it was with his town companions, who were the sons of the court people.

As a result, Morning Sun had already won the wrestling and spear-throwing championships. Nobody had won all three competitions since Green Field did it in his and Tall Oak's coming-of-age summer.

Additionally, Early Harvest, who belonged to a large and prosperous family of farmers living in the upper valley, had been Morning Sun's opponent in both the wrestling and spear-throwing championship games. Nobody, not even a teller, had heard of a prior year in which the opponents in all three championship games were the same two individuals.

Under the circumstances, few people speculated on the outcome of the final contest in that summer's coming-of-age games without going on to say what a shame it was one of the contenders would have to lose.

*****

So it was no surprise that people from all over the valley filled the town that full-moon holiday.

A large number of Early Harvest's relatives, including his father, Full Harvest, had come down the river on rafts and stayed the previous two nights in the home village. The upper-valley guests would stay the third night as well, before they left for home in the morning. Whenever they came to the town for holidays, they slept in home-village houses and barns.

In the last war, some marauding hill warriors, having found Early Harvest's mother and two neighbor women hiding in an orchard, raped and killed them. While the hill warriors were so occupied, the children reluctantly but wisely ran off, taking the infant Early Harvest with them.

Full Harvest was so badly wounded in the battle on sunrise pass that nobody who saw him expected him to survive. He nevertheless healed quickly. Being a man of good sense, abundant strength, and unusual stamina, he subsequently acquired more fields and livestock than any valley person before him had done.

Like Green Field, he could persuade children to willingly do the work they needed to do if they were to eat well, dress and sleep warmly in the winter, and fully participate in holiday activities. He'd achieved that with his son, as well as his many nieces and nephews who'd lost their fathers in the war. He'd insisted his land, buildings, and livestock belonged to them all.

The previous evening in the home village saw the feasting, dancing, and drinking the occasion required. People from neighboring villages needed no invitation to take part. Youthful tellers arrived from the town with their instruments to provide the music the villagers' feet could resist no more than their wheat and barley could remain unbending in a summer breeze.

Toward the end of the festivities, Gentle Brook asked Blue Sky if he didn't agree Early Harvest would be the best possible man for Rose Leaf to spend her life with.

Their cups were down to their final sips of wine. Most of their guests were sleeping.

"What about Morning Sun?" Blue Sky, feeling the wine in his head, couldn't resist asking.

Gentle Brook and Blue Sky were watching Rose Leaf dance a last dance with Early Harvest, whose desire for his dancing partner—making its existence known "under the loincloth," as their people liked to say—was difficult not to notice.

Early Harvest and his male cousins still wore their hair almost as short as the prince did.

"I'm waiting for your reply," Blue Sky said to his mother. "You don't think Morning Sun wants Rose Leaf as much as Early Harvest does?"

Gentle Brook closed her eyes and shook her head.

Blue Sky had seen females his age staring at Morning Sun, and apparently not just because he was the prince. Blue Sky had seen the prince looking over his admirers, too.

Lately, Blue Sky had seen the prince looking at Rose Leaf in the same way, often as if she might be the one he wanted most of all.

Blue Sky couldn't blame Morning Sun and Early Harvest—and apparently every other male their age who wished to go with women— for looking at Rose Leaf the way they did. They could've imagined her eyes, as dark and yet hopeful as the night sky before dawn, inviting them; her lips, soft and full and responsive, letting them know they could have what they'd decided they had to have; her body, lithe and slender, moving with theirs as in a dance, promising them more.

They also liked to stare, Blue Sky couldn't help but notice, at her ample breasts, almost as if they had in mind the needs of their and her hungry children, who would suckle from them.

Blue Sky had chosen to let his hair grow as long as Rose Leaf wore hers. He hadn't imagined any other males would wish to do that, but the young men and boys living in the villages near the town quickly did so. Not a few of them liked to let Morning Sun know how sorry they were a prince couldn't let his hair grow to any length he might desire.

"Rose Leaf can't have Morning Sun," Gentle Brook said firmly. "And he can't have her. You've heard the king himself say that. More than once, you've heard him say that."

"I've heard him say that more than once. But I don't know why he says it. Do you?"

Gentle Brook, drinking the last of her wine, chose not to reply to her son's question.

Still as lissome as her daughter, Gentle Brook often danced with Full Harvest. During the interludes when the dancers were supposed to embrace one another as lovers would, most of the older people, even those who were mates, merely narrowed the gap between themselves and their partners. Full Harvest and Gentle Brook, though, held one another the way younger people did.

*****

The racetrack was in a sunken area on the west side of the bluff. When the snow melted in the spring and the river rose, the hollow became a large pond. Late in the summer, though, it was dry. Most of the spectators took up places on the grassy slopes surrounding the track. The tellers who weren't officiating occupied the grassy infield, as if that was their exclusive right.

The runners chose the spectators who got to view the race nearest the finish line. Early Harvest's cousins were on one side of the line. Morning Sun's town companions, including his three first cousins, Sturdy Limb's sons, were on the other. Green Field, Full Harvest, Gentle Brook, Rose Leaf, and Blue Sky were in the middle of those groups, with the best view of them all.

The people from town were wearing linen for the competition. The visitors from the upper valley were wearing shirts, blouses, loincloths, and skirts made of hides. The farmers who lived near the town were divided on the subject, as Blue Sky's own family was. Gentle Brook and Rose Leaf were wearing linen. Green Field and Blue Sky, though, had vowed they'd never wear it.

The tellers, both the youngest and the oldest among them, gathering on the other side of the track near the finish line were wearing linen. Blue Sky imagined it would always be a point of difference between him and them.

Morning Sun had decided to wear a leather loincloth since that was what Early Harvest would be wearing. He told the court people the lighter linen they wanted him to wear might give him an unfair advantage.

He'd made the same condescending remark before he'd raced Blue Sky—and won.

The younger town and upper-valley males on the sidelines were soon exchanging the usual village-versus-town insults, along with well-worded doubts as to whether the manhood of the more vocal individuals in the other group had been, or could ever possibly be, achieved.

Whenever one of them made an especially cutting remark, his friends would promptly and loudly repeat it, so that nobody would miss out on something so clever and rude.

None of their gibes, though, was directed at either of the competitors in that day's contest.

Blue Sky thought it possible that Morning Sun and Early Harvest, after their many victories that summer, had earned too much respect, even from their opponent's backers, to be the target of insults—and certainly not on the occasion of their final competition.

But Blue Sky also knew the upper-valley partisans would never wish to insult the prince, not even in jest. He took their side in their dispute with the court people regarding the river people.

It was equally true that Full Harvest had fought alongside Green Field and Tall Oak in the last war. He was present on sunrise pass, badly wounded, when Tall Oak and Green Field were captured. Unlike so many others, he hadn't retreated to the town.

And the valley people favored the children of heroes.

*****

Blue Sky had decided that for most of his childhood, he'd judged Morning Sun's town companions too harshly. Despite their parents' high positions in the kingdom, they'd had hard work to do. The younger town children fetched water from the wells at the base of the bluff, and firewood from the timberland that shared the bluff top with the town. The older children, under the direction of their mothers, prepared and served the meals for the entire court.

They were also Blue Sky's relatives. The family Green Field descended from had originally lived in the home village, but it split into two branches many years ago. One went to live in the town with a new king, an ancestor of Tall Oak and Morning Sun's. The other branch remained in what then became known as the "home village."

Green Field, though, was more closely related to the town branch than he was to his village neighbors. Green Field's father, who'd been born in the town, had gotten into an acrimonious quarrel with his nearest relatives. His youth made him do what he did, the valley people said later. In any event, the king, Tall Oak's grandfather, ordered him and his new wife to leave the town.

They began their life together with almost no possessions. They did have their youth, though, and a willingness to work hard. They settled in the home village, accumulating solely through their and their two sons' efforts the fields, pastures, buildings, crops, and livestock Green Field inherited after his parents and brother died in the last war with the hill people.

The king who'd ordered Green Field's father and mother to leave the town had meted out the same punishment to a brother of Green Field's father who'd made the mistake of siding with the chief offender. The brother, wishing to put as much distance between himself and the town as he reasonably could, moved to the upper valley and fathered numerous children who lived to become adults. He and his mate called one of their sons Full Harvest.

*****

The officiating tellers came by announcing the race, as if those present didn't already know what was going on. Their formality was often that tedious. Many spectators openly laughed.

When the tellers announced the names of the contestants, all the spectators, whether from the upper valley, lower valley, or town— as well as the river people present for the race—loudly cheered for them both.

As Tall Oak and Rainbow Evening rose from their bench at the top of the slope above the finish line, the people abruptly stopped talking and laughing and rose with them. It was improper to remain seated during a competition. People unable to stand sat in the front row.

Tall Oak gave Law Keeper the order to begin the race.

Law Keeper was the first teller. The valley people considered his position the third most important in the kingdom, behind only the king and the chief warrior.

As the first teller made his way down the slope to the finish line, his high tellers somewhat too forcefully and rudely pushed a number of spectators to open a path for him.

At one point, Law Keeper himself gave Autumn Wine's younger grandson a shove. Autumn Wine and her two grandsons were Green Field and Gentle Brook's neighbors.

It was easy to see the boy was deliberately moving much more slowly than he could've.

His grandmother, who wasn't one to shrink from amazing a crowd, saw fit to reward the first teller with a retaliatory slap across his face. Even more surprisingly, the blow caused the man—no longer young, but still much younger than his assailant—to fall to the ground.

As the high tellers hurried back up the slope, stumbling, to restore their leader to his feet, the farmers, as well as the younger court people and tellers, laughed without restraint at the first-teller's strange comeuppance.

The older court people and tellers, though, stood expressionless. In the kingdom of their imagination, no farmer had cause to strike a high official—or escaped punishment for doing so.

The king and queen looked at one another and shook their heads.

Law Keeper hadn't needed to insist upon remaining in his seat next to the king and queen until it came time for him to start the race. He'd admitted, Rainbow Evening once told Blue Sky and Rose Leaf's family, he did that sort of thing solely to remind the people how important he was.

As justified as Autumn Wine might've been to strike her blow, and as much as the first teller's behavior might've deserved the crowd's laughter, Blue Sky couldn't help but pity the man. He was clearly failing to get what he wanted most: the high regard of the people.

*****

As Law Keeper, on his feet again, approached the part of the crowd near the finish line, the prince's companions from the town and the cousins from the upper valley, so recently trading invective but now working together, were clearing a broad way for him and his attendant high tellers to pass through, without any further need for an angry physical confrontation.

Solemn Promise, one of the sons of the family considered the wealthiest in the town and kingdom, and Good Harvest, Early Harvest's younger cousin and best friend, were in charge.

The companions and cousins were doing what they did ostentatiously, to be sure, but also gently, courteously, and effectively. They got what they wanted: the cheers of the crowd.

The first teller and his party, though, got from the crowd what they didn't want: loud recitations of the remarks of the gods on the folly and self-defeat of rudeness in high places.

*****

When Law Keeper reached the starting line, he greeted the amused contestants and loudly wished them both good fortune in the race to come.

A number of people had reported hearing the first teller say he was certain Morning Sun would win all three of his championship contests with Early Harvest.

If Law Keeper made his remarks thinking he could ingratiate himself with the king and the queen, as most people assumed he did, he'd seriously blundered.

Tall Oak and Rainbow Evening had referred to the matter in open court, making no effort to conceal their irritation.

The king sternly reminded the tellers, with Law Keeper present, that whenever they officiated at an athletic contest—and only the first teller could be the ultimate judge at a final coming-of-age contest—they weren't to have favorites. Under no circumstances, Tall Oak insisted, should they express a wish, or even a prediction, as to who might win.

Law Keeper thereupon effusively promised the king and queen, no matter what he might've been heard to say, his impartiality in the games between the prince and Early Harvest would be well beyond question.

*****

Morning Sun and Early Harvest crouched in starting position.

"Proceed to the starting line!" Law Keeper sonorously intoned.

The runners were already there.

"Position yourselves properly!" the first teller ordered.

Neither runner saw any need to make the slightest adjustment in his position.

Craning his neck, Law Keeper peered at the runners from every possible angle to make certain neither had any part of his body, not even his nose, over the starting line.

Apparently satisfied they were properly positioned, after what must've been an agonizing pause for the competitors, the first teller straightened himself up again.

"Prepare to run," he continued, squeezing every last drop out of his part in the festivities, "on my next order!"

The runners were at the starting line, properly positioned, and long-since prepared to run.

Finally, the first teller gave the only order he'd needed to give: "Go!"

Morning Sun and Early Harvest ran down the track, their sinewy, sweat-soaked legs thrusting them forward.

Rose Leaf, her arm around her brother's waist, audibly sighed.

When the runners reached the first bend in the oval track, they were neck and neck.

The spectators lustily cheered, but without making it apparent which runner they were cheering for. It was as if they were cheering for the sake of cheering itself.

Rounding the right end of the oval, neither Morning Sun nor Early Harvest appeared able to gain even a fraction of a step on the other.

The cheering of the spectators grew louder.

Morning Sun and Early Harvest ran on, across the backstretch from the spectators' right to their left, neither runner giving his rival the slightest advantage.

Like the thunder of an approaching storm on a sultry summer day, the clamor of the crowd increased.

The prince and his tall opponent were forcing each other to run as fast as they ever had.

Going into the turn at the left end of the oval, their hard upper legs reminded Blue Sky of his family's horses running in their pasture, their hoof beats scaring the lambs and kids.

The runners were still dead even.

Which is what the crowd belatedly realized it had come to see. Nobody, not even a cousin or companion, was calling out the name of either competitor.

The thunder of approval was now for the fitting closeness of the race.

Morning Sun and Early Harvest stayed together, stride for stride, into the final turn.

The people roared.

The runners charged down the homestretch toward the finish line, their fear of defeat and their lust for victory, as their families and friends watched, distorting their faces.

The full fury of the storm had come.

The rivals crossed the finish line.

And the excitement of the crowd immediately gave way to consternation.

"Who won?" the people not close to the finish line began yelling. "Who won?"

Those nearest the finish line couldn't say.

Even the companions and cousins shrugged their shoulders.

As the two high tellers on either side of the finish line looked at one another, somebody in the crowd yelled what many of the spectators quickly decided they wanted to hear: "Tie!"

"Tie!" the crowd yelled its agreement. "Tie!"

And as Law Keeper conferred with the finish-line officials, the people, momentarily laughing at their audacity, caught their breath and began shouting again.

"Another race!" they insisted. "Another race!"

If the tellers were to decide the race had ended in a tie, the rules required that it be run again, after the runners had a chance to quench their thirst and rest.

The crowd's demands for a tie decision and another race grew louder and louder.

Without a cloud in the summer sky, the storm had resumed.

A farmer who was called East Land, his wife, his two sons, the wives of his sons, and his grandchildren were standing not far from the finish line.

East Land had fought in the last war alongside Green Field, Tall Oak, and Full Harvest. He was also gravely wounded on sunrise pass and present when the hill warriors captured Green Field and Tall Oak.

"Green Field," he suddenly and loudly shouted, "wouldn't it be a shame if the tellers decided who the winner of that race was? Such a fine race! The tellers didn't run it! Why should they say who won it?"

The people, laughing, repeated his last two rhyming remarks.

Law Keeper and the finish-line tellers glanced sideways at the vociferous farmer.

"I certainly wouldn't want to be the one," East Land continued, as loudly as before, "to tell either of those young men he lost that race!"

The spectators roared their approval. The lovely summer storm raged on.

"Tie! Another race!" the crowd insisted, chanting. "Tie! Another race! Tie! Another race!"

Morning Sun and Early Harvest, having run a distance down the racetrack beyond the finish line as they'd slowed before coming to a halt, stood apart from the crowd, speaking quietly together as if the tumult had nothing to do with them, as if what Law Keeper and the high tellers were deciding was no concern of theirs.

The two of them could just as well have been off by themselves in a clearing hidden deep in the forest, on a raft floating slowly down the river, or atop a high mountain commanding a view of the valley.

Rose Leaf and Blue Sky were staring at the runners, and, like them, paying little attention to the crowd and the officiating tellers.

Law Keeper and his attendants began climbing back up the slope.

The crowd, giving them all the room they needed to pass by, fell silent.

When Law Keeper reached the summit, Tall Oak, Rainbow Evening, and Sturdy Limb rose from their benches.

"The high tellers and I," Law Keeper said, speaking as loudly as the outspoken East Land had, "have unanimously reached a decision."

He paused—doing so, no doubt, to let it sink in that the decision wasn't his alone.

Rainbow Evening glowered at the first teller.

She was as fond of Early Harvest as Gentle Brook was. She hoped, almost as much as her cousin did, Rose Leaf would choose him for her husband.

"What's your unanimous decision?" Tall Oak asked, his impatience showing.

"We've decided," Law Keeper replied, "neither runner was ahead at the finish line."

As was the custom, voices in the crowd repeated that news to the spectators farther away.

"Not even by a grown-man's nipple!" the irrepressible East Land shouted.

Voices repeated that remark as well.

"Therefore," Law Keeper shouted, attempting to raise his voice above the laughter of the crowd, "therefore, the runners must run the race again!"

Although the first teller made it sound as if the contestants had to be punished for not winning or losing the first race, the people, greatly pleased, bellowed their approval. They'd come expecting to witness one remarkable race, and now, having seen it, they'd get to see another.

Two young men had brought them a gift as unexpected as love itself. The people would talk about that day for a long time to come, and all those present knew it.

*****

The people began appeasing their thirst, too, but not, as the runners were doing, with water. When a number of the tellers inside

31

the racetrack oval started playing their instruments, many of the spectators on the other side of the track broke into song and dance.

The cousins and companions pressed around their heroes, showering praise upon them as if they were two gods who'd openly come to the human world as they used to do, for no better reason in this case perhaps than to amaze the valley people with their athletic prowess.

One might've expected the enthusiasm of their supporters would physically separate the contestants. But that day, Morning Sun and Early Harvest were bound together in their adventure as tightly as the valley and its protecting, imprisoning mountains were in theirs.

Blue Sky told Rose Leaf he had to go down to the track.

He was certain Morning Sun and Early Harvest would appreciate his quiet, understated praise more than the loud effusions the companions and cousins were subjecting them to.

Rose Leaf turned to her brother, laughing. "I'll have to go with you," she said.

She knew that would get the attention of the crowd. People who suspected—or hoped—an athlete might be in love with them weren't supposed to go near him immediately before or during a competition. The god or goddess to whom an athlete had dedicated his efforts, as he was required to do, would be greatly displeased if his lust for another human so distracted him that it made him lose.

Every other young, unmarried woman in the kingdom who wished to go with men was accordingly keeping her distance from the competitors that day. No such woman would want either of those two people to think she had no interest in him. Since Rose Leaf could only have one of them, the other women could keep their hopes alive for the one she didn't choose—and for both of them if, thank heaven, she chose somebody else.

So it was no surprise, as Rose Leaf and Blue Sky made their way down the slope to the track, the people paused in their dancing, singing, music-making, wine-drinking, and pontificating to turn and look. Was it possible Rose Leaf wanted neither Morning Sun nor Early Harvest for her mate and the father of her children?

Or had she simply listened too long to her brother? He'd openly told people he hoped the gods had far more important things to concern themselves with than a footrace, wrestling match, or spear-throwing competition. And despite the protests of the high tellers, he'd gotten away with it. Being Green Field and Gentle Brook's son, he could apparently say whatever he pleased.

Morning Sun and Early Harvest, seeing Rose Leaf and Blue Sky coming through the crowd toward them, excused themselves from their other admirers and took turns embracing the newcomers, blessing them with the smell and feel of hard-earned sweat.

Early Harvest didn't dare linger long with Rose Leaf. Not with so many tellers nearby stealing glances at his loincloth.

He instead commenced a conversation with Blue Sky.

As did Rose Leaf with Valley Defender, Sturdy Limb's eldest son, who was third in the line of successors to the king, behind only his first cousin and father. He was a year older than Morning Sun, Early Harvest, and Blue Sky. His encampment comrades and father had given him leave from guard duty to attend his cousin's final games. And to see Rose Leaf, Blue Sky gathered.

Was Valley Defender, the people had to wonder, the man Rose Leaf had chosen for her husband? Sturdy Limb's son and Green Field's daughter? Was that possible?

"So," Early Harvest began, "who are you and your sister cheering for today? Your upper-valley cousin or your prince?"

"We're cheering for you both," Blue Sky replied.

Early Harvest tried not to glance at Rose Leaf, but frequently did so anyway.

"She's become such a beautiful woman," he found himself saying to her brother.

"I'll let her know you think so," Blue Sky said, as if it were possible she didn't already.

Early Harvest looked at her again and smiled.

"Let her know something else," he said. "Let her know I'll win this next race for her."

With that, Morning Sun turned on his heel and faced them.

He'd obviously been paying more attention to what Early Harvest was saying than to the hyperventilations of his court companions.

"Farmer boy," he said, grabbing the front of Blue Sky's shirt, "you'll tell your sister I'll be the one who wins this next race for her."

Blue Sky smirked. "Maybe," he said, "I should inform Rose Leaf, no matter who wins the race, it'll all be for her. Little do the people know. They think it's for them."

Morning Sun and Early Harvest glanced around at the crowd and laughed.

"This farmer boy likes to remind people of their duties," Morning Sun said to Early Harvest, giving Blue Sky a bit of a shaking as he did so. "He'll make a good teller, won't he?"

*****

When Morning Sun and Early Harvest were rested and ready to run again, the officiating tellers struggled in vain to clear the track of the prematurely celebrating spectators.

Sturdy Limb himself rose from his seat on the bench next to the king and shouted at the people to get off the racecourse immediately.

Anybody who didn't, he promised, would be caged. And he'd make no exception for children or old people.

Rainbow Evening quietly shook her head and looked down at Gentle Brook and Green Field, as if for help.

It wasn't the first time the court people and tellers, nudging one another and whispering, had seen her do that.

The crowd on and near the track, though, having helped themselves to as much as they pleased of the king and queen's wine and beer during the rest period for the runners, paid the chief warrior no attention whatsoever. They'd just witnessed Green Field and Gentle Brook's daughter thumb her nose at authority. So why shouldn't they?

The chief warrior's deputies near the racetrack shouted at the revelers, repeating their commander's threats. But they wisely made no attempt to actually carry them out.

Eventually, though, the companions and cousins nearest the competitors, having embraced both contestants one last time, as Rose Leaf and Blue Sky had, stepped back from the course, inducing the spectators nearest them to do likewise.

Within moments, the crowd, taking the hint, parted, clearing the circuit all the way around.

The teller musicians laid down their instruments. The dancers stopped dancing.

Tall Oak rose. After thanking the people for their "kind, thoughtful, and prompt cooperation," and receiving in return their loud wishes for his life to be a long one, he gave the first teller the order to start the race.

*****

Law Keeper made his way down to the starting line unobstructed this time and yelled his instructions as dramatically as before, finally calling out his inimitable "Go!"

As they'd done in the first race, the runners took off stride for stride.

And the crowd roared.

Rose Leaf tightened her arm around her brother's waist.

As the runners rounded the bend at the right end of the track, Morning Sun took a slight but discernible lead.

Many of the intoxicated spectators reverted to their usual habit of cheering whichever competitor was winning, yelling "Morning Sun! Morning Sun!"

The previous evening, Early Harvest had spoken with Rose Leaf of the possibility of their marriage after his encampment year.

Now, heading into the backstretch with the prince, he was closing the gap between them.

Not surprisingly, some in the crowd began yelling, "Early Harvest! Early Harvest!"

Blue Sky had told Rose Leaf he was certain the prince would approve of her accepting Early Harvest's proposal.

As the runners neared the end of the backstretch, Morning Sun regained the lead.

And the crowd was once again yelling, "Morning Sun! Morning Sun!"

Of all the men in the kingdom, Blue Sky had assured Rose Leaf, Early Harvest was the one the prince would most want her to spend her life with.

That upper-valley champion, rounding the left end of the track, was closing the gap between himself and the prince once more.

Many in the crowd shamelessly switched their allegiance without pausing to take a breath. "Morning Sun!" they'd yell. "Early Harvest!"

As the runners came down the homestretch, Early Harvest took a lead of his own.

And the crowd rhythmically called out his name: "Early Harvest! Early Harvest!"

With the runners approaching the finish line, the deep-throated rumbling of the crowd became as godlike as thunder in a storm.

Morning Sun was unquestionably giving it his all, but Early Harvest was keeping his lead.

And the crowd couldn't yell the leader's name enough.

Early Harvest crossed the finish line a quarter of a stride, at most, ahead of Morning Sun.

And the crowd roared.

The runners, looking at one another and laughing at what they'd done, came to a halt well beyond the finish line. Their games together over at last, they embraced.

And the people—prepared to drink, sing, and dance again—loudly shouted their approval.

All except Rose Leaf, who was in tears.

*****

Four people knew what, in fact, had happened that day.

Blue Sky was one of them. For as long as he could remember, people had remarked on his exceptional eyesight. They told him he could see things they couldn't see. His arrows rarely missed their targets, even at great distances.

That afternoon he could see the prince had won the first race. Morning Sun's chest, which was what counted, was ahead of Early Harvest's by about the length of a grown man's hand, measuring from the bottom of the palm to the tip of the middle finger.

It wasn't much, to be sure, but it was still, contrary to East Land's claim, considerably more than the length of a grown man's nipple.

Blue Sky could also see that Morning Sun, his head slightly turned toward his opponent at the right moment, saw what Blue Sky had seen: he'd won the race.

The two high tellers on either side of the finish line also saw what Blue Sky had seen.

Blue Sky watched them look at one another and open their mouths as if they were about to yell "Morning Sun" together, as they were supposed to do. But they never got the words out.

The crowd was already making known its wish for a tie, another race, a more deeply felt inebriation—and the dancing, lewd remarks, obscene invitations, and license that would come with it.

After that, none of the four people who knew the truth chose, for whatever individual reasons they might've had, to argue with the crowd.

Chapter 3

There were two guard encampments at sunrise pass. At one, the new men among the court people's sons did their guard duty. That was where the prince would do his.

Blue Sky had decided to do his guard duty at the other sunrise pass encampment, the one for the new men who'd chosen to become tellers.

Men who wished to go with other men almost always became tellers.

Women who wished to go with other women could also choose to be tellers. But most of them declined to do so, remaining near their families but in houses of their own with a like-minded friend. A minority, usually those who preferred living in the town, became tellers.

Many families, particularly those with several children, were pleased if one or more of them wished not to go with an individual of the opposite gender and have offspring of their own to provide for. The children favored included those who wished to live as people of the gender they wouldn't physically appear to be with their clothes removed. Their families and villages readily treated them as they asked to be treated.

Childless women, including childless men living as women, were considered gifts from the gods. They often became mothers to children whose own mothers had abandoned them or died.

The men and women who became tellers helped grow crops on the lands set aside for the tellerhood. But they often went home and helped their families, too, especially during the times for planting and harvesting. Their shares from the harvest on the tellerhood lands ordinarily exceeded their own needs by a large margin. Most of them used at least part of the excess to keep alive the people in their families and birth villages who couldn't do it on their own.

It was also true that some of the warriors who fell on both sides in the last and previous wars with the hill people were, those who saw their unclothed bodies confirmed, women who'd been living as if they were men.

*****

Morning Sun knew the tellers well.

"Their damned lessons," he'd grumble. "Day after day, they come to the court with their lessons. The prince in this kingdom has to sit there and listen to them drone on and on. Nobody else does. Is that fair?"

The tellers and court people would say it might not seem fair to the prince, but it was necessary. The tellers gave lessons to all the children. But they had good reason to spend far more time instructing the prince and, to a lesser extent, his closest cousins, Sturdy Limb's three sons. It was to prepare for the day the prince would become the king. To rule wisely, the gods had said, a prince needed to know everything he could possibly know before that day arrived.

Rainbow Evening chose the teller who was responsible for the education of the prince and his cousins. She was a woman teller many of the people had insisted upon calling Fair Judge.

She'd assured Rainbow Evening that the prince was an attentive student. He was always asking questions, most of them pertinent. He seemed to enjoy arguing with the tellers and forcing them to justify what they told him. He also liked to let them know whenever he took up one of their questionable assertions with his farmer friends, to see what they might have to say about it.

Under the circumstances, his instructors didn't consider it a chore giving him lessons. They looked forward to their days with him. It almost always amused them to hear what the farmer friends, especially the hero Green Field's bizarrely outspoken son, had to say.

When Rainbow Evening repeated that news to Blue Sky's family, Morning Sun wrinkled his nose as if he'd smelled something rotten.

"It's the only way to keep it interesting," he said. "What am I supposed to do? Just listen to all that stuff and nod my head? That's what my cousins do—when they're not falling asleep."

Although the farmers enjoyed mocking the tellers, as they did the court people, they knew the tellers—like the town, the court, the court people, the royal family, and the king himself—were indispensable.

The tellers not only memorized and told the people their common stories. They listened to the people's individual stories as well, along with their complaints against their neighbors and other family members. They did so in place of the king.

Disputants could appeal the decisions of the tellers if they wished, for whatever good it would do them. They'd have to go to the town and see the first teller or a high teller in private or the king in open court. Then they'd have to hope whoever heard them gave them enough time to reveal everything needing to be known, especially when they were responding to an adversary's most outrageous lies.

The tellers traveled throughout the kingdom, going from village to village. They often stayed for a night or two, endlessly asking questions of everybody they met, even the children. Some of the tellers, especially those who frequently traveled in the upper valley, spent most of their time away from the town. They usually showed up in a village alone or in pairs. Occasionally, they were in larger groups. For the children, those visits were the most fun of all.

No matter who the children were, the tellers who regularly came to their village knew their names and ages. They also knew the names and ages of their parents, siblings, and other relatives. They knew if children were reaching adulthood, reminded them how soon it would happen, and insisted upon finding out what they were doing to prepare for it.

The tellers kept track of the seasons as well. They knew when it was safe to plant in the spring, and when it was best to harvest in the summer and autumn. They knew when it was time to turn the bulls loose with the cows, the rams with the ewes, and the billies with the nannies.

They also kept track of the breeding of the crops and livestock. They remembered how the farmers and their neighbors had mixed their seeds in the current and preceding years. They could predict how they might more profitably choose to mix them in the next and succeeding years.

They remembered which bulls had bred which cows, which rams which ewes, which billies which nannies, and they knew their ancestry as well. They could advise which young bulls, rams, and billies should be chosen for the future privilege of breeding, and which should be led to slaughter and consumed. They could also tell which bull calves should be castrated and trained to become oxen.

The children were especially glad to see the tellers, who could recite stories and sing songs that made them laugh one moment and cry the next. Beating on leather stretched over large pots and hollowed-out tree trunks, and blowing on dry reeds, horns, and bones, the tellers made people want to dance and forget their many worries and cares.

As Blue Sky and Rose Leaf grew older, Morning Sun passed on to them some of the more interesting things he'd learned from his instructors. There were times when Blue Sky wished he were the prince and spent his days with the tellers. He wondered if following the many rules the court people laid down for Morning Sun might've been worth finding out what the tellers knew.

The tellers also fought in the first ranks of the army. In a number of the valley people's stories, the gods particularly favored childless men, usually those who went with other men, who exposed themselves to danger in place of men with children.

*****

In the last years of his childhood, Blue Sky had come to realize he'd be a man who didn't go with women. Almost all the men among his people who didn't wish to go with women did wish to go with other men. He was one of them, although in his case the only man he wished to go with was the man the prince was becoming.

That was the other reason he'd decided to do guard duty with the apprentice tellers.

But unlike most of the tellers who went with other men, he'd be one of the few who didn't go with any person.

Although he was in love with Morning Sun, he knew he couldn't have him the way he wanted him. He was also certain nobody else could take the place of the prince in his life.

*****

During the festivities in the courtyard on the bluff following the two races between Morning Sun and Early Harvest, Blue Sky crossed the path of a young teller who'd become one of the people's favorites. In the ceremonies, he often sang the solo parts, the songs of the gods.

He called himself Spring Rain. The men living in the part of the valley he'd come from were as hard-bodied, and almost as tall, as Blue Sky, Morning Sun, Early Harvest, Solemn Promise, and their cousins, but they were leaner, too. Spring Rain was no exception.

Pleasantly surprising Blue Sky, he stopped and spoke with him.

Spring Rain said he'd heard a rumor that Green Field and Gentle Brook's son had decided to do his year of guard duty with the apprentice tellers.

Spring Rain lived in a house he and another young teller, who was called Many Numbers, had built in the part of the town where the tellers lived.

The last war with the hill people had left both of them, then four years old, without either a father or a mother. Because there were too few able-bodied adults remaining in their land-poor village to care for them—or so the claim went—their relatives took them to the town and placed them in the orphanage the tellers maintained.

Their uncles and aunts had originally decided to send away only one of the boys. Having become friends, though, neither boy would leave unless the other went with him. And neither would stay home if the other left. They got their way and went to the orphanage together.

"For days after they arrived, they clung to one another," Fair Judge told Rainbow Evening.

Fair Judge was in charge of the orphanage as well as the education of the prince.

Afterward, Spring Rain and Many Numbers' uncles, aunts, and cousins never went to see the boys or invited them home for a visit. Possibly ashamed of themselves for having abandoned their kin, they claimed the orphans had become "too much like town people."

Farmers elsewhere tended to laugh at that. Wouldn't a village that didn't want its children becoming "too much like town people" do everything it could to keep them in the village?

If the village Many Numbers and Spring Rain had come from had enjoyed the presence of a childless woman, or a childless man living as a woman, the orphan boys might've become her sons, working in her fields and tending her livestock.

As it turned out, though, because their relatives in their birth village chose to keep no connections with them, Spring Rain and Many Numbers were able to give the parts of their shares of the tellerhood harvest they didn't require to live, as well as their help with the planting and harvesting, to people anywhere in the kingdom who needed their assistance the most.

When Many Numbers was born, that wasn't the name his family gave him. But after the tellers found out how easy it was for him to remember days, seasons, and years and make calculations, even with large numbers, they decided he needed a new name.

Amid the singing and dancing in the courtyard, Spring Rain smiled at Blue Sky.

"The other apprentice tellers will be glad to have you with them," he remarked.

"But I won't be going with any of them," Blue Sky hastened to say.

Spring Rain smiled again. "You already have a friend?"

"Yes, but he won't be going with other men."

"Morning Sun?"

Blue Sky, nodding his head, assumed Spring Rain had already heard the story of the great hero Green Field's son falling in love with the prince. The young teller the people loved was too polite, though, to laugh at the youthful folly the story exposed.

Many Numbers, as pleasantly lean as his mate, joined them. He sang in ceremonies, too, often in duets with Spring Rain. They both—again, as their relatives did—had eyes set unusually close together. Blue Sky sometimes found himself wishing he looked more like them.

They also had with one another what Blue Sky wanted with Morning Sun.

Rose Leaf, seeing who her brother was with, made her way toward them.

She soon remarked on a ceremony song in which Spring Rain sang the part of the goddess of love and Many Numbers the god of war.

Rose Leaf and Blue Sky were recently paying more attention than they had as children to the songs the tellers sang in their ceremonies. In the one she'd referred to, Blue Sky had taken a liking to the lyrics the chorus sang, having realized they were gently mocking both the god and goddess for their partial views of the matter at hand, which was the loss in war of people beloved.

"You do that song so well," Rose Leaf said, "you make me cry. My mother and I sing it, and we try hard with the goddess of love's part. We feel what she's saying. But neither of us can sing the god of war's part and make anybody believe we mean it. My father and brother aren't very good at singing, I'm sorry to say. Not even as a chorus, which is all they'll ever attempt."

"We're afraid," Blue Sky said, "people might compare us to the orphan boys and laugh."

"I should imagine," Many Numbers said to Rose Leaf, taking her hand, "both you and your mother more than do justice to the goddess of love's part. The war god's part is silly anyway."

As was the custom for a male teller, Spring Rain sang his part as if the goddess had a male voice. But he made those who heard him believe the goddess's human lover, who died in the latest of the other god's wars, could've been their own, and they would've felt the lover's absence from their lives as much as she did.

And Many Numbers might've sincerely believed the war god's part was "silly," but that wasn't the way he sang it. He, unlike other people who tried it, came close to convincing his audience the conflicts the god brought about in the human world were inevitable. He forced his listeners to consider the possibility that any hopes they might entertain for long-lasting peace were doomed from the start—maybe even "silly."

*****

On the path from the town to the home village that evening, the inebriated cousins surrounded Early Harvest, heedless of his many hopeful glances in Rose Leaf's direction.

Rose Leaf, walking behind them with Blue Sky, couldn't stop talking about Spring Rain and Many Numbers. At one point, she went so far as to say those two men were as pleasing to her eyes as Morning Sun and Early Harvest. Blue Sky tried not to think too long about that remark.

Many valley people believed that children who spent their youth in the orphanage didn't amount to much as adults because, unlike children living with families, they grew up resenting hard work. Spring Rain and Many Numbers, though, had reputations for being among the most diligent workers in the tellerhood fields. Their shirtless bodies in summer proved the point.

"And they still find the time," Rose Leaf said, "to practice their singing."

"And their arithmetic," Blue Sky responded. "Their days, seasons, years. Their stories."

*****

One day between the last full moon of the summer and summer's end, Green Field and Gentle Brook's family took a cartload of wheat to the town for trade with the river people.

After the business was done, Rose Leaf and Blue Sky went to see the orphan boys.

The houses, granaries, and barns in their people's villages were joined together, sharing as many common walls as possible. So were the houses in the town. Spring Rain and Many Numbers, though, had built their house somewhat apart from those of the other tellers, near the path to the bluff-top woods.

In the summer and early autumn, visitors to the town often came by to see the house. Ivy entirely covered it then. After the orphan boys had finished building it, they dug up the ivy in the woods and replanted it all around the structure. Nobody had seen such a house before.

The orphan boys and their guests, Blue Sky and Rose Leaf, sat on benches outside the "ivy house," as it was known, drinking wine and exchanging greetings with passersby.

Spring Rain and Many Numbers confirmed the truth of one story Morning Sun had told Blue Sky and Rose Leaf. It was a story the tellers weren't supposed to pass on to the people.

When Blue Sky mentioned that, his hosts looked at one another and laughed.

"You're the son and daughter of Green Field and Gentle Brook," Many Numbers said. "Would Sturdy Limb even try to put us in his cages for telling you?"

"And why would we need to admit," Blue Sky asked, laughing himself, "you told us?"

The story concerned a bloody war their people had fought a few generations previously. The war wasn't fought against the hill people. It was a civil war, fought among themselves.

A king who went with men had died without any descendants or close relatives surviving him. The war was fought between the backers of two distant relatives with equally plausible claims to the kingship.

Blue Sky asked why the tellers didn't share the story with the people.

"They don't think it's appropriate for the people to know about something like that," Many Numbers replied. "We weren't fending off savage invaders nobody could fail to despise. We were fighting and killing one another."

"But shouldn't the people know their own stories?" Blue Sky asked. "Whatever the stories are, good or bad? Shouldn't the people know them?"

Spring Rain shook his head. "The tellers can't see what good would come from bad stories. We have no doubt about which of Tall Oak's relatives would become king if both he and Morning Sun were to die without heirs surviving them. We have it all figured out."

Indeed they did. Since Green Field and Blue Sky were distant cousins of the king and the prince, they were included in the tellers' calculations. Many Numbers said there were two times ten people before Green Field in the line to the kingship, and Blue Sky was next. Full Harvest and Early Harvest were immediately behind them. Many Numbers could name all the people in the line of succession in order, beginning with Morning Sun and Sturdy Limb and going well beyond Early Harvest and his cousins, and he could explain exactly why a person was in the line where he was.

In Blue Sky's former dream, with him and Morning Sun becoming mates, Valley Defender would've sired the next heir to the kingship. And Rose Leaf would've been the child's mother.

*****

Green Field and Gentle Brook's family ate that evening with the royal family in the king and queen's room. They sat at the dining table as they always had, with the king and queen in their chairs at either end, Green Field and Gentle Brook on the bench on one side, and the prince between Rose Leaf and Blue Sky on the other.

Sturdy Limb's two younger sons had volunteered to serve them. Like Morning Sun and their brother, Valley Defender, they weren't supposed to do any court work. Roiling their father— deliberately, Blue Sky assumed—they'd claimed that waiting on guests of the king and queen such as Green Field and Gentle Brook and their son and daughter was an honor, not work.

The lengthwise middle of the main court building, the great central hall, was open to the peaked roof above it, with fireplaces at either end. It was where the king held court during the winter and inclement weather, sitting on a dais with the queen and, during ceremonies, the prince. It was also where the court people set up tables and benches for indoor feasts.

Two floors of rooms lined the long sides of the building. Stairs on either side rose from the central hall to the balconies leading to the second-story rooms. One of the rooms, as large as some houses in the valley, was Morning Sun's. Another, twice that size, was the king and queen's.

When Morning Sun and Blue Sky were little boys sitting in the king and queen's room with their parents and Rose Leaf, they'd fidget until their parents finally gave in and let them go out to exhaust themselves in the courtyard. Rose Leaf, invited or not, would go along with them.

Valley Defender and his two brothers would often join them. Rose Leaf and Blue Sky liked the cousins and therefore never spoke of their chief-warrior father in their presence.

They knew the boys' mother had died giving birth to the youngest of them, and Rainbow Evening was the person most like a mother they'd ever known.

During visits to the court in more recent years, Morning Sun, Rose Leaf, and Blue Sky had usually chosen to stay in the king and queen's room. It was pleasant sitting in chairs softened by multiple layers of wool and talking with, and just as often back to, all four of their parents.

A good part of Blue Sky's and Rose Leaf's pleasure they owed to their host and hostess, who found out things other people weren't supposed to know. Most entertainingly, they could account for many of the instances of children failing to resemble the men who were supposed to be their fathers, like calves proving at a glance that a wayward bull, unwilling to let mere humans deny him what he wanted, had jumped over or broken through a fence to satisfy a cow in heat.

The king and queen always refused to confirm, though, the story concerning a number of individuals, including Good Harvest, who were said to be Full Harvest's nephews and nieces but were born too long after his brothers, the only men ever married to their mothers, had died in the last war with the hill people. That part of the story, the tellers whispered, was undeniably true.

The unconfirmed part of the story was that the father of them all was Full Harvest.

*****

"I've decided to do guard duty with the apprentice tellers," Blue Sky announced.

"And leave no heirs for your father and mother?" Tall Oak asked. "You're their only son. Is that what you intend to do?"

Some men who were inclined to go with men married women anyway and didn't become tellers. They were almost always the only children their parents had. If they didn't father children, they'd leave their parents with no heirs. Many of the men who attempted to do that ultimately failed. Even after their weddings, they either couldn't bring themselves to do what needed to be done, or they'd quit doing it before they produced a child who survived its infancy.

The valley people kept close track of their neighbors. If they saw a man spending too much time alone with the tellers when they came by, or with a neighboring man who was similarly rumored to have broken off with his wife, they drew the appropriate conclusions.

The court people and tellers laughed at the predicaments those men had gotten themselves into. And the tellers who went with the men were often the people making the remarks giving rise to the laughter. The people liked hearing that a wife of such a man had taken up with an available neighbor, perhaps a man whose wife had died, or one whose wife no longer wished to go with him.

"Rose Leaf has assured me," Blue Sky replied, "she wishes to go with a man."

Morning Sun looked at Rose Leaf and smiled.

Rose Leaf wasn't above returning the prince's smile.

The queen saw what they were doing and frowned.

"I don't have any reason to doubt," Blue Sky continued, "she'll provide my father and mother with all the heirs they'll ever need."

Morning Sun snickered. Rose Leaf laughed.

Rainbow Evening's frown deepened.

"All our fields, pastures, and livestock will be theirs," Blue Sky added.

"Yes, of course," Tall Oak said, looking at Rose Leaf almost as if he'd never seen or heard of her before. "They will."

"If I survive guard duty in the mountains," Blue Sky said, "Rose Leaf will never have to worry about providing for our father and mother in their old age."

"Yes," Tall Oak agreed again, drily, turning to Green Field. "This turn of events does give you that advantage."

"I'm very sorry, though," Rainbow Evening said, looking at Blue Sky, "you've decided not to spend your year in the mountains with Morning Sun."

"This farmer boy wants to take lessons from the tellers," the prince said. "Can you imagine anybody wanting to do that if they didn't have to?"

"I can," Blue Sky said. "They know a lot of things they don't tell the people."

"A lot of things they shouldn't tell the people," Tall Oak remarked.

"Even the story about the king who failed to produce an heir?" Blue Sky asked. "The story where half the kingdom fought a senseless, brutal war against the other half?"

"That story," Morning Sun said, an unusual tone of cynicism in his voice. "The tellers know all there is to know about that war. But when older people say their ancestors told them about it, the tellers rebuke them for talking nonsense. They have to insist that war never happened."

"That's how the tellers do it," Blue Sky said. "They lie."

"That's how they have to do it," Tall Oak said.

"That's nice," Blue Sky said, making his mother smile at his sarcasm. "The king and the prince and the tellers can know the truth, but the people can't."

Morning Sun shook his head. "I never asked to be the prince in this kingdom."

"Nevertheless," Tall Oak said, "you are the prince in this kingdom."

The prince glared at his father.

"The fate of our people rests on your shoulders," the king went on, daring the prince to differ, "whether you'd choose to have it there or not. Don't blame your mother and me. Any male child we had would be a prince. You happened to be the only one who survived his childhood."

Green Field looked at Morning Sun and nodded his head.

"And you'll also have to decide for yourself," he remarked, "as your father does now, how much the tellers should let the people know."

"How much they should let the people know," Tall Oak said, "without inciting them into another senseless, brutal war."

"Isn't that the reason they should tell the people the truth?" Blue Sky asked. "So the people can learn not to make the same mistake all over again?"

"The truth might not have that effect on the people," the king replied. "It might simply set them to plotting another war."

"So," Blue Sky persisted, "the best way for our people to deal with senseless, brutal wars is to forget they happened?"

"If you're ever in a war yourself," Tall Oak replied, "you'll be overjoyed to see the day come when you can forget it. But you'll learn something else instead: that day never comes."

He glanced at Green Field, who, despite having suffered grievous wounds in the war, walked unbent and without a limp. Although he was the same age as Tall Oak, he looked, with his farmer's body and full head of hair, a number of years younger.

"I understand," Tall Oak continued, "the survivors of that war especially wished to forget it. The tellers say that's why those people put it in our laws that nobody—except, of course, the tellers among themselves or with the king or prince—should speak of that war."

Gentle Brook laughed. "That law seems to have been ignored this evening."

"Luckily," Tall Oak came back, "the king can speak of and listen to anything he wishes."

"Still," Green Field said, "I really can't see why common knowledge of that war would set anybody to plotting anything in this day and age."

Tall Oak sighed. "You're probably right. But it's up to the tellers. If they decide they should start letting the people know about it, the law can be changed. All they have to do is ask me, and I'll issue an order."

"I should imagine," Green Field said to Tall Oak, "you could ask them to ask you."

"Yes," Tall Oak agreed, "I could. But where would we go after that? Surely, Green Field, you must agree there are some things the people shouldn't know."

Ignoring the king, Green Field looked across the table at Blue Sky.

"I believe," he said, "you should do guard duty with the apprentice tellers. I believe you should become a teller. I don't believe there's anything they know, or anybody knows, you shouldn't know."

Tall Oak, turning back to Blue Sky, sighed again.

"Nor do I," he said. "The tellers said you'd become one of them. Now I see they were right. As, of course, they so often are. About so many things. I'm sorry I didn't wish to believe them. I'd hoped the only son of Green Field and Gentle Brook would wish to give them heirs."

Green Field shook his head.

"He has no need to worry about that," he countered. "He's my son. He's a grown man now. I understand him. I trust him. He can do as he pleases. Rose Leaf wishes to have children."

"Well, then," Tall Oak said, turning to Blue Sky again. "If it pleases you and your father and mother, I agree, you should do guard duty with the apprentice tellers."

"That civil war secrecy," Rose Leaf interjected, "doesn't fool anybody anyway."

Morning Sun and Blue Sky laughed.

The king and queen looked at Rose Leaf with the solemnity her blunt remark required.

"Everybody knows there was a civil war," she continued. "Autumn Wine's parents swore to her there was such a war. Ancestors of hers, not very far back, were killed in it."

"The people just don't know the details," Gentle Brook added.

"They know the tellers are lying," Green Field said, "when they deny it happened."

Their parents had long ago told Morning Sun, Blue Sky, and Rose Leaf there was only one rule they needed to follow concerning their conversations with the king and queen, but it was an absolute rule, and there were no exceptions to it: they could never repeat to any other person anything they said among themselves.

Blue Sky turned to Tall Oak. "What would you have to do," he asked, "if I simply told the people the truth about that war? You'd have to order me put to death?"

Rainbow Evening looked at Gentle Brook, slowly shook her head, and closed her eyes.

"Death is the penalty for that," Tall Oak replied, as if he were Sturdy Limb.

Morning Sun laughed. "You wouldn't order him executed," he said. "Not for that."

Green Field smiled at the prince. "I'm sure your father knows a little defiance of authority isn't always a bad thing."

Tall Oak glared, briefly, at his longtime friend.

"Maybe it's not always a bad thing," he said. "But it's usually a dangerous thing."

Morning Sun shook his head, laughed again, and looked across the table at Green Field.

"The gods made a big mistake," he chose to remark. "Haven't I always said you should be the king in this kingdom?"

Tall Oak laughed, too. "I would that Green Field were," he said. "And actually being the king might cause him to talk somewhat less lightly about defying authority."

Morning Sun waved off that remark as if his father, the actual king, were a village fool.

"And you," he continued, turning to Blue Sky, poking him in his chest. "You should be the damned prince in this kingdom."

It was Blue Sky's turn to laugh. "No, thanks," he said. "I'll gladly leave that heavy burden on your strong shoulders. I've no doubt you'll do everything for our people you'll need to do. And they'll be as safe and prosperous under your rule as they are under your father's."

Rainbow Evening stared at Blue Sky. "Can we hope you'll help Morning Sun do that?"

She was said to have been even more disappointed than Tall Oak and the people were when Green Field opted to return to the home village after the last war.

"If the prince and the kingdom need me," Blue Sky replied, glancing at his father, whose choices in war and peace had set in motion the story they found themselves in, "I will."

Chapter 4

At the end-of-summer ceremony that year, Morning Sun stood with the sons of the court people, Blue Sky with the new men in the kingdom who'd chosen to become tellers.

After the ceremony, the prince and Blue Sky embraced, congratulating one another—as was the custom for new men on that day—for having stayed alive long enough to become a man.

Morning Sun's town companion Solemn Promise joined them.

The young man from the wealthiest family in the kingdom revealed that he was sorry the best friend of the prince wouldn't be spending his year in the mountains with the prince. He hoped Blue Sky knew he would've been more than welcome in their encampment.

Solemn Promise was a fairly close relative of Blue Sky's. Many Numbers said he was ten plus seven in the line of succession to the kingship, four places ahead of Green Field.

Solemn Promise also assured Blue Sky he'd take good care of the prince. After all, they'd be sharing a hut.

Initially, Blue Sky was as receptive to that news as he would've been to a blow to his head.

He said nothing, though, because he had nothing to say. He soon realized his resentment would've arisen in the presence of any person who'd announced he was sharing a place to sleep with Morning Sun. And it could never be a worthy feeling, whoever that person was.

The prince had to share a hut with someone. Blue Sky thought Solemn Promise was certainly bright enough to be a companion of the prince, and he was honest as well. Unlike many of the court people— his own family included—he'd never seemed too impressed with himself.

Morning Sun would someday need people capable of helping him rule the kingdom. Why shouldn't one of those people be Solemn Promise?

Blue Sky thanked Solemn Promise for what he'd said. He told him he was pleased knowing a person such as he would be sharing a hut with the prince—who'd chosen well.

*****

That same morning, the new men said their good-byes to their families, neighbors, and friends, and with their mothers and sisters in tears, set out for the mountains.

Gentle Brook hadn't been able to conceal her disappointment that Morning Sun and Blue Sky wouldn't be spending their encampment year together. She was certain their not sharing a hut on cold winter nights would be a bitter loss for both of them.

Although Blue Sky felt like asking his mother how she thought he was supposed to lie huddled together through winter nights with a person he was in love with and not be able to do anything about it, he put no such question to her.

The encampments for the apprentice tellers and the sons of the town people were on either side of the great canyon at sunrise pass. In addition to being the hill people's favorite site for launching their invasions, it was also where most of their recent hostile encounters with the valley people took place.

The valley tellers believed the hill people's king often pitched his tents near a plain that was said to be within a two-day walk from the pass, which would be the closest and easiest place for his warriors to probe the farmers' defenses. The summer just ended had brought his latest attempt, leaving two of his warriors dead and the valley warriors without a wound.

One of the valley people's kings a few generations back had decided the apprentice tellers and sons of the court people should bear the burden of defending sunrise pass. He thought the people who ran the kingdom should always be the first to sacrifice their able-bodied males for it.

Although they traveled in two separate groups, the apprentice tellers and sons of the court people took the same route east from the town for most of their three-day journey.

People looking through the window openings in the royal rooms in the court could see the valley people's only bridge over the river far below. They could follow the path beyond it until it came to a fork. The branch to the left and north led to the home village, which they could make out on a sunny day if, like Blue Sky and Rose Leaf, they knew where to look.

The branch to the right led to the eastern mountains and sunrise pass.

When the path went through the highest pastures in that part of the valley, grazed by the livestock belonging to the people in East Land's village, the new men found themselves with less to say to their companions.

Reaching their people's high wall of boulders and logs separating farmland from forest to keep the wild animals where they belonged, the new men had nothing to say. As they cleared the gateway and restored it after both groups had passed through, they worked in silence.

Their people feared the forest. They felled trees for construction and gathered firewood in it, but only at its edge. Hiding from the hill people in the last war and traveling to and from the encampments were the only reasons for them to go into it to the point where they were no longer in sight of farmland. And they almost always went into the forest in groups, the larger the better.

In the worst dreams of Blue Sky's childhood, he was always hopelessly lost deep in the forest, and the hill people—ghastly creatures, half human, half animal—were pursuing him.

"We all have those dreams," his mother would say. "The gods want us to have enemies."

*****

The new warriors slept two nights at the usual stopping places in the mountains, grateful the waxing moon was up and the sky cloudless.

Blue Sky was surprised to see some of his new companions, so recently strangers to one another, lonely farmers' sons from the farthest reaches of the kingdom, having bathed in a brook and freshened their mouths with mint leaves they'd picked in the forest, already pairing off.

He thanked those who asked him to go with them. But he also thought it best to let them know he wouldn't be going with anybody all through the year they'd be together.

Most of them seemed less disappointed by his response than amused. Like Spring Rain, they'd no doubt already heard the story concerning the hero Green Field's son, who'd unwisely let himself fall in love with his boyhood friend—who was the prince no less, making it the kind of tale few people could resist repeating.

One of his new comrades, a son of poor farmers from the upper valley called Noon Breeze, hearing from Blue Sky his vow of celibacy, laughed and wished him good luck with his hand.

He said Blue Sky should let him know if he ever got tired of that and changed his mind.

Noon Breeze was short and scrawny, having known hunger in winter more than once.

Blue Sky told Noon Breeze his invitation flattered him, but they could never go together.

Noon Breeze, who didn't look old enough to be a man, even found that amusing.

Several tellers were chosen each year to accompany the apprentices to their encampment and spend four seasons teaching them to be tellers, as well as guards and men in good standing in the kingdom. One of the tellers going to the encampment that autumn was Spring Rain.

Because Blue Sky and Spring Rain shared a desire not to go with any of the men in the encampment, they also decided to share a hut.

Many Numbers had remained in the town and would only be able to come up to the mountains during full-moon holidays. Spring Rain promised him he'd wait for his visits.

Two orphan boys had what a hero's son who was the best friend of the prince wanted most.

*****

The third-day's climb up the mountains was entirely through evergreen forest, which provoked even greater dread in valley people than the more familiar leaf-losing forest below.

The tellers liked to say that fearing the gods, and what they could do to mere humans, was the only way people could enjoy their beauty. Blue Sky wondered if for him the same notion applied in the case of the forest. Perhaps more so since it, unlike heaven, was a place he could actually visit.

And when he did, he could see how clean, hard shafts of sunlight pierced its darkness like arrows, but without disrupting its essential mystery. A wolf or bear—or an even more lethal human—could've been hiding in its shadows waiting to kill him.

*****

Reaching sunrise pass near the end of that third day, the new men finally saw what they'd heard lay beyond: hill after rocky hill. Most of the landscape was treeless, much of it barren.

The encampments controlled all the heights surrounding the valley. One purpose was to keep hill warriors from infiltrating the forest on the valley side of the mountains. Otherwise, they could, and no doubt would, launch raids at will on the villages nearest the forest, and sooner or later render life in the valley untenable for all the people to whom the gods had promised it.

Commanding the mountain passes also provided warning of an invading army well before it reached the valley. The time-honored response of the guards was to sound the alarm to the neighboring encampments, and thus to all of them, and to send their speediest messenger down the mountains to the valley to alert the people.

If the invading force was large enough, as Tall Oak's father had erroneously assumed it was in the last war, the army would fall back to the town to fight a defensive battle on the bluff. If the hill people's warriors were too few, as Green Field and Tall Oak saw they were, the invasion would end on whatever pass the hill people's king chose to attempt to cross over.

Since that war, though, the hill people had made no further attempt to invade the valley. They instead harassed the encampment warriors, especially those at sunrise pass, with what the valley people took to be probes, testing whether the valley people had forgotten the last war yet and were falling asleep in their guard posts.

For the probes, whatever their purpose, the mountaintop encampments provided an essential advantage to the valley people: the hill people could only attack them from below.

The skirmishes occurred when a group of hill men would venture too high on their side of the mountains and get too close to the encampments. The guards, spotting them from above, would start yelling at them, in the process alerting the neighboring encampments.

The hill people would almost always reverse their course as soon as they heard the guards and saw them in their guard posts aiming arrows at them. Occasionally, though, they wouldn't heed the guards' cries and turn back but would continue coming up the mountain.

If the hill people weren't carrying shields, the guards would take up previously assigned positions behind boulders, exposing their bodies as little as possible, and fire away with their bows and arrows when the enemy came within range. The first or second well-aimed arrow usually turned the intruders around, dragging their wounded comrades with them.

But occasionally, the hill warriors would crouch behind boulders themselves, shooting arrows at the guards. That kind of fight usually ended with few injuries or dead on either side. A brief while of it would convince the hill warriors they had nothing to gain, and they'd go away.

But if the hill warriors had their shields with them, the guards would dispense with the archery as a waste of time, effort, and arrows. They'd instead converge on the steepest, narrowest, and therefore most defensible position the enemy would need to break through if they were going to enter the valley and cause whatever havoc they had in mind.

In the case of the apprentice tellers' encampment, the designated position was on higher ground than the guard post. And that was where the guards practiced fighting with spears, taking turns posing as hill warriors. The battleground became familiar to them but not to the enemy.

The guards would accompany their positioning with loud cries for help across canyons to neighboring encampments, where the guards would repeat the alarm to comrades farther away, and run with their weapons to the place where the encampment under attack fought its battles.

Thus summoned, the guards almost always quickly outnumbered the hill people's warriors. If the enemy warriors still wished a close fight with spears, they'd drop their bows and arrows and continue coming up the mountainside.

When they got close enough to let the guards dispense with their bows, arrows, and shields, they'd drop their shields as well. The guards and the hill warriors would then skirmish spear tip to spear tip, daring one another's opponent to step forward from the protection of his line and die.

It didn't take a lot of practice to see how much easier it was for the warrior on the higher ground to unbalance his lower-ground opponent, leaving him momentarily vulnerable to a quick, precise, and fatal blow, often delivered by the valley warrior's nearest comrade, sighting out of the corner of his eye an opportunity to kill an enemy— and become a hero.

At the same time, the three ablest valley guards would go up and down behind their line looking for the hill people's smallest, slowest, or least agile fighter. When they found their man, they'd give him a descriptive nickname, such as "Missing Teeth," "Broken Nose," or "Crossed Eyes," and call it out, over and over, so everybody would know for certain who he was.

Suddenly, on the lead guard's signal, their line would surge forward together, closing upon their quarry from all sides, separating him from his companions, letting him as well as them in on the secret: they'd selected him for an example of what the valley guards could do.

After the guards had him behind their line, one of their ablest fighters would swing his spear, batting the doomed man's spear away. A second warrior would thrust his spear into the hill warrior's belly, opening it up for the world to see. A third would mercifully slit his throat as he staggered to the ground.

Having witnessed the methodical slaying of their comrade, the other hill warriors would usually flee. There were times, though, when even two or three of their fighters lying in the dirt, red in death, their guts exposed, couldn't make their comrades turn and run.

The guards' instructions were to continue as they had, using their next ablest and most rested fighters to separate yet another of the hill warriors, and then another—and as many as it took—to show them the gods had given the farmers the valley and would help them kill anybody who attempted to take it away from them.

What the valley people prized most in warfare, and what they considered an even greater gift from the gods than the valley itself, was their discipline.

There were occasions, though, when the brutality of battlefield death—even when the death was an enemy warrior's and the brutality their own—overcame the guards' sworn commitment to do only what they were trained and ordered to do. The fight would become the skirmish they never wanted to find themselves in: a senseless free-for-all.

Still, the guards had the advantage of greater numbers fighting a defensive battle on higher ground. Always, eventually, the hill people's warriors would turn and flee. But not until maybe one or two or more of the valley guards also lay in the dirt dead or dying.

The people would fill the town the day of their burial. Into the night, the tellers would sing mournful songs of youths becoming men, dying in battle, and missing out on their manhood.

Even some of the grown men, practiced in concealing their grief and fear, would weep.

The guards remaining in the hills would vow on their knees never to let it happen again.

Those who'd fought in the battle, witnessed the needless deaths of their comrades, and later came home, would have it to remember, and vainly attempt to forget, for the rest of their lives.

*****

Across the wide and deep canyon separating the encampments, the apprentice tellers and the sons of the court people could see one another.

Although it was difficult to distinguish individuals at that distance, Blue Sky was quite certain which one of them was Morning Sun. It was mostly the way he walked, holding his head high and his back straight as the court people had taught him to do.

When Rose Leaf and Blue Sky were younger, they thought it great fun to mimic the prince walking, showing him how well they could do it themselves, exaggerating freely, caustically instructing one another as they'd imagined the court people did their unfortunate friend.

"You could've spent the year over there with the prince," Spring Rain said. "His comrades told me they would've been glad to have you with them. I'm sure they meant it."

It was their first evening in the encampment. Spring Rain and Blue Sky were doing the first duty of the new men in the guard post. They'd volunteered for it. The others were busy reveling.

Blue Sky had told Spring Rain all about falling in love with the prince. He'd even admitted he'd wanted with Morning Sun what Spring Rain had with Many Numbers.

"I wish to become a teller," Blue Sky said. "That's why I'm here—and not over there."

Rainbow Evening had asked Spring Rain to be Blue Sky's tutor. She and Fair Judge had gotten Law Keeper to agree to it. Blue Sky wouldn't have to take lessons with the others.

"We can go faster and further," Spring Rain had said, cinching the deal for Blue Sky.

The town guard who'd appeared to be Morning Sun was no longer in sight.

Blue Sky turned to Spring Rain.

"Can we start my lessons now?" he asked.

Spring Rain laughed. "There's no reason why not."

"I want to know how the tellers know when the farmers can safely plant their crops."

"'If the people please heaven,'" Spring Rain sang, "'the gods whisper in the tellers' ears.'"

They both laughed. That was how one of the tellers' songs explained it.

"I'll tell you," Spring Rain said. "I'll tell you anything I know that you might want to know."

"I'll keep you busy with my questions."

"Please do. But first I've got to make sure you know where to look to see if any hill warriors are coming this way. And what to do if you see them."

They'd be awake in the guard post until dawn.

Spring Rain showed Blue Sky where their predecessors had fought the skirmish the previous summer that left two hill warriors dead. The guards from Morning Sun's encampment, Valley Defender among them, had run over and joined the apprentice tellers in the fighting.

The king and queen were accordingly preparing a homecoming celebration at the court for the guards from both encampments, inviting all their families as well. During the feast in the great central hall, Tall Oak, Sturdy Limb, and Law Keeper themselves would serve the guards.

For the time being, though, the heroes of the battle last summer were still in the mountains, mostly dirty and tired from the day's work, mostly complaining. The previous-year's guards would stay in their encampments until the next full moon, all that while showing the new guards what they had to do to keep their encampment safe and the hill people away.

After the old guards left, the new guards would be on their own.

*****

When Noon Breeze found out Blue Sky would be sleeping in a hut with Spring Rain, he confronted Blue Sky during preparations for an evening meal.

"Do you know what you're doing?" Noon Breeze asked.

Blue Sky chose to say nothing. Any truthful reply would've included the word no.

"You're making yourself the first teller's enemy. That's what you're doing."

Law Keeper's unwanted advances on young tellers, which were well known to the male tellers but hardly at all among the people, had sparked a great deal of mirthful repartee on the part of Blue Sky's new comrades. Much of it was in the form of speculation as to which of them would be the first teller's next victim and which of them had no reason to fear the man.

The first teller's long and strenuous pursuit of Spring Rain despite his prey's attachment to Many Numbers had once come close to being known beyond the tellerhood. Law Keeper had promised to make life miserable for both of the young men if Spring Rain continued to resist him. Only a personally and privately delivered threat from Tall Oak—to remove Law Keeper as first teller and appoint a new one—could make the man give up his obsessive pursuit.

Noon Breeze had learned all that in just three days as an apprentice teller.

Blue Sky shrugged his shoulders. "I guess I'll have to take my chances."

Noon Breeze stared at Blue Sky. "You're brave," he said.

Blue Sky laughed. He wasn't brave. He was Green Field and Gentle Brook's son.

*****

When the first full moon of the autumn came, Blue Sky went to see Morning Sun.

During the two days and three nights of the full-moon holiday, the guards had no drills or lessons to attend, no required work to perform. They had only to keep people in the guard posts. They shared that duty in equal portions, but before and after, they were free to do as they pleased.

Spring Rain, who'd gotten Blue Sky to admit, over wine two evenings before, that he did in fact miss seeing the prince, took him to the path that led around the top of the canyon to the encampment for the court people's sons.

With the autumn sun on his shirtless back that day, Blue Sky set out by himself, wondering if his childhood was truly over.

The evening he and Spring Rain had drunk wine in their hut, he'd begun kissing his tutor.

At first it was just that, but he soon felt he had to have more.

When he came to his senses again, he begged Spring Rain to forgive him.

Many Numbers would arrive the next afternoon.

After Spring Rain and Many Numbers became men, they had the supervising tellers in their encampment bless their marriage. They'd made the usual promises to the gods that they'd go with nobody else as long as they were both still living. But that evening, drinking with Blue Sky, Spring Rain merely smiled and told his hut-mate he'd enjoyed what they'd done.

Blue Sky had to weigh that remark carefully. As long as he wasn't Law Keeper, Spring Rain, who was invariably polite, might've said what he said whether he meant it or not.

*****

Upon Blue Sky's arrival at the encampment for the new men from the town, he spotted Morning Sun's hut-mate and asked him where he could find the prince.

"I believe he's at the women's huts," Solemn Promise replied, smiling uneasily.

Blue Sky laughed. "I should've known. Where else would he be?"

Solemn Promise, who was almost as polite as Spring Rain, reluctantly smiled again.

It wouldn't have surprised Blue Sky if all the eligible court people's daughters had come to see the prince and throw themselves at him, their brothers having shown them how it was done.

"I'm going down there," Solemn Promise said. "It's just a short distance. Why don't you wait here? I'll tell Morning Sun you've come for a visit. I'm sure he'll be glad to see you."

Solemn Promise knew Blue Sky wouldn't want to show up at the women's huts looking for the prince. That was another reason for Blue Sky to be glad the man was Morning Sun's friend.

*****

All the encampments except the apprentice tellers' had a site nearby, ordinarily in a clearing in the forest, where the guards maintained a separate group of huts. These were for use by the young women who volunteered to lead the oxen pulling the carts filled with the people's supplies for the encampments.

The supply treks—or "journeys of the full moon," as they were known—were how many of the new men and women in the kingdom decided who they'd live with for the rest of their lives. As a result, most of the weddings in the valley took place in the autumn, soon after that year's guards returned from their encampments.

It was also true that the journeys provided opportunities for new men and women to go with a person who wasn't yet their spouse blessed in a ceremony presided over by the tellers.

Quite a few of the autumn weddings were done at the insistence of grandparents-to-be of grandchildren-to-arrive who might otherwise have embarked upon life as bastards and become the king's responsibility. Those ceremonies were often hastily performed, in some cases without even an opportunity for relatives living nearby to gather for the usual feast.

Sometimes the man and woman involved were still reluctant to become husband and wife despite the insistence of their families. They could, after all, end up paying a lifelong price for what might've been the folly of a single night.

Sometimes one or both of them continued in their refusal even after the king sent tellers and court people to add his strenuous encouragement to that of their families. At which point the king could threaten to take the child when it was born and give it to the tellers to raise in their orphanage, with the families of the father and mother paying tribute for the child's upkeep until it became an adult.

In almost all cases, though, the king didn't have to do that. Instead, either the father's or the mother's family would take the child as if it had been born to a properly married member of the family. The other parent's family would then share with the adoptive family a portion of its harvest each year until the child came of age.

Sometimes an extra child in the family to work in the fields was an advantage and welcomed. Sometimes, even with the extra help to be had, it wasn't.

When it wasn't, people heard stories of the adopting family, as well as the one paying tribute, strenuously reminding the child's parents of all the trouble their careless and wayward behavior had brought down on them. Most of the people wished not to let that happen.

Blue Sky had always refused to pay any attention whenever the tellers came around instructing the older children how to prevent the arrival of a child they didn't want.

He'd been hoping he and Morning Sun would never have to worry about that.

*****

"You must have a lot of them to choose from," Blue Sky said.

He and the prince were sitting in the sun on a bench outside the door of the hut the prince shared with Solemn Promise. They were drinking the first of that autumn's wine.

"I'm sure you can have whichever one you want," Blue Sky persisted. "I mean, whoever becomes your wife not only gets the most beautiful man in the kingdom, she gets to be the queen in the bargain. Her children will be princes and princesses. One of the boys will be our king after you die. With that kind of good fortune, she'll praise the gods for the rest of her life."

Morning Sun rolled his eyes and shook his head.

"What are you going to do?" Blue Sky ventured forth. "Give them each a try? You could do that. You're the prince. You could say you just want to make sure you've found the right one to spend the rest of your royal life with. And when you're the king, you won't have to stay faithful to your wife the way your father does. You can have other women on the side. They won't say no to you. If your wife doesn't like it, too bad for her. What can she do about it? You'll be the king."

Morning Sun was still shaking his head. "I never asked to be the prince in this kingdom," he remarked once more. "I don't want to be the king either. To be honest, the only thing I look forward to in that is the day I get to order your execution."

"And I wouldn't blame you if you did. I've never paid you the respect you're entitled to as a prince. I wouldn't like it one bit if I were you. I'd insist on seeing that person dead."

Morning Sun wasn't amused. "Your sister," he said, "is at the women's huts."

Rose Leaf could've gone on a full-moon journey as soon as she became a woman the previous spring. Everybody knew Morning Sun's cousin, Valley Defender, had invited her to the encampment for the court people's sons. They also knew she'd politely declined his invitation, telling him she wasn't quite ready for a journey of the full moon.

"That's a surprise," Blue Sky said. "I thought she'd go where the men in our village go. Early Harvest told her he'd do his encampment there, so it would be easy for her to see him. Did you know he asked her to be his wife? I was hoping she'd accept his proposal. I really think he's the right man for her. I told her so. I told him that, too."

Not yet used to the combination of wine and high mountain air, Blue Sky plunged on.

"Which of your comrades here does Rose Leaf want?" he asked.

Without attempting to reply, Morning Sun gave him another hard look.

Blue Sky couldn't help himself. "Well, if she wants one of the men from the town, I'm hoping she chooses Solemn Promise. Did he go to the women's huts to see her? He'd make a good husband for any woman. Wouldn't it be nice if they had a wedding next autumn? I was hoping she wanted Early Harvest, but I can see where Solemn Promise could be just as right for her. She could live with him in the town. They'd be close to the home village for visits. I could accompany them and their children back and forth. I'm sure he'd be a good father for my nieces and nephews."

At that point, the prince was giving Blue Sky a look heavily tinged with anger, like a cloud at sunrise or sunset taking on the red of the sun.

"Don't you think Solemn Promise would be a good husband for her?" Blue Sky asked.

"No," Morning Sun replied sharply, having had enough. "I don't."

"What's wrong with him? You think she should be Early Harvest's wife? Valley Defender's? I think any of those three would be good for her. I must say she's fortunate she has so many to choose from. All our young women should be so favored by the gods. Or lucky."

"Oh, shut up," the prince snarled, sending a stone flying with his foot. "I don't want to hear about those people. I'm sure they'll be the most wonderful husbands and fathers our kingdom has ever seen. I'll look forward to throwing a feast in their honor when I become the king. I'll ask you to speak. You can praise them to your heart's content. You'll reduce us all to tears. But we aren't talking about them right now. We're talking about Rose Leaf, your sister."

Blue Sky thought it was a good time to take another sip of his wine.

After he did so, the prince put his hand on his shoulder and looked him in the eye.

"Rose Leaf came here to see me," he said.

Blue Sky chose neither to blink nor look away.

"You knew she was coming to see you?" he asked.

"Yes."

"You and she arranged it?"

"Yes."

"Is she coming back to see you again?"

Morning Sun stood up and nodded in the direction of the path leading to the women's huts.

"You'll have to ask her about that," he replied.

Rose Leaf was close enough by then to have heard Blue Sky's last question.

"Yes," she said. "I'm coming back to see Morning Sun."

Blue Sky set his cup down, stood up, and embraced her.

"Do our parents know why you came here?" he asked.

"They will," Rose Leaf replied.

Blue Sky turned to Morning Sun.

"Do the king and queen know?" he asked.

The prince looked at Rose Leaf and smiled. "They will," he replied.

After the drama in the village orchard, their parents seldom mentioned the impossibility of her marriage to the prince again, but whenever they did, it was only to affirm that the prohibition existed, it was absolute, and it could never be discussed in the presence of any other person.

Blue Sky stared at Rose Leaf. He'd been aware she was becoming a woman even as he and Morning Sun were becoming men. Suddenly, though, her actually being a woman startled him.

Blue Sky realized Solemn Promise must've assumed he was a fool, somehow unaware that his best friend and sister wanted each other the way lovers did. Solemn Promise didn't know that Blue Sky, no matter what he'd seen, wasn't allowed to think that was possible.

"You'll defy our father and mother?" Blue Sky asked Rose Leaf.

"Yes," she replied without hesitation.

Blue Sky turned to Morning Sun.

"And you'll defy your parents?" he asked. "You'll both defy the king and queen?"

"Yes," the prince was answering even before Blue Sky finished his questions. "We will."

"Did you hear my last question?" Blue Sky asked. "You'll both defy the king?"

"Look," Rose Leaf said, "I wish to live with Morning Sun for the rest of my life. I wish to have his children."

Morning Sun extended his arm around her shoulders.

"And I wish to live with Rose Leaf for the rest of my life," he said. "That's all there is to it. What she wants and I want are the same thing. And nothing will stand in our way."

He was the prince, after all. Why shouldn't he have her?

Why, for that matter, shouldn't Rose Leaf, of all the eligible women, have the prince?

"The king," Blue Sky said, "can refuse to let you do that."

"So be it," Morning Sun came back. "I don't give a damn. So what if mighty Tall Oak won't let the tellers bless a marriage between Rose Leaf and me? Rose Leaf and the prince will live together without the benefit of their blessing. We don't need it."

"I wish to have children with Morning Sun," Rose Leaf said. "I don't wish to be royalty."

The people, though, would want to see their union blessed in a proper ceremony.

"And the children you might have?" Blue Sky asked.

"They'll live with us," Morning Sun replied. "Whether Rose Leaf and I are properly married or not. Legally, they can be my father and mother's children. Or they can be Green Field and Gentle Brook's children, your brothers and sisters. What difference will that make to us? Rose Leaf and I will still be their mother and father."

"What about the kingdom?" Blue Sky persisted.

"When my father dies," Morning Sun replied, "I'll become king. The first thing I'll do, I'll order the tellers to bless the marriage between Rose Leaf and me. Then we'll take our children back. They'll be our sons and daughters after that. One of our sons, or a son of a daughter, will become king when I'm gone. The kingdom will go on."

"But the people won't like that," Blue Sky insisted.

"They'll survive," Morning Sun said. "The kingdom will survive."

"But what if your father disinherits you?" Blue Sky asked.

Morning Sun laughed. "You mean I don't become the king when my father dies? That's okay. They can make Valley Defender the king. He'll do the job as well as I could. Probably better. He's thoughtful and kind. More so than I am. You like him. You can be his first teller. You can tell him in private what to do. Like your father does my father. The same as you'd do for me. The kingdom will survive very nicely. You'll see."

"Our children," Rose Leaf said, "don't need to be princes and princesses. Valley Defender and his wife can raise those. Many Numbers, Spring Rain, and you can give them their lessons."

"But the people," Blue Sky said, repeating himself, "won't like that at all. They want Morning Sun to be their next king. They've got this idea he's the best prince our people have ever had. They won't like it if he doesn't become their next king."

Morning Sun looked at Blue Sky, making no attempt to conceal his irritation. "Has anybody ever given you a good reason why Rose Leaf and I can't marry?"

Blue Sky once asked his father and mother if Rose Leaf and Morning Sun were somehow sister and brother. They insisted that wasn't the case and told him not to ask the question again.

The king and tellers refused to let siblings marry and have children. In one of the stories the tellers told, a man and woman married to other people had a son who was then raised separately from one of his half-sisters. When the brother and sister, who were unaware of their true relationship, decided to become husband and wife, the tellers, knowing the truth, told the king, who promptly forbade the marriage. The end of the story never failed to leave many who heard it in tears: the lovers went deep into the forest together, found a tree with a strong horizontal branch, tied leather-and-vine ropes to it, and simultaneously hanged themselves.

Blue Sky did raise the question again, though, in the presence of all four of their parents, who stared at him, refusing to speak.

"Is that the real reason they can't have children together?" Blue Sky had asked.

Unfortunately, Morning Sun had chosen just then to laugh.

"Rose Leaf won't ever want me," he'd scoffed. "She told us she wants a good-looking man for a husband."

"That's what I want," Rose Leaf had quickly agreed. "I'm certainly not going to have children with a man just because he happens to be the prince."

Their parents maintained their silence—hiding, Blue Sky dared imagine even then, behind the opportune levity of the two people in question.

"You haven't answered my question," Blue Sky had said to the four adults present.

"There's no need to answer your question," Green Field had said firmly.

"But there must be a good reason," Blue Sky said to Rose Leaf and Morning Sun a few years later on a warm and sunny autumn afternoon in the mountains. "Our parents aren't fools."

"Then why don't they let us know what that good reason is?" Rose Leaf asked. "Aren't we entitled to know what it is?"

"What if the people side with our parents?" Blue Sky asked. "What if the court people side with the king and oppose you? What if the tellers side with the king and oppose you? What if the farmers side with the king and oppose you? It'll be the two of you against the world."

"No," Rose Leaf said, taking her brother's hand. "If it comes down to that, it'll be the three of us against the world."

Blue Sky looked at Morning Sun. He couldn't imagine why Rose Leaf wouldn't want to be with him, of all the men in the kingdom, the rest of her life. The rule laid down by their parents, which apparently applied only to Rose Leaf, did seem arbitrary, to say the least. Why, without knowing the reason for it—if there was one—were they supposed to go along with it?

Rose Leaf couldn't have Morning Sun for one reason, and Blue Sky—having secretly dreamed of being a Many Numbers to his Spring Rain—for another.

Blue Sky's barrier, though, was in the nature of things. As some men did, Morning Sun wished to go with a woman. As other men did, Blue Sky wished to go with a man. That was simply the way things were. Blue Sky's vexation was his own affair, nobody else's.

Rose Leaf's impediment, on the other hand, was wholly artificial.

She and Morning Sun wanted to be together. If they weren't sister and brother, a good reason why they shouldn't have what they both desired couldn't exist.

If they were sister and brother, and their parents remained friends despite the commission of the acts that had brought the relationship about—which sometimes happened among their people—why wouldn't they tell their maturing children that was the case and be done with it?

Blue Sky felt he had no choice. His sister and the prince were the two people he'd spent his childhood with. The injustice they faced was as clear as a sunrise without clouds.

"Yes," Blue Sky agreed. "It'll be the three of us."

Chapter 5

Early in his lessons, Spring Rain told Blue Sky what he thought was the most important thing the tellers understood and other people didn't: there was an astonishing consistency in nature. And that was the real proof the gods existed and ruled the world humans lived in.

For most of the valley people, a season or a year went on until the tellers said it was time—say five days after the next full moon—for it to end and a new season, or year, to begin. The gods somehow communicated those things to the tellers so they could let the people know.

The people were also convinced the gods' years and seasons were often longer or shorter than usual. They sometimes seemed filled with days that went on and on, especially in the heat of summer or cold of winter. Yet others seemed short of days, when everyone swore that, despite what the tellers were saying, cold or heat, snow or thaw, had simply come too soon or too late.

But the tellers, Spring Rain assured Blue Sky, knew the lengths of the seasons and years never actually changed. The gods simply wouldn't let them change.

The people also assumed the tellers, after being properly trained, could hear the gods speak, even if it was just the faintest whisper in the wind or the song of a bird high in a tree. Although the tellers encouraged the people to think that was what happened, the gods didn't in fact speak to humans the way other humans did, or even the way the breeze or a bird would.

Instead, they'd long ago decreed that, contrary to what the people might sometimes believe, it would always take the same number of days for a season or a year to come and go. If people were careful enough in their observations and had a good memory, they could figure that out themselves. They didn't have to be an amazing Many Numbers to do it.

That was how, Spring Rain insisted, it was really the gods who declared the end of one year or season and the beginning of the next. That was how the gods communicated with humans. One could see it in the patterns they'd laid down. That was what they intended for humans to see. They didn't need the breeze or birdsong to do it.

The tellers had two ways to be certain when a new season or year was to begin. First, they counted the days of each year, and kept the total of them gone by in their minds, just as they kept count of a person's years. To guarantee their accuracy, whenever they encountered another teller for the first time in a day, they'd both state what they thought the number of the day was.

It amused the people that the tellers would wish to greet other tellers with a meaningless number they, for some reason, gave a day rather than a comment on what the day really was or might well be—such as hot or cold, rainy or dry, pleasant or unpleasant—as everybody else did.

Some tellers did it well, Spring Rain said. Some tellers had no gift for it at all. Most mornings, Law Keeper needed correcting by at least the first two or three tellers he saw. But certain tellers could always be counted on to know what day it was, how old somebody was, and how far into a season a year was. Other tellers, knowing their own limits, deferred to them.

There was a second way the tellers could decipher the intention of the gods, who had also long ago decided the sun and the moon would move across the sky in a regular and consistent manner. The people knew, of course, the sun was higher in the sky when the weather was hot and much lower, hanging over the southern end of the valley, when snow and ice came.

But they didn't know that for each corresponding day of a season, or from one year to the next, the sun rose and set at the same point on the horizon, as long as the place where you were standing was the same from one year to the next. And from one day to the next, the rising and setting points were slightly different, moving along the surrounding mountaintops toward the upper valley during winter and spring, toward the lower valley during summer and autumn.

One year came to an end and a new one began on the day the sun reached the rising and setting points on the horizon in the southeast and southwest it always refused to go beyond, like an unreasonably obstinate ox tempting its owners to sharpen their butchering blades and call their relatives and neighbors in for an unanticipated feast.

The first season, winter, ended when the sunrise and sunset points were precisely halfway between their most extreme points on the horizon. The second season, spring, ended with the day when the points were as far north as the sun, like a stubborn ox again, would ever rise and set. When the third season, summer, ended, and the fourth, autumn, began, the points were back where they were when winter ended and spring began.

The people were right about one thing, Spring Rain acknowledged. Years weren't always exactly the same length. But the difference didn't amount to much. The valley people's ancestors had noticed every few years an extra day turned up. They'd originally assumed that, as good as some of the tellers' memories were, they must've lost proper count. Then somebody realized the extra day accumulated after every four years. Many tellers thought the gods must've had a good reason for this strange anomaly, but nobody had ever thought one up that made much sense.

Others assumed it was just a godly prank, like the sudden darkening of the sun or the full moon. Those things sometimes happened, but nobody could predict when they would. They always frightened the people. And the tellers just as often took the opportunity to warn the people the gods were reminding them to behave themselves. But otherwise, a darkening neither failed to end promptly nor made a difference in peoples' lives. Maybe the gods were simply having harmless fun with humans.

The court was more than the place where the royal family and many of the court people lived, the army stored its tribute, and the chief warrior caged his prisoners. It was also the means by which the tellers kept track of the seasons. Tellers had designed it for that purpose long ago. From either end of the two-story main court building, and perpendicular to it, two long single-story buildings stretched to the north, where another such building connected them end to end, enclosing the rectangular courtyard where the tellers conducted their ceremonies and the king and queen held court in good weather.

A monolith in the center of the courtyard, as high as a grown-man's eyes, was the one certain place in the kingdom where the tellers observed sunrises and sunsets. In order to confirm the endings and beginnings of the seasons, the tellers had fastened three widely spaced spears—so large only a god could wield them—atop the roofs on both the east and west sides of the courtyard.

When tellers took turns standing at the monolith at sunrise or sunset on the first day of summer and clouds didn't obscure their vision, they'd see the first rays of the rising sun and the last of the setting sun at the tips of the northern spears. On no other day would they see that. On the days when summer turned to autumn and winter to spring, they saw the rising and setting of the sun above the middle spears, due east and west of the monolith. On the day when winter came—and on no other day—they saw the sun rise and set above the southern spears.

By keeping track of the number of days having passed since the last season-changing day, and by remembering what previous years had taught them, the tellers could give the farmers the advice they needed for growing their crops and raising their livestock.

Spring Rain was pleased beyond doubt with that.

"Only the gods," he said, "can make the seasons proceed, the sun and the moon move across the sky, and the years progress, with such certainty. That's how they speak to us."

"Then the gods don't speak to the tellers," Blue Sky said. "They're saying the same thing to everybody. A teller is just a person who wishes to listen."

Spring Rain smiled. "A person who has the time and wishes to make the effort."

"Shouldn't the people know this?" Blue Sky asked. "Would you tell people who aren't tellers or apprentice tellers what you've told me?"

Spring Rain thought for a while. The first rule of the tellerhood was that only the tellers were to know such things. That was how the gods supposedly wanted it.

"I'd tell the people," he finally replied. "I don't think any harm would come from it."

"Then why don't we tell them? Why are tellers so special?"

Blue Sky knew most of the tellers would've warned him not to ask those questions.

"Do the people really want to know?" Spring Rain asked. "Do you think they'd enjoy counting the days of the seasons, or seeing the tiny difference between one day's sunset point and the next? Would they enjoy memorizing those things—and all the stories behind those things?"

Blue Sky, who found his tutor's lips more essential than "those things," remained silent.

"Don't you think," Spring Rain asked, "they're happier making wine and roasting beef?"

"And dancing," Blue Sky replied.

Spring Rain laughed. "And dancing."

*****

Many valley people prospered. Others didn't.

It often seemed as if the gods decided such matters whimsically. Only a small fraction of the people survived childhood, avoided illnesses and accidents, didn't get killed or maimed in a war, and lived long lives. Morning Sun, Rose Leaf, and Blue Sky had older siblings who'd died in their infancy. Their parents had shown them their graves.

All of a man and woman's children might die early, leaving them to enter old age with only their own feeble efforts to count on for survival. They'd end up trading parcels of their land year after year for food, hides, and firewood. Life could be just as woeful if the gods gave a man and woman more children to raise than their land, despite their best efforts, could support—or could be divided into equal portions when they died without leaving each of their heirs too little.

But it often also seemed as if the people, with no help or hindrance from capricious gods, made the difference themselves. The prosperous among the people especially liked to make that claim, ascribing their lot in life to their willingness to engage in arduous work and noting the lack of it on the part of almost all those with little or no land, livestock, or goods for trade.

There were farmers who gave themselves excuses not to venture forth on cold spring days to prepare and plant their fields, even well after the tellers said it was safe to do so. They reaped the diminished harvests they had every reason to expect.

Blue Sky could remember in his childhood two families in his village having less in their barns, granaries, and storage pits than they needed to feed their livestock and themselves through the winter. They came to his parents, seeking a part of what they had, which everybody could see was more than enough to feed their family and livestock no matter how long it would take the next spring and summer to arrive. The neighbors had only the following year's use of a portion of their land to give in return, but Green Field and Gentle Brook were happy to take it.

That maneuver, though, only reduced the neighbors' chances of seeing a bountiful harvest the next year to make up for the past year's deficit. For several years thereafter, they could only request the bounty of Green Field and Gentle Brook's family, and always on the same terms as before. And they were aware, from the beginning, that after their benefactors had worked the land ten years, with the tellers doing the counting, the land became Green Field and Gentle Brook's.

Nevertheless, one of those families did gradually increase its harvests and multiply its livestock to the point where they no longer needed to seek anybody else's surplus. They regained their land and soon became prosperous themselves. The second family, on the other hand, failed in their efforts and ultimately lost all their land to their neighbors.

Few valley people contemplated the failure of others in their kingdom without wishing they didn't have to think about it. Whether the cause of the poverty was a trick of the gods or the unwillingness of the impoverished to work as hard as they needed to do, the people not so situated often did what they could to keep the suffering of their neighbors to a minimum.

This usually took the form of other family members and neighbors helping to do some of the work for the unfortunate people. This was help, but with the limitations of help not bargained for. If the helping people thought the beneficiaries of their labors were merely improvident or indolent, or both, the helpers would be certain to schedule the beneficiaries' planting and harvesting after that of the helpers' own. Those helped therefore couldn't expect to reap a harvest as abundant as that of those who helped them.

The help included tending the livestock of those in need, especially if they were elderly and feeble or had fallen ill. Fortunately, the need for this kind of assistance usually came in the winter, when the helpers, having no fieldwork to do, had sufficient free time for it.

Green Field and Blue Sky would often spend portions of their winter days caring for the livestock of neighbors in need—taking the animals feed and water, cleaning out their pens, and putting down new straw for them to lie on—and not just for the neighbors in their own village. In doing those deeds, though, they never jeopardized the welfare of their own livestock.

In fact, when their neighbors were enjoying periods of good health in the winter, their family could sit near the hearth in the evening, sometimes with visiting neighbors, doing little more than telling one another stories. For Blue Sky, those nights almost made winter agreeable.

Some of the people had no land, no livestock, and little ability or willingness to work for those who did have land and livestock. Many in this group were excessively fond of wine and beer. But if they were pleasant enough and didn't cause unnecessary trouble, their neighbors, who were usually their relatives as well, would ordinarily let them live in an unused house—or even build a small, simple structure for them—and give them just enough food, hides, and firewood to get by.

Few valley people wished to live that way. But some of those who did nevertheless seemed to take pleasure in their lives. They could hardly claim they had insufficient time for telling stories.

There were other individuals who had to be taken before the king. Those who stole, cheated, or wouldn't keep their agreements had to make their victims whole. If they didn't, the king would order enough of their livestock or land taken to do so. If the miscreant had no livestock or land but was able-bodied, the king might order that person to work off the debt.

Those who committed violent acts, other than in war or self-defense, required sterner measures. The king had to order murderers put to death. He could have other criminals killed, but neither Tall Oak nor his father had ever ordered an execution for any crime except murder or attempted murder. In this, they'd departed from the practice of previous kings, who'd had people executed for nothing more than openly criticizing some decision the king or other high official had made.

Many of the murderers were people who'd discovered, or suspected, their partners were going with other people, the victims being the partner, the other person, or both.

A few of the people thought the king shouldn't execute those murderers if their partners were in fact going with other people. But most of the people would laugh whenever they heard somebody make that argument. If the king started to sympathize with those murderers, they'd say, a great many people in the kingdom would be dead before the next day was done.

The king sent to the chief warrior's cages people who committed unjustified violent acts other than murder. Most of these offenders were young men who beat up their wives or children.

Sturdy Limb's cages barely allowed a prisoner room to stand or lie down. They were said to be hot in the summer and cold in the winter. Prisoners invariably complained the food Sturdy Limb's deputies gave them wasn't fit for a rat.

They'd be back before the king on their knees promising they'd never beat up on anybody again. Then the king might have to hear the victims insist the prisoner would never reform and should be kept right where he was.

A few years back, Sturdy Limb's cage-keeping deputies sometimes tried to convince Tall Oak that a prisoner had learned his lesson and would keep his promises.

They were usually wrong, but that hadn't stopped the king from listening to them.

It was obvious to many people the deputies simply wanted less work to do, and Sturdy Limb took their side of the matter because they were his cronies and did his bidding.

And yet Tall Oak stubbornly insisted that his brother would never do such a thing.

Then a released prisoner the deputies had vouched for went home and, wielding his spear, immediately killed his wife in front of their three young children.

Blue Sky could remember hearing Rainbow Evening vehemently agree with Green Field and Gentle Brook, who'd bluntly told Tall Oak that the people were right to be outraged.

Sturdy Limb attempted to rectify the situation by personally spearing the man the moment the king gave the order for his execution, and then refusing to let anybody slit his throat—Green Field had offered to do it—and put an end to his agony, even though it took the man two long days to die.

Although some of the court people and high tellers predictably praised the chief warrior, most of the people were quick to let him know he'd egregiously failed to mollify them.

Some quietly blamed Green Field for refusing to become chief warrior in the first place.

"He never would've let it happen," Blue Sky heard them whisper.

After that, in matters concerning a prisoner's release, the king refused to listen to the deputies, and sometimes he even cut his brother off in the middle of his remarks.

"I'm quite certain of one thing," Sturdy Limb said to Tall Oak on such an occasion, as his allies among the court people and tellers held their breath. "You'd pay a lot more attention to what your chief warrior had to say if Green Field had accepted the position. And he's not your brother."

*****

In the encampments, it didn't make any difference whether a guard's family was prosperous or poor, admirably well behaved or quite lacking in judgment. Day after day, whether he was destined to become a king worthy of adoration in the memory of the people or a murderer facing a prolonged execution as a drunken crowd jeered, he did the same work his comrades did.

When the guards weren't manning the guard posts watching for invaders, they were practicing for battles they prayed to the gods would never come. In the waking time remaining after those guard duties, they had the daily work of the encampment to do: fetching firewood from the forest and water from the nearest spring, preparing food for the encampment table, washing and mending their clothes, and keeping the wind, rain, and snow out of their huts.

*****

In the entrance to the deep ravine below the apprentice tellers' guard post, there was a thicket of gnarled and stunted leaf-losing trees and bushes, now the vivid yellow and red of another autumn come, another summer gone, and another winter on its way.

That was where Blue Sky and Spring Rain first spotted the hill men with their beards and long, dark, curly hair. Maybe ten men in all were walking single file along the bank of the brook the guards could sometimes see sparkling down there when the sun hit it just right.

The hill men carried spears, bows, and arrows, but no shields.

The guards knew hill people were nearby. They'd seen their campfire smoke. One campsite, just beyond the far end of the thicket, had been used, off and on, all summer.

"Hill warriors in the ravine!" Spring Rain yelled to his and Blue Sky's comrades, sounding the alarm as they were instructed to do. "Hill warriors approaching! No shields!"

Within moments, their comrades, scattered about doing their daily chores, repeated the warning. Having seen the campfire smoke and fearing the worst, they'd remained close to the encampment that day.

The hill men, who were beyond the range of the guards' arrows, seemed to be paying no attention to the commotion above them. They remained silent, peering into the thicket.

"Hill warriors!" Blue Sky and Spring Rain's comrades were yelling toward the encampments on either side of them, hoping the wind was right and their comrades in at least one would hear. "Hill warriors attacking the apprentice tellers!"

Because the hill men weren't carrying shields, Spring Rain and Blue Sky remained in the guard post, ready to let their arrows go when the intruders came within range.

The hill men began talking among themselves, now gesturing toward the guard post.

Shouting orders and warnings, the supervising and apprentice tellers were assembling at the place above the guard post where they confronted the enemy. The guards in Morning Sun's encampment were yelling to one another. Some were already running around the canyon rim.

The hill men, though, began walking, single file again, back along the brook the way they'd come. Jumping over the stream, they disappeared behind the lower end of the thicket.

"A lot of times this happens," Spring Rain said. "The yelling scares them away."

He turned and rose to his feet so their comrades farther up the slope could see him.

As he did so, Blue Sky watched a deer leap out of the thicket and over the brook.

"They left!" Spring Rain yelled to the comrades. "They left!

"They knew they'd die!" the comrades yelled back.

The deer, apparently startled by the new outburst of noise, took one look in the direction of the guard post, saw Spring Rain standing upright waving his spear above his head, and bounded back over the stream and into the thicket.

Deerskin, Blue Sky thought. The hill men were wearing deerskin.

At the edge of a clump of bushes surprisingly close, perhaps half the distance between the lower entrance to the ravine and the guard post, and well within the range of Blue Sky's arrows, something or someone was making the lower branches move.

A hill man was crouching there. He seemed to be looking in the direction where the other hill men had gone. Maybe from his position he could still see them.

Blue Sky pulled his arrow back against the string of his bow and took aim.

He wondered why the hill man didn't know he could be seen from the guard post.

Spring Rain and their comrades, Noon Breeze the loudest and most persistent of them all, were still shouting back and forth.

Blue Sky was aiming for the hill man's back, looking for the largest gap in the brush on his side of the man. He didn't want a branch deflecting his shot. The poor fellow had made a mistake, exposing himself to the guard post, and now he'd die for it. His constant moving about on his hands and knees, though, wasn't making the job easy.

Blue Sky also wondered how the hill man could've gotten to where he was without having been seen from the guard post. It didn't appear to be possible. The clump of shrubbery the hill man was in stood all by itself, with barren rocks and gravel surrounding it.

Spring Rain, keeping up his loud conversation with their comrades, still didn't know an enemy was so close to them. Nor could the comrades, from their angle, see the hill man.

Blue Sky could've let his arrow go. With his good aim and the gods, or luck, on his side, he might've wounded the hill man fatally.

But how could he shoot a man in his back? The man wasn't posing a threat either to Blue Sky or his comrades. He appeared to be alone. If he tried to attack the guards by himself, they'd have no trouble subduing him.

Then the hill man turned, looking up at the guard post, and Blue Sky saw his face.

Almost ashamed of himself, Blue Sky pointed his arrow at the ground.

For several moments, he and the hill man stared at one another.

The hill man, who looked surprisingly like a Spring Rain or Many Numbers, but with a beard and long hair, could tell Blue Sky was letting him go.

Blue Sky glanced up at Spring Rain and motioned with his hand to the hill man, urging him to get out of sight before his comrade turned around and spotted him.

Still crouching, the hill man retreated, disappearing into the undergrowth.

But how, Blue Sky asked himself, did he get there in the first place?

Suddenly, the main group of hill warriors, now clutching shields, came charging back around the lower end of the thicket, each of them jumping the brook in one bound as the deer had.

"They're back!" Blue Sky and Spring Rain's comrades yelled.

Spring Rain turned and saw them.

"Retreat!" the comrades yelled down to the guard post. "Retreat!"

The shields could only mean the hill warriors were attacking. Spring Rain and Blue Sky weren't supposed to fire useless arrows at them and leave themselves exposed to the enemy's. They were required to retreat behind their shields and join their comrades at the place where they'd fight the hill warriors with their spears—and kill as many of them as they needed to.

Spring Rain grabbed Blue Sky's shirt.

"Come on," he said. "We've got to go."

Blue Sky didn't move. "They're hunting."

"What?" Spring Rain asked, incredulously, looking at the hill men.

"They're after a deer. It's in the thicket."

"You're crazy. They don't need shields for hunting."

"They got their shields because they're afraid we'll shoot arrows at them. When they come within our range."

And they were coming within the range of any arrows shot at them from the guard post.

"We've got to go," Spring Rain insisted.

"Go. I'm staying here. I want to see if they get their deer."

Spring Rain stared at the hill men advancing toward them behind their shields.

Somebody in the ravine was shouting at the top of his voice.

The hill men were now within range of arrows from the guard post.

"Retreat! Retreat!" Blue Sky and Spring Rain's comrades yelled at them.

Blue Sky briefly glimpsed, at the bottom of the ravine, the man he'd seen in the bushes. But how had he gone from the one place to the other without being noticed by any of the guards?

"We've got to retreat!" Spring Rain insisted. "They'll kill us!"

"What good would that do them?" Blue Sky asked. "Do they eat humans?"

In a few of the valley people's stories, the hill people did. Almost all the people who lived in the town and many of the farmers, including Green Field and Gentle Brook, didn't believe the hill people, as odious as they were, practiced cannibalism. In support of their view, they'd cite the opinions of the river people, who ridiculed the idea. Some of the farmers, though, especially those far removed from the town like the orphan boys' relatives, could still be heard claiming the hill people would roast farmers and eat them, especially their tender children, if they got the chance.

One hill man dropped his shield and raised his arrow to take aim at the guard post.

Spring Rain and Blue Sky already had their arrows aimed at him.

"Don't fire," Blue Sky whispered to Spring Rain. "We don't need to fight with these men."

Blue Sky could see the hill man was acting on impulse. Even with his comrades on either side of him attempting to cover him with their shields, more of him was exposed to Spring Rain and Blue Sky than either of them, behind their stone wall, was to him. And he faced two arrows, while his adversaries chanced only one from him.

Blue Sky realized the man who'd been in the bushes was the person yelling at the hunters.

Spring Rain and Blue Sky's comrades had given up shouting at them to retreat.

One of the hill men, apparently their leader, motioned for his comrade to lower his arrow.

As the hill man complied, Blue Sky lowered his own arrow—and reached out and lowered Spring Rain's for him.

The lead hill warrior said something to his comrades.

The man who'd been in the clump of bushes had stopped yelling.

Walking backward behind their shields, the main body of hill men slowly retreated. When they were well beyond the range of arrows from the guard post, they lowered their shields, turned, and left the ravine again.

"They didn't get their deer," Blue Sky said to Spring Rain. "They must be disappointed."

On the other hand, their comrades above and behind them, watching the hill men go, broke into cheers.

Chapter 6

The hill men didn't come back.

Blue Sky and Spring Rain were rewarded for their disobedience. Even though they'd clearly failed to follow orders, their comrades considered them heroes.

They'd faced the enemy, arrow to arrow, all by themselves, and the enemy chose to flee.

Blue Sky insisted his comrades were giving them far too much credit. The hill men were hunting, he said. They were after a deer. He'd seen it leap out of the thicket and, scared by the clamor from above, back into it. He was certain the hill men had reluctantly decided to break off their pursuit of the deer rather than come any closer to the guard post and get into a pointless fight.

Spring Rain agreed with Blue Sky they'd done nothing heroic. But he also said he'd seen no deer jumping out of or into the thicket, or anything else to indicate the hill men were hunting.

Morning Sun, who'd taken his position on the battleground and was now down at the guard post with all the others, looked at Blue Sky and laughed.

"Farmer boy," he said, "deer hunt or not, you and Spring Rain got us out of that one. And the rest of us are damned glad you did."

He threw his arms around Blue Sky's shoulders.

"And we don't want to hear another word about a deer hunt," he said. "You and Spring Rain made the hill warriors go away, and we're still safe. That's all there is to it."

*****

The guards from both sides of the canyon chose to hold a celebration that evening at the apprentice tellers' encampment, drinking extra wine for the occasion.

The prince himself, and only the prince, could wait upon Spring Rain and Blue Sky.

Noon Breeze sat across the table from Blue Sky and smirked, campfire flames reflecting in his eyes like dawn sunlight on the brook at the bottom of the ravine.

"The prince made you shut up," he said. "I didn't think anybody could do that."

Morning Sun, seated next to Blue Sky but speaking with Solemn Promise on his other side, pretended he wasn't paying any attention to Noon Breeze. So did Solemn Promise.

"You're still in love with him," Noon Breeze continued, knowing Morning Sun, Solemn Promise, and most of the other celebrants could hear what he was saying.

Noon Breeze also knew Blue Sky would be too embarrassed to even attempt a reply.

Spring Rain, on the other side of Blue Sky, glared at Noon Breeze.

"It's so obvious," Noon Breeze added, snickering. "You're hopelessly in love with him."

Under the table, where nobody could see, Spring Rain took Blue Sky's hand.

*****

Spring Rain and Many Numbers told Blue Sky they hadn't bothered to wait until they became men before they went together. They started in the woods outside the town one spring day when they still had more than another year of boyhood ahead of them.

That autumn, they went from house to house in the town and in the nearby villages, asking people for any old hides they had and no longer needed.

Blue Sky could remember hearing that two orphan boys came to the home village and spoke with his mother while Green Field, Rose Leaf, and he were harvesting lentils. Gentle Brook gave them a number of scarcely used hides. She also insisted the boys use two of her family's horses and one of their carts to haul back to the town all the hides they'd collected that day.

Many Numbers and Spring Rain sewed the hides together and hung them from the girders around the part of the orphanage where they slept.

Law Keeper, who ordinarily took little interest in what happened in the orphanage, thought they shouldn't be allowed to do that, and his high tellers were quick, as usual, to agree.

Fair Judge spoke up, though, insisting the two boys wouldn't do anything wrong.

"They're like brothers," she said.

Among the high tellers and their acolytes, Law Keeper heaped ridicule on that idea, portraying Fair Judge as a deluded mother who couldn't believe her little boys, who weren't so little anymore, were capable of gross misbehavior.

He nevertheless chose to drop the matter. Many of the younger tellers believed he did so only after one of his high tellers was brave enough to drop hints that the people might not care for his seeming to pay too much attention to what two boys in the orphanage were doing.

If Many Numbers and Spring Rain had been caught, they would've ended up in Sturdy Limb's cages, probably until they came of age. They told Blue Sky nobody in the orphanage had ever followed them during their many evening walks into the woods or lifted up their wall of hides to see what they were doing behind it.

Blue Sky suspected none of those things had happened mostly because nobody had wanted to see something they'd have to report to Law Keeper and Sturdy Limb.

"If I'd been in the orphanage with you," Blue Sky told them, "I would've looked under your hides. I would've followed you into the woods, too."

Many Numbers laughed. "I'm sure you would've," he said.

"But you never would've told anybody what you saw," Spring Rain said.

"No," Blue Sky agreed. "I never would've done that. But I would've looked."

He and Morning Sun had touched one another one day when they were both aroused. He'd hoped something like that would happen again, but it never did.

*****

During the next full-moon holiday, Tall Oak and Green Field traveled with Rose Leaf, Many Numbers, and the other young women and tellers bringing supplies to sunrise pass.

The king sent a messenger around the canyon rim to summon Blue Sky to the encampment for the court people's sons.

Before Rose Leaf had left at the end of her first full-moon holiday on sunrise pass, she'd told Morning Sun she wished to inform their parents she and he intended to have the tellers bless their marriage when autumn came again.

Morning Sun, though, had insisted he should be with her when they made their wishes known. But that wouldn't be possible before he could go to the town as a messenger. And his turn to do that, determined by a drawing of straws, wasn't until spring.

His comrades enjoyed the chance to be a messenger and make a visit home. Certainly, though, they would've let their best friend the prince go out of order. But Morning Sun, being the prince he was, wasn't going to ask them to do that.

So instead he asked Rose Leaf to wait.

Rose Leaf smiled at Morning Sun, kissed him good-bye, embraced her brother, and went into the forest with the other women and tellers as they began their descent into the valley.

One full moon later, Morning Sun met Blue Sky on the path around the canyon rim.

"Rose Leaf told our parents," the prince said.

Blue Sky knew she would. Their parents would've soon found out anyway.

When the women and tellers who'd traveled with Rose Leaf returned to the town, they quickly let it be known that the prince had spent most of his holiday with her. And few people failed to understand it was past the time when the two of them could still claim their meetings were those of childhood friends. In fact, the prince and Rose Leaf had made no attempt to do so.

"And what did our parents say?" Blue Sky asked.

"Nothing. They simply told her our fathers would come here with her during the next full-moon holiday. They told her they'd say what they needed to say in front of all three of us."

As soon as the messenger had shown up at the apprentice tellers' encampment, Blue Sky took off, running most of the way. He looked forward to the encounter as much as he dreaded it.

Morning Sun knew he wasn't supposed to fall in love with Rose Leaf. But he'd done it anyway, putting himself ahead of all the other men who wanted her—maybe even taking pleasure in beating them out. He might've been a prince as worthy as the people thought he was, but Blue Sky also knew he wasn't above that.

Blue Sky looked at Morning Sun and shook his head.

"Why do our parents think this is any concern of mine?" he asked.

Morning Sun laughed. He had Blue Sky as cornered as he had everybody else.

"Because it is," he replied. "You're the farmer boy who taught Rose Leaf and me everything we know about misbehaving. And now you're going to pay the price for that."

*****

Tall Oak, Green Field, and Rose Leaf were beyond the encampment huts and as close to the edge of the canyon as their people would go. They were gazing at the steep hills and chasms that lay beyond the mountains encircling the valley as if they were seeing them in a dream.

When Morning Sun and Blue Sky drew near, the three visitors turned and embraced Blue Sky. They'd already embraced the prince.

"Your mother and Rainbow Evening are well," Tall Oak said. "They send their greetings. They miss you."

"Yes," Green Field agreed. "We all miss both you and the prince. Greatly miss you."

It was always the seven of them, the five people present and Gentle Brook and Rainbow Evening. They could say anything they wished. Even the children could tell the king he'd chosen perfect fools to be his chief warrior and first teller. Tall Oak would sigh and once again note that the people who should've been in those positions had turned them down.

The person who'd refused to be the first teller was Fair Judge's older brother, now deceased. He would've taken the job if Green Field had agreed to become chief warrior. He had no interest, though, in attempting to run the kingdom with Sturdy Limb.

Tall Oak turned to Blue Sky. "Our people were glad to hear you and Spring Rain held off the hill warriors. Doing it by yourselves was remarkable. The people admire your courage."

After the incident with the hill people, the sunrise pass encampments sent two messengers to the town, as they were required to do.

"We weren't courageous at all," Blue Sky said. "The hill men were chasing a deer. They didn't want a fight with us. They wanted a deer. For their families to eat. For their children to eat. I saw the deer they were after. We kept them from getting it. What was courageous about that?"

Tall Oak looked at Green Field and gave him the usual indulgent smile.

Blue Sky was Green Field and Gentle Brook's son. Therefore, even the great king himself would listen to what he had to say, no matter how absurd it got at times.

Rose Leaf and Morning Sun looked at Blue Sky. They knew as well as he did that this was a mere prelude. The five of them had something far more important to talk about than hill people and their insistence on hunting—if that's what they were doing—where they weren't allowed to do it.

Tall Oak turned to Blue Sky again. "At court we've discussed your version of the attack. So have your father and I. I personally believe you're quite wrong. Hill people will take any opportunity they can to kill or harm our people. They therefore only need to understand one thing: if they come too close to our valley, we'll kill them. It's as simple as that."

Blue Sky knew it wasn't as simple as that. How were they to justify killing people who weren't trying to kill them? Who was the hill man in the clump of bushes trying to kill?

"It doesn't matter what brings them into the ravine," Tall Oak added. "They've got to understand how far they can come. They've got to know if they go beyond that point, they'll die. It's as simple as that."

Green Field nodded his head. "The people are convinced the attack was another probe. Like all the others—testing our defenses, looking for a soft spot."

"Maybe some of their attacks have been probes," Blue Sky said. "Maybe other times they're not. Maybe usually they're just looking for animals to kill. Now would be the time to stock up for the winter. Maybe they're from far away. Maybe they aren't that familiar with this area. Maybe they don't really know where they're allowed to be."

"That's a lot of maybes," Tall Oak said. "Maybe, as I said before, we don't give a damn what they're doing. We just want them to stay away."

Green Field had his eyes fixed on his son's. When he was younger, he could see what Blue Sky saw. So could Gentle Brook. All their older neighbors and relatives said that.

Blue Sky once got his father and mother to agree the hill people must at least think the way their people did. What was logical to valley people would be equally logical to hill people. That was clearly the case for river people. Why should it be different for hill people? When Fair Judge heard the argument from Rainbow Evening, she agreed it made sense and might even be right.

Green Field turned to Tall Oak.

"There could be some truth in what Blue Sky is saying," he said. "We've always assumed the hill people are testing us. Maybe they aren't."

"Well, even so," Tall Oak asked, with his usual sigh, "don't we have to assume every attack is a probe and not just some deer hunt gone wrong? How are our guards supposed to tell the difference? Are they all so clear-sighted and perceptive as your son, Green Field?"

"Of course they are," Blue Sky interjected. "I can only see what they see."

Morning Sun looked at Blue Sky and shook his head. "That's isn't the truth, and you know it."

Green Field chose not to respond to Tall Oak's question.

Tall Oak, frowning, looked at Blue Sky again.

"The people admire what you and Spring Rain did," he said. "So do I. Standing your ground was brave. Please tell Spring Rain I said so. On the other hand, as your king, I'm telling you to obey the orders you're given. When you're supposed to retreat, you must retreat. Please let Spring Rain know that as well. The people love him. They love you, too. He and you have to set a good example for your comrades. I'm sure you know that."

Blue Sky could scarcely believe the opening the king had given him.

"You're right," he said. "I understand that's what the heroes Tall Oak and Green Field did in the last war."

Valley people paying their first visit to sunrise pass almost always asked to see the exact spot where the hill warriors had captured Green Field and Tall Oak, who were standing on it now with their grown children.

Full Harvest was the one yelling the loudest to his comrades that the hill warriors had gotten the prince. Otherwise, the hill warriors might've considered Green Field and Tall Oak, despite their fighting prowess, nothing more than two unlucky warriors they had to eliminate, the sooner the better, opening up their bellies with spear thrusts and throwing their bodies into the canyon to finish them off.

But that time the hill warriors held their spears back and instead shouted what seemed to be instructions to the two men they'd surrounded. Green Field somehow guessed he and Tall Oak could choose to become prisoners or be killed. He also guessed he and Tall Oak had to lay down their spears if they wished to become prisoners. They did so.

Valley people could see something else when they got to sunrise pass. Holding off the hill people there would've saved the lives of a great number of people they loved.

The valley people had long since agreed Tall Oak and Green Field were correct in wanting to defend the kingdom in the mountains, and Tall Oak's father's order to retreat to the bluff had created the horrific disaster the war became.

"Is this the first time you've come back here?" Blue Sky asked his father and the king.

"Yes," Green Field replied.

When the hill people came up the ravine that day, the valley people's rear ranks, unable to see for themselves that the number of enemy warriors attacking them wasn't overwhelming, changed their minds and made their fateful decision to retreat with the king.

Only two of the warriors who'd remained with Tall Oak and Green Field to the end survived the fighting on sunrise pass: Full Harvest and East Land.

"The queen and I," Tall Oak said to Blue Sky, "would be grief-stricken if you were killed or seriously injured up here. You're like a second son to us. You know that."

Green Field looked at Blue Sky and put his hand on his son's shoulder.

"There's one person in our kingdom who doesn't admire your bravery," he said. "That's your mother. Since she heard what you did, I've often found her with tears in her eyes. She says you're too damned brave—you'll get yourself killed up here, and she'll never see you alive again."

Rose Leaf, nodding her head, looked at Blue Sky. Tears welled in her eyes.

"It's been very difficult for her," she agreed. "She doesn't deserve having to live in fear."

Morning Sun was looking at Blue Sky, too.

"You should do what you're told to do," he weighed in. "Nobody wants to see you dead."

Tall Oak turned to Morning Sun as if his remarks had surprised him.

"Thank you for saying that," he said to the prince. "I can only hope he'll listen to you."

Blue Sky thought it best to say nothing further as to the likelihood—or unlikelihood, more likely—of the hill people's evil intentions in the ravine and his bravery in the guard post.

*****

"Now," Tall Oak said, looking at the prince, "I'll get to the next thing we need to discuss, and then Green Field and I'll be gone."

When the king and Green Field had showed up with the young women, Morning Sun's comrades asked them to stay for a full-moon meal in their honor. But the unexpected guests declined. The comrades assumed that their seeing again the place where they'd been captured in the last war weighed too heavily for them to stay any longer than they needed to.

"First," Tall Oak continued, "as you all three know, you must never discuss this matter with any other person. Never."

The king looked beyond the prince at the encampment.

"I asked your comrades to remain well beyond earshot," he said. "Please thank them for complying with my request."

The comrades thought the king and Green Field had come to chastise Blue Sky for his blatant disobedience. They all knew by then Spring Rain had nothing to do with it. The king and Green Field would surely make a greater impression on Blue Sky than the chief warrior and first teller he openly despised could ever hope to.

Tall Oak looked at Morning Sun again.

"You and Rose Leaf may not marry," he said. "Rainbow Evening, Green Field, Gentle Brook, and I have always made it clear you and she may not do that. Under no circumstances will you do so. I absolutely forbid it. And don't hope I'll ever change my mind on this matter."

Tall Oak turned to Rose Leaf.

"I'm sorry," he said. "I don't blame you for wanting to become Morning Sun's wife. It isn't difficult to see the entire kingdom is in love with him. His mother and I are extremely proud he's become the prince he is today. But you simply can't marry him. We've always made that clear to you, too. Your parents, Rainbow Evening, and I deeply regret you and he wish to disobey us."

Morning Sun defiantly put his arm around Rose Leaf.

"Then we'll live together without the benefit of a wedding blessed by the tellers," he said.

"You'll never do that either," Tall Oak countered.

"Some people in your kingdom do that," Morning Sun said.

Tall Oak looked at Morning Sun as if the prince were a child again.

"My father," he said, "saw no reason to punish ordinary people for doing that. Nor do I. But you're the prince. You and Rose Leaf will neither marry nor live together. I absolutely forbid your doing either of those things."

Morning Sun looked at his father as if the man had struck him.

"Rose Leaf and I will have children together anyway," Morning Sun said. "Even if we choose to obey your ridiculous order and don't live in the same house. You can't stop us from having children together."

"I know you and Rose Leaf won't do that," Green Field interjected. "Neither of you would bring an unwanted child into the kingdom. Neither of you is that uncaring."

Blue Sky could remain silent no longer. "Why would any child of theirs be unwanted?"

Tall Oak glared at Blue Sky. "Why would anybody not want to avoid more trouble than this kingdom could possibly bear?" he asked.

"What are you talking about?" Blue Sky asked the king. "How could a child born to Rose Leaf and Morning Sun possibly cause more trouble than the kingdom could bear?"

Tall Oak had his eyes fixed on Blue Sky. "I was born to rule this kingdom," he said.

"Nobody disputes that," Blue Sky said.

"As your king, I'm telling you the trouble for the kingdom will greatly outweigh whatever Morning Sun and Rose Leaf gain from what they wish to do."

"That isn't possible," Blue Sky countered. "They wish to live together and have children. If any two humans wish to do that, no king worthy of the title should attempt to stop them."

Morning Sun's comrades were turning to look. They couldn't hear what the king and the four people with him were saying, but they could tell the prince and Blue Sky were vehemently arguing with their fathers.

"Morning Sun is the prince," Tall Oak insisted.

"It doesn't matter who he is," Blue Sky said. "He and Rose Leaf wish to marry, live together, and have children. I don't care if you are the king. You can't stop them. The people won't let you stop them."

"I understand," the king said, "the people are as fond of you and Rose Leaf as they are the prince. But I also know their affection won't lead them into treachery."

"We won't call it treachery," Blue Sky said. "We'll find some other name for it. The gods will bless us. They'll be kind, as they always are, to people seeking justice in this world."

Green Field, who'd greeted those remarks with a scornful look, turned to Morning Sun.

"Rose Leaf," he began, "says you and she wish to have a wedding ceremony next autumn. That'll give you and her three seasons to think about it. In that time, I'm confident you'll both decide you wish to act responsibly. I'm also quite certain you'll both find happiness with other people in our kingdom."

Rose Leaf's eyes were flashing angrily, like lightning in a storm.

"What if we nevertheless decide to disobey you and the king?" she asked.

Green Field turned to Tall Oak, who was looking at Rose Leaf, choosing his words.

"Only the tellers can say," the king replied, almost whispering now, making certain nobody else could hear him, "how many generations it's been since our kingdom has seen a person sacrificed. And I don't wish to be the next king to order our chief warrior's men to perform such a deed. But I can assure you, if any child is born to you and Morning Sun, I'll order it put to death."

Their arms around one another, Rose Leaf and Morning Sun looked as if the king had just ordered them put to death.

"That's the most disgusting thing I've ever heard," Blue Sky said.

The comrades in the distance could see Blue Sky was livid and the prince and Rose Leaf frightened.

"You can't possibly mean what you're saying," Blue Sky continued. "The people will never let you get away with it."

Tall Oak looked at Blue Sky without making a response.

Blue Sky turned to his father. "This king has obviously taken leave of his senses."

Green Field also chose not to respond.

"Did you hear what he said?" Blue Sky asked his father. "He said he'd order the death of an innocent child—his and your own grandchild no less."

Blue Sky looked at the king, making no effort to conceal his contempt.

"Some of our people," he said, "believe the hill people sacrifice their children—and eat them, too. If we're going to be doing the same horrific things they do, why don't we invite them to live in the valley with us? We should get along with them quite well. We'll all be happy savages, killing and eating children together whenever we choose."

Green Field shook his head. "Tall Oak will never order a child killed."

"Are you losing your hearing?" Blue Sky loudly asked his father. "When Rose Leaf and Morning Sun have a child, this king will order it killed. He just promised us he would."

Rose Leaf and Morning Sun still speechlessly clung to one another.

"But only if they have a child," Green Field countered.

Such a child might've already been on its way. It was Blue Sky's impression Rose Leaf and Morning Sun had already done everything that needed to be done to create one. He had no idea, though, what steps they'd taken to keep from having a child before their wedding.

"I'm certain Tall Oak's well in command of his senses," Green Field continued. "And make no mistake about it, he does mean what he's saying to the prince and Rose Leaf. Our kingdom depends upon their doing as he says. And your behaving yourself, too."

Green Field looked at Rose Leaf and Morning Sun, his lower lip trembling.

"And that means, I'm sorry, but you'll have to find other people to have children with."

For a moment at least, he pulled himself together again.

"We all know you can both have anybody else you want," he said.

Morning Sun straightened himself up as well, glaring at Green Field.

"We don't want anybody else," he said. "We want each other."

Blue Sky looked at his father as if he were seeing him for the first time.

"And neither you nor the king," Blue Sky said, "have given us one possible reason why they shouldn't have each other."

Green Field shook his head again.

"I agree with you that individuals in our kingdom are important," he said. "Most of the time, they should be able to do as they please. But even you have to agree the kingdom comes first, and people can't always do as they please."

Blue Sky shook his head as vigorously as his father had.

"That's not a reason," he said, loudly, "why Rose Leaf and Morning Sun shouldn't want and have each other. What's your reason for saying they shouldn't? Tell us. Now."

"It's for the kingdom," Green Field replied.

"Their being together," Blue Sky came back, "is for the kingdom!"

"It won't be," Green Field said, quietly again. "When they think about it long enough, they'll change their minds. They'll do the right thing."

His face was wet with tears.

Blue Sky couldn't go on. He chose not to speak.

"Never forget this," Tall Oak said, his gaze shifting from Blue Sky to Rose Leaf to Morning Sun. "Never forget what Green Field and I have told you today."

Abruptly, he and Green Field said good-bye to their children and walked past the encampment comrades, who were shocked into silence and immobility, to the edge of the forest, where the king's two oxen were waiting hitched to a cart partly filled with jars of honey.

Morning Sun and his comrades had come across a beehive in a tree, got it down without suffering an inordinate number of stings, and they were sending a good portion of its contents home for the families of the women they were pursuing.

Tall Oak and Green Field walked beside the oxen into the late-autumn darkness beneath the evergreens. They didn't look back at the place where they'd been captured in their youth—and where their children, grown now, remained, finding it nearly impossible to believe they'd heard the two exceptionally decent men who were their fathers say what they'd said.

*****

Blue Sky turned to Morning Sun and Rose Leaf.

"I only hope," he said, "you don't change your minds. The people will never let anybody kill your children. I'll gladly die to keep that from happening."

"I'm not changing my mind," Morning Sun said, staring at the forest, his eyes glazed.

"Nor am I," Rose Leaf agreed, tasting her tears again.

"This is the way it will be," Blue Sky said. "When Tall Oak tells the people he'll kill your child, they'll have to choose. They can let a clearly addled king order your child killed—and never forget the horror of it as long as they live. Or they can ask the tellers to declare Morning Sun their king—and enjoy their lives ever after, roasting beef, baking bread, drinking wine."

Spring Rain had told Blue Sky a story not well known. One of their people's kings, having lived far more years than most of their people did, had lost his mind. Although he was breathing, eating, drinking, talking, and ambling to and fro, the tellers decided he was dead, at least to the point where he could no longer rule. They made the prince the king. The people, after seeing the old king themselves, readily agreed that what the tellers had done was proper.

In the case of Blue Sky, Rose Leaf, and Morning Sun, though, if the people chose not to agree with them that Tall Oak had lost his mind, they'd be guilty of treason. And end up—even if they were the children of heroes—dying for their misbehavior.

Chapter 7

The nights grew colder. When Blue Sky and Spring Rain slept, their bodies touched, sometimes from head to toe. Blue Sky began to regret Spring Rain already had another man.

Rose Leaf came back to sunrise pass every full-moon holiday that autumn. She and Morning Sun often paid visits to the apprentice tellers' encampment.

Rose Leaf got the guards to show her how they practiced fending off invading hill warriors. She borrowed their spears so she could learn how to open an opponent's belly without first taking a fatal thrust in her own.

She'd sit in the guard post with the supervising and apprentice tellers while they told her all the stories they'd been told of the battles fought in the ravine, explaining where the hill men had come from, how many there were, and how they'd fought, died, and fled.

She competed in running and spear-throwing contests with the guards as if she were a man. They were surprised she could sometimes beat them. Blue Sky and Morning Sun, her long-time opponents who already knew she could, lustily cheered her on.

She even wrestled with Noon Breeze, who was no taller than she and just as slender.

She'd had no previous experience with that sport, though. When she, Blue Sky, and the prince were children, she'd wanted to wrestle with them, but they'd declined to do that. Blue Sky, because she was his sister. Morning Sun, because he was a boy and she was a girl. When they grew older, he told Blue Sky he was afraid he might end up inside her and not be able to stop himself.

Rose Leaf nevertheless won her match with Noon Breeze.

Only the prince and her brother could serve her that evening.

She and Spring Rain sang the goddess of love's song together, while the young tellers played their instruments. Although Rose Leaf and Spring Rain sang the same words, their gestures toward one another made it clear she was taking the part of the goddess, and he that of the fatally wounded human warrior she'd fallen in love with.

Some of those listening to them struggled not to dilute their wine with tears.

Before their encampment, most of the apprentice tellers had only seen the prince sitting up high with the king and queen on ceremony days. Some of them from the far reaches of the valley—

Noon Breeze was one—had never seen him at all. Now they took every opportunity they could to wrestle with him.

Rose Leaf told them she didn't dare compete in athletic games or practice warfare with the guards in Morning Sun's encampment.

"She thinks her female companions wouldn't care for that," Morning Sun explained.

"In this encampment," Noon Breeze hastened to interject, "we don't allow jealousy."

He could say that, but Blue Sky had seen it erupt more than once.

Blue Sky, Spring Rain, and Many Numbers helped Rose Leaf and Morning Sun build a hut in a clearing halfway between the two encampments. Most of their people would've feared being so alone in the forest. But Rose Leaf and the prince said they liked being off by themselves, as Spring Rain and Many Numbers were in their ivy-covered house on the bluff.

Rose Leaf and the prince would sit at the encampment table and talk at length with the supervising and apprentice tellers. Morning Sun's pose of indifference toward what the tellers knew was gone.

Rose Leaf was especially interested in hearing them tell and retell the stories most of the people seldom or never heard.

Once, when Spring Rain said the words "the end," as the tellers always did when they finished a story, she shook her head.

"That story hasn't ended," she insisted.

"The tellers have always ended that story there," Many Numbers said.

"But it can't end there," she argued. "We're still here. No story of our people can ever end—not as long as we're still alive making it go forward."

The supervising and apprentice tellers looked at one another and shook their heads.

"But we're not in that story," Spring Rain said.

"Oh, but we are," Rose Leaf gently disagreed, taking his hand. "We are."

The story Spring Rain had told was the one where the tellers made the prince the king while the old king, claiming to be in the grasp of ghosts and other fearsome creatures nobody else could see or hear, was still alive.

*****

"The people are looking forward to a certain wedding ceremony next autumn," Many Numbers said. "The one involving a certain person's sister and the prince."

"And the days of feasting and drinking that'll go with it," the "certain person" added. "That's what the people are looking forward to."

Many Numbers laughed. "But there appears to be some question whether the king and queen will provide the food and wine for it—or even allow the ceremony to take place."

It was the first night of the third and last full-moon holiday before the winter solstice. As soon as Many Numbers had arrived that afternoon, he and Spring Rain did what they needed most to do, while Blue Sky helped prepare an evening meal. And had to put up with Noon Breeze's repeated insinuations that Blue Sky wanted to do with Spring Rain what they both knew Many Numbers was doing in the hut with him at that very moment.

Blue Sky finally decided to humor Noon Breeze and concede that was the case. In fact, because he couldn't have either the prince or Spring Rain, he was a broken, inconsolable man. His life would undoubtedly end early in some disaster of his own making. His story would be a bleak tragedy, meant to teach those who were fortunate enough to hear it a lesson not to be forgotten.

But now the broken man and his two orphan friends were viewing the start of that night's revel. The supervising and apprentice tellers were singing and dancing around the campfire, attempting to decide which of their comrades they wanted to go with when the music stopped.

"The court people's daughters have given up on the prince," Many Numbers revealed. "Graciously, too. When I come up here with them, I can't help but hear them talking. Seems now they're hoping they can at least get themselves a Valley Defender or a Solemn Promise."

"They'll be getting a good man," Spring Rain said, "if they get either of them."

"But they're not the prince," Many Numbers countered.

"Anybody who isn't the prince should be glad he isn't," Blue Sky said. "Someday Morning Sun will have to order people executed. Valley Defender and Solemn Promise won't. We won't."

Many Numbers shook his head. "The court people and the tellers don't see it that way."

"They should," Spring Rain said. "I wouldn't want to be the prince either. When he's the king, he'll have to listen to all those people dissatisfied with the decisions the tellers make."

The people often asked Fair Judge, Many Numbers, Spring Rain, or another of Fair Judge's followers to hear their complaints. They grumbled that many of the other tellers paid too little attention to what they said, hurried them along, and made them leave out significant details. There were times when both sides to a dispute ended up unhappy, forcing the king to hear them.

"I never had any doubt about it," Blue Sky said. "I knew the people would want to see Morning Sun and Rose Leaf marry and have children together."

Many Numbers looked at Blue Sky and smiled.

"And we all know the reason why they would," he said.

"The people like Rose Leaf," Spring Rain interjected. "She sincerely cares about them."

Many Numbers, smiling again, looked at Spring Rain. "That's a sweet thought," he said, "and true. But we shouldn't overlook that Rose Leaf is Green Field and Gentle Brook's daughter."

"What does that have to do with it?" Blue Sky asked. "You're saying the people favor Rose Leaf because she's a daughter of farmers?"

Many Numbers apparently found those questions as amusing as Spring Rain's remarks.

"You could say that," Many Numbers agreed. "You could also say the people know Tall Oak listens to Green Field. That's why the people are grateful Tall Oak is their king. They also know Tall Oak listens to Gentle Brook and their children. In private, I understand, they're free to say anything they please to both the king and queen. And the prince is right there with them. Gossip has it Green Field's son sometimes gets into heated arguments with the king."

Many Numbers was looking at Blue Sky with a smirk on his face.

"I understand," he continued, "they did it up here on sunrise pass during the last full-moon holiday. Rumor has it they were arguing whether the king should allow Morning Sun to marry Rose Leaf. But nobody has been able to figure out why the king shouldn't want them to marry. If the two people in question are somehow sister and brother, why are their parents still such good friends? The court people and tellers are totally mystified."

Rose Leaf had started the "rumor" with the young women during their return to the town after the last full-moon holiday. But she, Morning Sun, and Blue Sky had decided it was too early to bother the people with talk of child sacrifice and treason.

"Even Morning Sun's rivals admit he deserves Rose Leaf," Many Numbers remarked.

"I feel sorry for them anyway," Spring Rain said. "What man who wanted to go with a woman wouldn't want Rose Leaf?"

Many Numbers looked at Spring Rain, laughing now.

"You might be able to advise her how to deal with that," he said. "Noon Breeze tells me every last man in our kingdom who wants to go with a man wants you. I suppose you also feel sorry for all those men."

Spring Rain, gazing at the revelers around the fire, chose not to respond.

Being one of "those men," Blue Sky took his hand.

"They say Early Harvest at first tried to act as if the news made no difference to him," Many Numbers went on. "But later, when somebody in his encampment happened to mention Rose Leaf, he burst into tears."

"Early Harvest wept in front of his comrades?" Blue Sky asked.

"That's what they say," Many Numbers replied. "Most of them his cousins, too. They tried to console him. Some of them told him Morning Sun got Rose Leaf only because he's the prince. But Early Harvest turned on them and told them to shut up. He said he wouldn't tolerate anybody putting down the prince or Rose Leaf. He said their marriage will be good for the kingdom, and that's all that matters. He said the people are right to be pleased. Then he broke down again."

"That's sad," Spring Rain said. "He would've been a good mate for Rose Leaf."

"She can't have two," Many Numbers remarked, drily. "Somebody has to lose."

Many Numbers, unsmiling now, turned to Blue Sky.

"Let's get to the heart of the matter," he said. "Do you have any idea why the king wouldn't want the prince to marry your sister?"

"No, I don't," Blue Sky replied. "I can't come up with a reason. Neither can Morning Sun or Rose Leaf. But we'd like to know, more than anything else, what it is."

*****

Several times after Blue Sky and Spring Rain heroically saved the kingdom from marauding hill warriors, Blue Sky could tell the hill man he'd seen in the clump of undergrowth was there again. Sometimes he could glimpse a shadow not ordinarily present, sometimes a sudden brief movement in the shrubbery he couldn't imagine the wind causing.

Once, after Spring Rain made a sarcastic remark concerning Noon Breeze, Blue Sky thought he heard the hill man laugh.

Blue Sky dismissed the thought. Hill people couldn't understand them.

Whenever Blue Sky believed the hill man was present, he seemed to be alone, as he was the day he came close to feeling the sting of a farmer's arrow. Blue Sky never saw more than one shadow, or the multiple movements in the bushes he'd expect two or more people to cause.

The hill man had to have some way to get to where he was without being seen from the guard post. He also had to have some reason to wish to be there.

Then one day a steady rain followed by a cold and strong north wind stripped the last leaves off the shrubs and bushes in the thicket as well as the clump standing by itself.

Afterward and all through the bare-branches time of the year, Blue Sky neither saw nor heard anything to make him think the hill man was nearby.

None of the guards around the valley reported sighting hill people that winter, although at sunrise pass they could sometimes see smoke rising in the distance from what they assumed were the hill people's campfires. The cold season was always like that, the previous year's guards and the supervising tellers said. They warned the new guards not to let it breed complacence—which could be deadly in the spring, when the hill people were certain to return.

*****

"They don't have any reason to be in the mountains in the winter."

That, over wine with Spring Rain and Many Numbers, was Blue Sky's opinion. And he could see Many Numbers, his smile bordering on a sneer, wouldn't be easy to convince.

"We're here," Many Numbers said. "Wouldn't that be reason enough?"

They were in the hut Blue Sky and Spring Rain shared, listening to the wind. It was the second night of the last full-moon holiday of that autumn. The three of them would sleep together just as they sat before the fire: Many Numbers and Blue Sky on either side of Spring Rain.

Guards sleeping in a hut in the mountains on such a night were after all the warmth they could get from the person or people they were with. Their fire could never provide enough, or they'd be taking a chance their hut would go up in flames. If they were lucky and got out of it before it did, they might also watch the entire encampment burn down, while their comrades considered accomplishing their execution without waiting for an order from the king.

At least once, that had happened. Luckily, the king at the time was kind to the volunteer executioners. Although the tellers argued he couldn't do it, he made his execution order apply retroactively and appointed as executioners the guards who'd killed their reckless comrades. It might've helped that one of the executioners was a prince.

"I'm sure the hill people know we're here," Blue Sky tried to answer Many Numbers. "We can see their campfires. They can surely see ours. But ours just mark for them the mountains they can't cross over, the valley they can't enter. Otherwise, what interest in us might they have?"

Even as he asked the question, he wondered if one hill man might have some other interest.

"The wild animals go down the mountains in the winter," Blue Sky attempted.

Their people could see that on their treks to and from the encampments. In the winter, they almost never saw deer or wild cattle, sheep, or goats up high, and down below they ran across far more of them than they did in the summer.

"Grapes left on the vine freeze," Blue Sky added.

Spring Rain laughed and turned to Many Numbers. "The wine makes him talk like that."

"The deer go down the mountains," Many Numbers said, looking at Blue Sky. "The grapes freeze on the vine in autumn. What's all that supposed to mean?"

"Those savage hill people don't have any reason to be here in the winter," Blue Sky replied. "They wouldn't come up here just to take a look at us."

"They'd come up here to attack us," Many Numbers countered.

"Why?" Blue Sky asked. "Just to lose again? Just to see another comrade or two killed? Just to give up and run away again? Just to lose one more time? In the middle of the cold, snow, ice, and hunger of winter? Why would they do that?"

Spring Rain's thigh, touching Blue Sky's, was distracting him.

"You assume they think the way we do," Spring Rain said.

More than anything else, Blue Sky wanted to kiss Spring Rain again.

"Why would you assume they don't think the way we do?" he asked instead.

"They live there," Spring Rain said, nodding his head in the direction of the hills. "We live here. They hunt for wild animals and plants to eat and use. We raise and grow our own."

Blue Sky touched Spring Rain's face with his hand, caressed his lips with his fingers.

"That doesn't make them different," Blue Sky said, softly, thinking of the hill man in the bushes. He'd had Spring Rain's slender build, close-set eyes, even his pouty mouth.

"You might have a point," Many Numbers said. "It's possible. They come up here when it's warm to hunt deer and pick berries. Our people would do that, too, if we didn't farm."

Blue Sky removed his hand from Spring Rain's lips and turned to Many Numbers.

"I'm sorry," he said. "I'm no better than Law Keeper. I don't have a man to go with. That's my only excuse. I'm sorry."

Many Numbers laughed.

Blue Sky was alone in a hut with his two heroes, and he was making a fool of himself.

"It's the wine," Spring Rain offered again.

"That's okay," Many Numbers said, turning to his mate. "He has no need to be sorry. Noon Breeze tells me your beauty is so overwhelming no teller or apprentice teller in the kingdom hasn't been tempted by you. And you and Blue Sky share a hut. I can only feel sorry for him."

Blue Sky stared at Many Numbers.

"Would you rather Spring Rain and I didn't share a hut?" he asked.

"I'd expect you and Spring Rain to share a hut," Many Numbers said. "You've become such good friends. He's helping you get over the prince."

"But he isn't helping me get over myself," Blue Sky said.

"I can see that," Many Numbers said. "I was only hoping you'd tell us more about your plans for overthrowing Tall Oak and removing Sturdy Limb. Law Keeper, too. That's what I want to hear. To hell with those hill people and their problems."

"Treason?" Spring Rain asked Many Numbers. "You want to talk about treason?"

Many Numbers laughed again. "Why not talk about treason?" he asked. "You've never considered how delightful disloyalty might taste?"

Many Numbers, smirking once more, turned to Blue Sky.

"We're talking about Morning Sun and Rose Leaf," Blue Sky insisted.

"We're talking about the prince," Many Numbers agreed, "and the woman he loves."

"And treason," Spring Rain added.

"And treason," Many Numbers affirmed.

*****

One summer when Morning Sun, Rose Leaf, and Blue Sky were still children, they spent a full-moon holiday with their parents visiting their uncles, aunts, and cousins in the village their mothers had grown up in. Sturdy Limb had reluctantly let Valley Defender and his two brothers go with them. Their deceased mother and Rainbow Evening were sisters.

During the meals, the six children sat at the head table with Tall Oak, Rainbow Evening, Green Field, and Gentle Brook. The relatives would have it no other way. They ignored Blue Sky's insistence that he and Rose Leaf weren't royalty.

A brook ran through their village orchard. Gentle Brook had gotten her name from it. That was what the aunts, uncles, and cousins told them it was, most of the time: a gentle brook.

It emptied into the creek that eventually wound its way past the home village.

The day of the feast, Morning Sun and Blue Sky started a water fight in the orchard, and they kept it going for a good part of the afternoon. All the boys—and most of the younger men and women and the girls, including Rose Leaf—got themselves soaked.

The older relatives and guests from the neighboring villages were openly astonished that the prince and Blue Sky did what they did—and their parents made no attempt to stop them.

The two ringleaders heard several of their cousins telling their parents, aunts, and uncles they were only participating in the fight to please the prince.

When those cousins got back into the fray, though, Morning Sun, Blue Sky, and the other hard-core fighters, who by then included the usually well-behaved Valley Defender and his brothers, loudly called them liars. And how dare they try to make a scapegoat of the prince!

As their punishment, the apostate cousins suffered yet another drenching of brook water.

They were getting out of it what they wanted the most: the attention of the prince and his closest cousins and companions.

Only the tellers, when they showed up with their instruments and the music making, singing, and dancing began, could stop the fighting.

Two of the older boys from the orphanage were with the tellers. When that summer ended, they'd become men and apprentice tellers and go off to spend their encampment year on sunrise pass. People who'd heard them perform agreed they already made music and sang more pleasingly, and uniquely, than tellers with lifetimes of training behind them.

Fair Judge was with the tellers. She brought the two boys to the head table to meet the king and the other head-table guests.

They'd already met Rainbow Evening, Fair Judge having introduced them.

They'd met the prince and his cousins, too, despite the unusual claim of the chief warrior and first teller that their people had never permitted contact between royal children and orphans.

It turned out that the two orphan boys had also previously spoken with Gentle Brook.

They were shirtless that day. Blue Sky could tell from looking at them they must've been doing more than their share of the work in the tellerhood fields. Despite their slender physiques, it wasn't surprising they'd both gone far in all three of the summer games that year.

The orphan boys remarked on how wet the prince, his cousins, and his best friend were.

"Did you get a rainstorm here before we arrived?" the one who'd soon be known as Many Numbers asked them, glancing up at that day's cloudless sky.

"But the trees aren't wet at all," his companion noted. "And look, the one they call Rose Leaf is as soaked as the boys."

Even then, he preferred to be known as Spring Rain.

The orphan boys stood in front of the king and queen and the others at the head table, making them laugh, laughing themselves, two youths about to become men, each with a hand lightly touching the small of the other's back.

Whenever Blue Sky saw them after that, usually during ceremonies in the town, it was difficult for him to take his eyes off them.

*****

Many of the tellers changed their names. No child in the kingdom had ever been known as Law Keeper, Fair Judge, or Many Numbers. Law Keeper's friends, who later became high tellers, gave him his name when Tall Oak appointed him first teller. Others, including Spring Rain and Noon Breeze, chose new names on their own.

A few of the people who weren't tellers changed their names, usually by accepting names people thought more appropriate than their original names. Autumn Wine had done so, as had Solemn Promise. Good Harvest changed his name to honor the people who were officially his uncle and cousin but might've been more closely related to him than those terms would indicate.

Most of the valley people, though, kept their names throughout their lives. Gentle Brook, Green Field, Tall Oak, Rainbow Evening, Morning Sun, Sturdy Limb, Valley Defender, East Land, Full Harvest, and Early Harvest were all born with those names.

*****

During the first full-moon holiday after the winter solstice, it was Blue Sky's turn to go home. It was past sunset when he arrived in his village, but his father was still working in the barns.

Rose Leaf was in the mountains with Morning Sun. Blue Sky understood that Rose Leaf spent all of her time between full moons helping their parents and their ill and elderly neighbors. She did much of the work he used to do. She never went to the town. She worked, ate, slept, and went to see Morning Sun during the full-moon holidays.

Gentle Brook, who'd gone outside to empty a jar in the waste ditch, began weeping when she saw her son coming down the path from the forest in the moonlight.

Blue Sky embraced her.

"I won't scare you again," he promised, his arms still around her. "I'll do as I'm told."

A grateful smile broke through his mother's tears like sunshine at the end of a shower.

They went into the house and sat by the fire.

They drank that autumn's cider, which was pleasantly hard by then—and soon they spoke of what mattered most that winter.

"I want to tell Rose Leaf and Morning Sun one thing," Blue Sky said. "I want to tell them why Tall Oak says they can't marry and have children together."

His mother stared at him, saying nothing.

"Are they brother and sister?" he asked. "Yes or no? Are they or aren't they? What difference would it make if they and I knew that? We'd never tell anybody else."

Gentle Brook sighed. "I can assure you, they aren't brother and sister."

"Then why can't they marry? Why can't they have children together?"

"You wish to know too much."

"That's impossible. Nobody can ever know too much."

"Nobody needs to know why they can't marry."

"Rose Leaf and Morning Sun need to know," Blue Sky disagreed. "They want to become husband and wife. They want to have children together. They want to live the rest of their lives together. And they want to know why the king says they can't."

"I know what they want."

Blue Sky could see on his mother's face the pain their conversation was causing her.

"Rose Leaf sat here and told me what she wants," she continued. "Who can blame her? Morning Sun has become an honest and good man. A beautiful man, too. I think it would be wonderful if he could be Rose Leaf's husband and the father of her children. And live with her the rest of their lives. But they can't do that. Tall Oak says they can't. The king says they can't."

"And Rose Leaf and Morning Sun can't be told why they can't?"

"Tall Oak and your father are wise men. And I don't say that because the one is the king and the other my husband and your father. I say it because I know it's true. I know it with my own eyes and ears. I know it from the many years I've known them. I say it despite the mistakes both of them have made."

"Mistakes," Blue Sky spat. "Sturdy Limb and Law Keeper."

His mother shook her head before she resumed. "The king and your father say I shouldn't tell you why Rose Leaf and Morning Sun can't marry or have children together. I believe they're right about that. So you can ask me all you want, but I can never tell you."

Gentle Brook had tears in her eyes again.

"I never thought this would happen," she said, looking at Blue Sky. "I thought Rose Leaf felt she was as much a sister to the prince as she was to you. Maybe I was just hoping that's how it was. Whatever the reason, though, I was wrong."

Gentle Brook and Full Harvest were dancing close together once when Blue Sky saw she was crying. He assumed she was feeling sorry for the man because his wife, Early Harvest's mother, had been killed in the war, and he'd never found another woman who could replace her. The older people, though, said he, quite unlike Sturdy Limb, could've married any number of women who'd lost their husbands in the war.

"I was very, very wrong," Gentle Brook continued. "I'm sorry, but I never saw just how wrong I was. I know now I should've seen it. But I didn't. They were children."

Blue Sky and his mother had openly hoped Rose Leaf would become Early Harvest's mate. But those expectations were fatally flawed. They left out the fact of Morning Sun himself, growing into his manhood. Blue Sky and Gentle Brook were asking Rose Leaf to have the strength, which both of them entirely lacked, not to fall in love with the prince—not to dream they could somehow be the one he loved.

Gentle Brook took Blue Sky's hand. "I don't blame you for wanting to know. If I were you or Morning Sun or Rose Leaf, I'd insist on knowing. But I'm sorry. I can't tell you."

Blue Sky embraced his mother again and asked nothing more of her that evening.

*****

His father was in the horse pens working by torch light. One of the mares had given birth.

Green Field was ready to cut the foal's cord with his blade.

Blue Sky helped him hold the foal down.

When Green Field was done, they stood up over the foal and looked at one another.

"I thought," Green Field said, "you'd go to the town with Solemn Promise and the others."

It was also Solemn Promise's turn to go home. Blue Sky had come down from the mountains with him and two men from neighboring encampments.

Tall Oak had invited them to a banquet in the great central hall. The purpose was to honor Blue Sky. With only Spring Rain at his side last autumn, he'd stood his ground against ten hill warriors and made them turn away. The farmers had insisted upon his being recognized.

In his response, Blue Sky had promised that since he'd done nothing deserving recognition, he wouldn't attend. The king and queen canceled the event.

Solemn Promise had agreed to give to the court what little news, all of it of little worth, Blue Sky had from the apprentice tellers' encampment.

"I thought," Blue Sky said to his father, "I'd have a better use for my time—better than listening to the imbecilities of people like Law Keeper, Sturdy Limb, and Tall Oak."

Green Field winced when he heard his son include the king in that remark.

"When I was a child," Blue Sky continued, "I was led to believe you weren't like them. But that was before I saw who you really are. Before I became aware you approved the king's banning a marriage for no good reason at all. And anybody can easily see the two people involved truly love one another."

Blue Sky was hurting his father even more than he'd hurt his mother.

"That was also," he added, "before I knew you approved killing innocent children."

Green Field closed his eyes.

"I don't approve any of that," he countered. "Tall Oak has a good reason for banning the marriage you have in mind. It's irresponsible for people to give birth to unwanted children. Rose Leaf knows she can't have children with Morning Sun. He knows that. They've always known that. And that's why they should make certain they don't have children together. They can both have all the children they wish with other people."

"They don't wish to have children with other people. They wish to have children with each other. Why, may I ask, can't they do that?"

"I can't tell you."

"Tall Oak ordered you not to tell me."

"That's right. He did. He thinks you'll tell the people."

"He doesn't want the people to know."

"They don't need to know."

"You don't want them to know either."

With the torch light in his eyes like the sun at dawn, Green Field stared at Blue Sky and made no response.

"Tall Oak will suffer the consequences of this," Blue Sky said. "Rose Leaf and Morning Sun will have children together. If Tall Oak orders a child of theirs killed, who'll dare to obey such an order? Nobody. And Tall Oak will no longer be our king. The people will demand that the tellers determine he's lost his mind. I'll lead the rebellion myself if I have to. But I truly think an order to kill a child will be all the leading the people will need. Morning Sun will be the new king."

Green Field let the foal's cord drop to the barn floor.

"Just to say any of that is treason," he said.

"Is it? Many Numbers and Spring Rain tell me a prince once became the king before his father died. The king's mind had died, but not his body. That appears to be the case with Tall Oak."

"Many Numbers and Spring Rain agree with you? A king can be deposed like that?"

"The tellers can recognize Morning Sun as the king if his father has lost his mind."

"Sturdy Limb will never let the tellers do that."

"Even if the people demand it? Even if they think the chief warrior's life isn't as worthy as that of Morning Sun and Rose Leaf's child? Sturdy Limb would side with Tall Oak against the people? Why would a coward who feared for his life wish to do that?"

The foal was attempting to stand up.

"You think the people will side with you against the king?" Green Field asked.

"They'll side with Morning Sun and Rose Leaf against the king. That's what I think. Unless they're given some good reason not to. Do you and Tall Oak have one?"

"Yes, we do."

"What is it?"

The torch light still dancing in his father's eyes was the only answer Blue Sky got.

"You can't tell me," Blue Sky said. "You can't tell Morning Sun and Rose Leaf. You can't tell the people. That's the same as having no reason at all."

Blue Sky knew he was causing his father agony, but he also knew he could only go on.

"A king who's lost his mind can no longer be king," he said. "That's what the story says. The gods won't allow it. Nor will the people."

The foal stood next to its mother. Blue Sky was glad his words meant nothing to those innocent creatures.

"I'm leaving now," he said. "I'm going back to the encampment."

"Alone? In the forest? In the middle of winter? At night?"

Ordinarily, Blue Sky would've begun his return to his encampment with Solemn Promise and the other men the morning after the next day.

"I can do more for the kingdom in the mountains," he said, "than I could ever do here."

When he turned to go, his father caught the sleeve of his coat and held him back.

"I know this seems wrong to you," Green Field said. "I know why it does."

He held Blue Sky close to himself, as if his son were a lover he was attempting to talk out of an abrupt leave-taking in the middle of a quarrel.

"It would seem wrong to me, too," Green Field continued, throwing the words in Blue Sky's face. "But Tall Oak is the king. I promised him my loyalty long ago. That means I go along with his decisions. Even if his decisions might not always be the same as mine. He says we can't tell you why Morning Sun and Rose Leaf can never have children together. There is a reason for it. But I can't tell you, Rose Leaf, Morning Sun, or the people what it is and remain loyal to Tall Oak."

Blue Sky shook his head. "There's no possible reason why the people shouldn't be told."

"You don't understand," Green Field countered. "The world isn't as straightforward as you think it is. There are some things the people shouldn't know. For their own good."

"And this is one of those things?" Blue Sky asked. "And the people are just supposed to take your and Tall Oak's word for it that it is?"

Green Field let go of Blue Sky's sleeve.

"You and Tall Oak will find out," Blue Sky said, "the people aren't as stupid and unconcerned as you think they are."

"And you'll lead the people into treason against their king?"

"If that's what you and the present king wish to call it, yes."

"You won't like where this is taking you. Believe me, you won't."

Although what Green Field said could've been interpreted as a threat, the look on his face turned it into one last plea—which did him no good.

"When you were a youth," Blue Sky said, "rebelling against a misguided and fearful king was called bravery. Those who did it are still, to this day, considered heroes. And rightly so, in my opinion. When they were young, they were fearless. But sadly, as they grew older, they let fear rule their lives and the kingdom. I'll have nothing further to do with you. I'll say good-bye to my mother now and be gone. You, though, can forget you ever had me for a son."

Blue Sky walked alone in the forest all through the night. In the morning, snow began to fall. He walked all that day and through another night without sleeping. When he reached sunrise pass the next morning, the snow was as deep in the mountains and the valley as it got that winter.

Chapter 8

When Many Numbers came to sunrise pass for the second full-moon holiday after the winter solstice, he brought news from the town.

Blue Sky, Spring Rain, and he were sitting on the bench outside their hut getting as much warmth as they could from the midwinter sun and the wine they were drinking.

"Does Tall Oak know what the people think?" Blue Sky asked.

"Without a doubt," Many Numbers said. "You should see him in court. His mind appears to be somewhere else. He and Rainbow Evening are constantly whispering."

"How much does he know?" Blue Sky asked. "Do you think he's heard any talk of his being forced to let Morning Sun marry Rose Leaf?"

"He must've," Many Numbers replied. "Just the other day, Sturdy Limb was making one of his pointless speeches in court. He was going on and on describing the punishments for different crimes. When he got to treason, Tall Oak suddenly interrupted him, saying traitors have always been dealt with harshly in this kingdom, and if anybody had a story to the contrary, he'd like to hear it. He was looking at me when he said that. Everybody knew what he was talking about."

"Just as I thought," Spring Rain said. "He'll order all of us executed. Sturdy Limb will enjoy doing it, too. He'll prolong the execution of Green Field's son. He'll love that."

Blue Sky gave Spring Rain an unusually stern look. "Only if we don't succeed," he said.

"Most traitors don't succeed," Spring Rain noted. "That's how it's supposed to be."

Blue Sky didn't have to say he didn't want to hear any more of that kind of talk.

*****

People said Blue Sky must've inherited his good eyesight from his father and mother.

When he came of age, though, he had an undeniable edge over his father. The night they'd argued in the horse barn, he could tell his father wasn't aware that Autumn Wine's grandsons were on the other side of their common barn wall, listening to them.

The grandsons had seen Blue Sky coming down the path from the forest. They'd no doubt attempted to hear through the common house wall what he and his mother were saying, probably without success. But they could hear him leave the house and go to the horse barn.

They'd gone into their cattle barn without torches. Blue Sky could still see, through a tiny crack in the wall, when they opened their barn door and briefly let in the light of the full moon. He could hear them walking on the fresh straw they'd laid down that morning. He could hear the cattle moving out of the way as the grandsons approached the wall where they could best eavesdrop on their neighbors.

Blue Sky was certain, despite his people's dislike of traveling in winter, it hadn't taken long for the grandsons' news to reach the town or even the upper valley: the king was absolutely opposed to Morning Sun's mating with Rose Leaf. Hearing no good reason for the opposition, Rose Leaf's brother was so angry he was prepared to ask the people to remove Tall Oak as king in favor of the prince they'd come to love. And when Tall Oak fell, Sturdy Limb, Law Keeper, and all their high deputies and tellers the people had come to despise would go down with him.

*****

Shortly before the two orphan boys became men, and soon after the water fight in the orchard, Law Keeper summoned one of them, Spring Rain, for a private and, he promised, "earnest" conversation. It was lengthy, too, since most of what he said concerned Spring Rain's "extraordinary beauty." Although the first teller was said to be attractive himself in his youth, by the time of the conversation the valley people had agreed he was, like Tall Oak and Sturdy Limb, the unfortunate victim of the physical inactivity that often came with a high position.

Law Keeper's point, when he finally got to it, was this: he wished to groom Spring Rain to become the kingdom's next first teller. All he required of Spring Rain was his agreement to live with him after he returned from his apprentice year on sunrise pass.

Spring Rain flatly and indignantly turned the man down, insisting he'd be living with Many Numbers, and nobody else, for the rest of his life.

Law Keeper must've believed Spring Rain wasn't too bright. His promise was patently bogus. The king appointed the first teller, and neither Tall Oak nor Morning Sun was likely to appoint anybody Law Keeper had prepared for the position, and certainly not somebody the man had enticed to be his lover in exchange for his sponsorship.

It was easy to imagine what the king and queen's high-minded farmer friends Green Field and Gentle Brook would say, making no attempt to conceal their outrage: "Those high tellers are even more corrupt than we thought they were!"

They'd get the other farmers to agree with them that the situation was shameless, and the king, whoever he was, would simply have to rectify matters.

Smarting after Spring Rain's swift rejection, Law Keeper told his underlings the two apprentice tellers from the orphanage were not to share a hut during their encampment. He claimed Fair Judge's failure to discipline them had brought them to manhood as hardened troublemakers. He cited their outrageous wall of hides as a prime example of their willfulness.

Despite the first teller's order, Many Numbers and Spring Rain shared a hut. The supervising tellers on sunrise pass had no wish to enforce Law Keeper's order and made no effort to do so. The valley people had long adhered to the rule that encampment warriors chose for themselves the person they shared a hut with.

When Law Keeper and the high tellers showed up for their annual visit, two other apprentice tellers were only too happy to pose as the hut-mates of Many Numbers and Spring Rain. They had their arms around the orphan boys in surprisingly open displays of affection and need.

The high tellers figured out from the laughter what was going on. But they chose to pretend, as Law Keeper did, his order had gone into effect.

When word of the ruse got back to the court, it produced more laughter.

As soon as Fair Judge heard about it, though, she went to Law Keeper and told him the tellers and town people were laughing at him behind his back, and she didn't blame them.

The first teller saw fit never to mention his bizarre order again.

Hearing the story, Blue Sky found himself taking pity on Law Keeper once more. The two orphan boys who'd gone around collecting old hides became the ceremony singers the people praised the most. And the first teller had to pretend he enjoyed listening to them as much as everybody else did.

*****

After Blue Sky had spoken with Spring Rain in the courtyard and confirmed his encampment-year plans, Spring Rain decided he wished to spend the same year on sunrise pass teaching the apprentice tellers.

Some of the tellers enjoyed spending a year in the mountains with the new men.

Many Numbers had an explanation for it that Blue Sky at first considered excessively cynical: young men, especially new men, were easier to manipulate than older men.

Neither Many Numbers nor Spring Rain had ever spent a "supervising year" on sunrise pass. Many Numbers never had any desire to do so, but he readily agreed that Spring Rain should do it, as long as they could see each other every full-moon holiday.

Blue Sky was, Many Numbers noted, Green Field and Gentle Brook's son and Morning Sun's closest friend. People also said he wasn't afraid to argue with the king himself.

A teller who was scheduled to spend that year in the mountains was willing to let Spring Rain go in his place. Many of the tellers and court people were already whispering behind the man's back that he was getting somewhat old for yet another grueling year in the mountains with the apprentice tellers.

Law Keeper, though, flatly refused to allow the substitution.

"Just to please Green Field's arrogant son?" he supposedly asked.

Nobody had laughed with less restraint than Blue Sky when Autumn Wine's slap landed the first teller on the ground. It was impossible to be present later that day and not hear Blue Sky's loud praise for his elderly neighbor's "warrior-like" prowess in "hand-to-hand combat."

Fair Judge spoke with Rainbow Evening.

Neither of those two slender high officials was a victim of physical inactivity.

They spoke about Spring Rain's encampment request.

Law Keeper suddenly found good reason to change his mind.

The following winter, even the farmers were hearing stories about their first teller that caused more than a few to openly wonder why such a person would be left in his position.

*****

Two years earlier, when Autumn Wine's older grandson had been in the encampment the new men of age from his neighborhood usually went to, Green Field and Blue Sky had done most of Autumn Wine's fieldwork, as neighbors were expected to do when the only man in the family was in his encampment year.

A sister of Solemn Promise's had taken a liking to the older grandson and made journeys of the full moon to his encampment.

Her father, her mother, and most of her siblings were opposed to her liaison with Autumn Wine's grandson from the moment they found out about it. They let their daughter and sister know it was hopeless to imagine him being a suitable husband for her.

Autumn Wine had scarcely enough land and livestock to provide for herself and her two grandsons. The addition of grandsons' wives and great-grandchildren to the family might well eventually leave all of them with nothing.

Several years previously, though, the grandsons had taken to gathering firewood in the forest and carting it to farmers and town people who were willing and able to exchange grain, lentils, and livestock for it rather than going to the forest or woods on the bluff and getting it themselves. Ordinarily, "wood people," as those who delivered firewood were known, were landless people who weren't much better off than the individuals who chose to do very little or no work and lived on the charity of their relatives and neighbors.

Autumn Wine's grandsons, though, were unlike the usual wood people, who seldom showed up unless it was convenient for them to do so—meaning they had no rain, snow, high-summer heat, or deep-winter cold to contend with.

When the grandsons made an agreement to deliver a cartload of wood, they arrived with it the day they'd promised it, and there was no argument as to whether the cart was actually as full as it should've been. As a result, the grandsons were accumulating grain and livestock most people knew nothing about.

During the year when the older grandson was in his encampment, Green Field, Blue Sky, and Rose Leaf had also helped the younger grandson meet his firewood commitments.

On more than one occasion, the prince, having come out to the village for a visit, became a wood person himself, pleasantly surprising the people who took delivery of his cartloads.

"The prince brought us our wood," they could cheerfully tell their neighbors. "Has he ever done that for you?"

There was an elderly couple in the village whose three sons, the only children they'd had, were all killed in the last war with the hill people. They had no grandchildren or even nephews or nieces to help them do their work. They'd long since eaten all their livestock and crops, even their lentils. After that, they traded away their land year after year, usually to Green Field and Gentle Brook's family, to stay alive.

Lately, Green Field and Gentle Brook had declined to take the elderly couple's land, suggesting they bargain with Autumn Wine's grandsons for it instead. This, too, wasn't well known among the people.

Unlike his other siblings, Solemn Promise went out of his way to befriend his sister's farmer lover. He often told Morning Sun he'd consider it an honor to have Autumn Wine's older grandson as his sister's husband. The prince and Blue Sky always relayed those remarks to the person he was speaking of.

Solemn Promise was openly and unmistakably dismayed when his sister chose to give in to their parents, broke off her relationship with the farmer who loved her, and married a town man who was several years older than she and whose family's wealth hadn't yet found him a mate.

It soon became obvious the marriage wasn't a happy one—to the point where Solemn Promise's sister commenced seeing her former lover again.

Questions arose as to who the father of her first child was. According to every teller familiar with the matter, the girl was born far too long after the man who was supposed to be her father had complained—to the king, in open court—that her mother had ceased going with him.

Now she was with child again, despite her husband's having prevailed upon Sturdy Limb and Law Keeper to warn the interloper not to have anything further to do with her unless he wished to be executed for adultery.

Those worthies had somehow overlooked that neither Tall Oak nor his father had ever chosen to punish anybody for that particular crime.

Blue Sky envied Solemn Promise's sister. Having wrestled with Autumn Wine's older grandson in village competitions on a number of occasions, he well knew what a strong young bull her lover had become.

*****

As the days grew longer, even the high drifts of snow on sunrise pass began to melt. To the left of the guard post, the run-off collected in a stream tumbling over boulders as it fell down the mountain slope, creating miniature versions of the great waterfall in the upper valley where the lake overflowed and the river began.

One morning, following the run-off stream down the mountain with his eyes, Blue Sky rethought his question regarding the hill man he couldn't bring himself to kill the previous autumn.

He sat all during that day's guard duty staring at it. He invited Spring Rain to continue his work with the garments he'd brought with him to mend. Blue Sky said he'd keep watch.

Spring Rain being Spring Rain, he also started mending the garments Blue Sky had brought to work on.

The run-off stream flowed behind the clump of undergrowth the hill man hid in. After that, Blue Sky couldn't tell what happened to it.

A deer, unusually high in the mountains for that season, leapt into a small gully to the right of the guard post and stood staring at the guards in it, as deer sometimes did. Although they ran from the hill people down below, they didn't seem to fear the guards.

Spring Rain looked at the animal and laughed.

"Maybe that's your buck," he said. "The one the hill people didn't kill last autumn. Maybe he wants to let us know how grateful to us he is for saving his life."

"Maybe he's a god," Blue Sky said, "here to tell us something we should know."

The valley people liked to believe the gods came among them in the shape of other things—even if the tellers were the only people who knew, in hindsight anyway, when, how, and why the gods had made their appearances.

And even if what they said was often too general to be of any real use. As in their insistence that neighbors should love one another as they wished to be loved themselves. At least a god's coming to the human world and saying it was reassuring, Blue Sky supposed.

He turned away from the deer when he realized the melt stream to their left could empty into a hidden gully. The water could feed from the gully into the brook—which was swollen now, far below—somewhere before the brook came into view from the guard post.

When the gully was dry, the hill man could've come up it to the clump of bushes, and nobody in the guard post would've been able to see him.

The gully probably didn't exist when the valley people's ancestors chose the site for the apprentice tellers' guard post. Blue Sky could imagine the rain and melting snow hadn't yet started to chisel that particular gully into the mountain slope.

The surfaces of mountain slopes changed over time, his people had noticed—as the course of their river did, adding or removing a bend during a single spring or other flood time.

Water, whether in the form of rain, snowmelt, or the river, was the reason. Unlike air, unlike solid ground, it was a liquid that always went downhill, wherever it could, pushing things aside if it had to. Spring Rain had instructed Blue Sky that the nature of a liquid was something else the gods had decreed.

And after the valley people's ancestors had built the guard post, there was a reason their people hadn't seen whatever couldn't be seen from the guard post. One of their laws prohibited anyone from proceeding down the outer slopes of the mountains surrounding their valley farther than the guard posts. If a person did so and got into a fight with the hill people—as would surely happen if any of them came upon the scene—the guards were under strict orders not to endanger themselves by going to the defector's rescue.

A number of years ago in another encampment, a guard—excessively inebriated after his prospective mate had failed to appear for a full-moon holiday, word being that she'd chosen to take up with another man—had wandered down the wrong side of the mountain.

The law in his case required his comrades to watch from their guard post, doing nothing but screaming as the hill people killed the man. And, in the horrifying days that followed, viewing a scene from hell itself—as vultures, wolves, and other creatures devoured their comrade's flesh.

*****

Blue Sky hadn't been dreaming a child's dream when he saw the hill man in the clump of bushes. He realized his people had to go down the ravine to the clump of bushes and take a look. If there was a gully behind it in which intruders could lurk, the guard post should be relocated to some other position, probably just above the clump of bushes, where the gully could be kept in full view at all times.

During the remainder of that guard duty, Blue Sky showed Spring Rain what he saw. What appeared to them at several points to be bushes were, he'd come to believe, the tops of small trees growing in the gully. There were also places where the ground seemed to rise abruptly, perhaps the length of a grown person's leg. Blue Sky was convinced they were looking at the upper level of the opposite wall of the gully. When the sunlight hit the ravine at certain angles, he could more readily explain what he was talking about.

Squinting his eyes in the cold wind, Spring Rain was nodding his head.

"You could be right," he said. "A lot of snowmelt and rain would do it."

Blue Sky confessed to Spring Rain he'd seen a hill man in the clump of bushes the day they were proclaimed heroes. But he still couldn't admit he'd chosen not to kill the man. He claimed instead the man saw him and got away before he could take good aim at him.

Blue Sky went on to say he hadn't previously mentioned the hill man because he was ashamed he hadn't killed him.

"He's the one who was doing all the yelling," Blue Sky said. "He must've been warning his comrades not to come any further up the mountain."

Spring Rain looked at the ravine below them.

"Somebody down there that day was yelling," he said. "I couldn't figure out which of the men we could see was doing it. You're saying it was the man you saw in the bushes? I grant you that would explain why I didn't see anybody yelling."

When their guard duty came to an end that day, Spring Rain insisted they should make Blue Sky's discovery known to the other supervising and apprentice tellers in their encampment. They'd have to send a messenger to the town. Spring Rain would demand they send Blue Sky.

*****

Their comrades, though, made it obvious from the outset they weren't at all pleased to hear what Spring Rain and Blue Sky were telling them.

They particularly didn't want to hear Blue Sky's story of a hill man appearing out of nowhere far closer to the guard post than he was supposed to be.

They looked at one another and rolled their eyes.

"There's no gully down there," one comrade said.

"I've never seen a gully there," a second comrade said.

Spring Rain turned to Blue Sky.

"You've got to show them," he said. "You've got to show them what you showed me."

He turned to the others.

"At the guard post he'll show you," he said. "You'll see what we're talking about."

Their comrades, though, had many duties to perform, most of which, even that late in the winter, focused on keeping a good fire going in their huts, and warm and dry hides and skins on their bodies. They clearly didn't welcome the thought of traipsing down to the guard post and back again without having a good reason to do it.

Only a few of them, seemingly the most skeptical, ventured forth with Spring Rain and Blue Sky, and by the time they reached the guard post, they weren't hiding their anger.

"Those two," Blue Sky heard one of them muttering. "They know so much more than other people. Ask them anything you want, and they've got the answer. We're not as bright as they are."

Blue Sky didn't care for those remarks, but he could understand why the comrade might believe they were true.

"Neither of them," Noon Breeze saw fit to note, "goes with another man often enough. The one, not at all. Maybe that's their problem."

Noon Breeze might've been short and skinny with a boyish face and silly smile, but at the end of a revel he almost always seemed to get the encampment comrade—other than Spring Rain and Blue Sky—he wanted to go with.

The major drawback in the presentation of Blue Sky's case was his having to prove in a few glances from his put-upon comrades what had taken him most of a guard duty to convince Spring Rain of. And Spring Rain had the advantage of being willing to sit with him and stare at the details of an otherwise unremarkable mountainside.

Also, when Blue Sky made his argument to Noon Breeze and his fellow skeptics, it was late in the afternoon, and the guard post and possible gully were in the shadow of the mountains.

And beyond all that, the others simply couldn't see as well as Blue Sky could.

"There's no gully down there," the comrades scoffed.

"Then how," Blue Sky asked, blundering badly by then, "did that hill man get so far up the mountain without being seen?"

"Maybe you should ask yourself and Spring Rain that question," a younger supervising teller, one whose judgment Blue Sky had come to respect, replied. "The two of you were supposed to be keeping watch for hill people that day. You chose not to tell us about this hill man in the bushes until now. Maybe you weren't as watchful as you should've been."

Noon Breeze, giving in to temptation, laughed.

"Maybe," he offered, "they weren't paying any attention at all. Maybe, despite what they say, they were doing something else."

The comrades, snickering as they climbed back up the mountainside to the encampment, greatly enjoyed that remark.

Blue Sky imagined what they were thinking: "The people's favorite ceremony singer and the great hero's son—look at them now."

Spring Rain and Blue Sky were left with the current guards on duty, who made no attempt to conceal their own amusement and gratitude for the strange interruption in their otherwise all-too-ordinary turn in the guard post.

One of them was bold enough to ask if Blue Sky and Spring Rain could stay awhile and show them what they'd been doing that glorious day the previous autumn.

Blue Sky and Spring Rain, once heroes in the eyes of their encampment comrades but now apparently buffoons at best, retreated to their hut.

Blue Sky took comfort in the fact that, of all the men in the encampment, Spring Rain was the one he spent his days talking with and his nights sleeping next to. Noon Breeze's snide innuendo only made Blue Sky regret it didn't point to the truth of the matter.

*****

During the third and last full-moon holiday of the winter, Spring Rain and Blue Sky had guard duty in the morning.

As soon as Many Numbers had arrived the previous afternoon, their comrades told him that his friends had let their imaginations run wild and seen a gully, of all things, where there was none.

"The hill people," one of the apprentice tellers said, "can use it to walk right into our encampment and our valley, and nobody will be able to see them. Can you imagine that?"

Maybe, Noon Breeze hinted, Blue Sky and Spring Rain were drinking too much wine. Although, he chose to add, looking them up and down, one of the usual reasons for doing that—to assuage the guilt infidelity invariably created—surely wouldn't apply in their case.

Many Numbers, looking the culprits up and down himself, laughed at those remarks.

The taunts of the comrades, though, impelled Many Numbers to demand that Blue Sky and Spring Rain show him their imaginary gully.

Having nothing better to do, he was willing to remain at the guard post with them and listen to their argument in all its many details. He also viewed the landscape in the sunlight and could see the subtle shadowing on which their reasoning ultimately rested.

"Sturdy Limb needs to know about this," he said. "I wouldn't call that an imaginary gully. We've at least got to go down there and find out for sure."

"Can he let us do that?" Spring Rain asked.

"If he can't or won't," Many Numbers replied, "I'll speak to Tall Oak in open court."

"What if Law Keeper won't let you?" Spring Rain asked.

Tellers were always supposed to request the first teller's permission before addressing the king in open court. Failure to do so could get a teller sent out of the town permanently.

Many Numbers laughed. "I'll tell him to go to hell."

After Law Keeper's humiliation in all matters concerning Spring Rain, Many Numbers might've gotten away with that. The first teller would be wise to let Many Numbers speak to the king just to keep him from starting another confrontation—and reminding the other tellers and court people of the results of their previous skirmishes.

"You're going to confront the king with our imaginary gully?" Spring Rain asked.

"Why not?" Many Numbers replied. "We know it's there. We can visualize it, even if your comrades can't—or won't. We'll eventually win the argument, and all those who choose to oppose us will reveal themselves to be the fools they are."

Blue Sky wondered if there was in fact a war god, and if he'd come to visit the world of humans as Many Numbers.

Chapter 9

The spring equinox came. The undergrowth on sunrise pass turned green again.

Doing guard duty one afternoon, Blue Sky saw something he'd paid no attention to the previous autumn: grass grew on either side of the snowmelt stream. It was already knee-high.

He made no mention of his new discovery to Spring Rain.

Although Spring Rain would never admit it, his association with Blue Sky wasn't doing him any good with their comrades. They'd lately found cause for ridicule in Blue Sky's contention, and Spring Rain's allowance he might be right, that hill men would look like themselves if they didn't have beards and long hair.

Some of their comrades, Noon Breeze foremost among them, argued that if Spring Rain and Blue Sky fully took part in their revels, they'd have no reason to outrageously imagine that those "savages" in the hills might ever be as pleasing to the eye as valley men were.

After dark, but before the moon set that night, Blue Sky went to the place where he'd observed the part-time brook coming out of the forest. He got down and crawled along the stream bed on his hands and knees, keeping his rear end as low as he could.

As he'd assumed, the stream bed was deep enough in the ground, and the grass on either side of it sufficiently high, to keep him hidden from the guards on duty in the post below him, as well as from his comrades in the encampment above him.

As slowly and cautiously as he proceeded, he still bloodied his hands and knees scraping them against the unfamiliar stream-bed rocks. Although he couldn't be certain how far down the mountainside he was, he eventually decided he had to be well past the guard post.

Reaching the bushes, he found what he'd convinced himself he'd find: a gully. It wasn't a shallow ditch either. He could stand up in it without fearing his comrades might see him.

Now the danger was from the other side. If he encountered hill warriors here, his people, Spring Rain included, would have no choice but to leave him to his fate.

He'd dragged his spear, bow, arrows, and shield along the stream bed with him. He picked them up and became a warrior.

A few days previously, the guards had reported seeing, for the first time since the last autumn storm, campfire smoke at the other end of the thicket. They'd often noticed it ever since.

Blue Sky wanted to know if it was the campfire of the hill man he'd chosen not to kill. If it was, why had he come back? The tellers believed the hill people didn't care to stay high in the mountains for long, even during the warmth of summer. That was one reason their occasional appearances near the encampments caused such alarm.

Although the god of fear was gaining in his eternal struggle with the god of curiosity—if they weren't goddesses—Blue Sky moved down the gully. He stayed on the dark side, out of the moonlight, looking down at every step he took to see where he was placing his feet.

He hadn't been able to get out of his mind what he'd seen when he'd aimed his arrow at the hill man crawling under the bushes: how pleasant the man's body would be to touch, to put his arms around, as he'd done with Morning Sun wrestling and Spring Rain sleeping. He'd gotten away with as much as he could with both of them, but it was never enough.

He was certain he would've killed the hill man if he'd let his arrow go. He could've made it fly between two branches and pierce the man's back. But Blue Sky couldn't bring himself to do it.

He sometimes wondered if all the old rules were meant to be broken.

Proceeding down the gully step after tiny step, he thought it odd that he couldn't see the brook. In fact, near the point where he'd supposed the snowmelt and rain would meet the brook, there appeared to be a rock wall.

But if the water, stopped by the wall, couldn't empty into the brook, where did it go?

A hard and prolonged rain had fallen two days earlier. Some of that run-off should've still been trapped where Blue Sky was standing, perhaps to a height over his head. But the pebbles beneath his feet were dry to the touch.

More closely approaching what he'd thought was an impenetrable wall, he saw what it really was: a pile of large boulders wedged together in the gully entrance. At times in the past, they must've broken loose from the mountain above and rolled down the slope. Taking the path of least resistance like the water, they would've found their way into the gully, rolled to its end, which was level, and come to rest. The snowmelt and rainwater emptied out of the gully through small gaps between the boulders, which passersby on the other side might've assumed were springs.

Bending down and peering through the gaps, Blue Sky could see the brook—and smoke rising from the campfire that had brought him down the mountain.

He hoisted himself up to the top of the wall of boulders.

On a high bank between the brook and the thicket, the hill man was standing outside his tent, his back to Blue Sky again. He'd apparently cooked his evening meal in a pot resting on stones above his fire, which was just inside the entrance to his tent. He ladled a portion of his supper into a bowl—the inferior kind the potters among the farmers made, not the more durable sort some of the valley people had acquired from the river people in exchange for their surplus wheat and barley.

Kneeling on top of the boulder wall, Blue Sky watched the hill man sit down on a flattened log and eat his supper with a wooden spoon carved in the style the valley people carved theirs—and the river people laughed at for lacking the useless embellishments of their own eating utensils.

The hill man appeared to be alone. Did that mean, Blue Sky wondered, he had no wife or children? Did it mean he went with men? Did it mean he'd go with the valley man who'd declined to kill him the previous autumn?

A waterfowl landed on a widened stretch of the brook behind Blue Sky.

Hearing the brief soft splash in the still night air, the hill man turned to look.

Blue Sky realized, too late, he, like the hill man, was in the moonlight.

The hill man stared at him.

Blue Sky had left his weapons on the gully floor.

The hill man, who couldn't know that, nevertheless made no attempt to pick up his own weapons, which were at his feet.

He merely watched Blue Sky while he ate, taking his eyes off him only to refill his spoon, sometimes seeming to nod and smile as if to let Blue Sky know he recognized him.

It wasn't impossible, though, that the hill man's hunting comrades were nearby, aiming arrows at a strangely dislocated valley man who'd soon find out how arrowheads felt piercing his body.

Thinking those thoughts, Blue Sky quickly got himself down from the boulder wall.

After retrieving his weapons and shield, he ran up the dark side of the gully, crawled over the snowmelt stream bed, and sneaked back to the encampment the way he'd left it.

*****

Entering the hut, Blue Sky inadvertently woke Spring Rain, who soon asked him where he'd been.

"You don't want to know," Blue Sky mumbled as if he'd been at the scene of a murder.

Spring Rain wrapped his arm around Blue Sky and chose not to ask what he meant by that, perhaps assuming he'd finally gone into the forest with one of their comrades.

Blue Sky was ashamed of himself. The hill man had left himself open to him, hardly seeming displeased by his sudden appearance. But Blue Sky had given in to irrational fears and proven what a coward the hero Green Field's son was. If there were unseen hill warriors aiming arrows at him, where were their tents and campfires?

*****

Blue Sky made his way down to the gully the next night, too, after the sun had set but while the moon was still hanging in the western sky. This time he dragged only his spear and shield with him. He knew, no matter what else might happen, he'd have no use for his bow and arrows.

He proceeded into the gully as cautiously as he had the previous night.

He imagined the hill man somehow causing even the faintest whisper of the spring breeze, even the slightest vibration of a leaf in the light of the moon.

Suddenly, far down the gully, just inside the blocking wall of boulders, came a sound and a movement no breeze could explain.

Blue Sky quickly got himself behind a large rock.

A deer poked its head out of the shadows and, seeing nothing to frighten it, leapt up to the top of the wall of boulders and down, apparently to the bank of the brook on its other side.

Ashamed of himself again, Blue Sky stood up—and immediately saw, out of the corner of his eye, he'd also blundered again.

The hill man was standing above him in the gully, having the advantage of higher ground. He must've been hiding in the dark. He knew the terrain. Blue Sky didn't.

The hill man had his spear, pointing down, in one hand, and his shield, off to the side and concealing nothing, in the other. The hill man had also shaved off his beard.

The night was unusually warm for that early in the spring. The upper part of the man's body was bare. He had a loincloth around his waist, deerskin no doubt, but that was all he had on.

Blue Sky's eyes hadn't fooled him the previous autumn. The hill man's body was as hard and pleasing to see as Spring Rain's or Morning Sun's.

As the god of fear battled mightily with the god of lust, Blue Sky stepped backward.

The slope, though, was steeper at that point than he'd expected it to be. The gravel gave way beneath his feet. He fell, dropping both his spear and shield.

Valley warriors learned that was the precise moment they should drive their spear through their opponent's belly. Pinning him to the ground, with no hope of getting up again, they'd grab his spear and finish him off by slashing his throat with his own weapon.

The hill man, though, stayed where he was. He watched and did nothing as Blue Sky picked up his spear and shield and scrambled to his feet again.

Blue Sky moved in the other direction this time, up the slope.

The hill man, holding his ground and enjoying himself now, smiled at Blue Sky.

Blue Sky drew close to the space where either of them could've suddenly batted aside the other's spear and driven his own spear home, striking a lethal blow to the other without fear of retaliation.

When Blue Sky moved into the space, the hill man remained motionless.

Blue Sky got so close to the hill man he could hear him breathing.

And sometime since Blue Sky saw him the previous night he'd shaved off his beard.

Blue Sky laid his spear and shield on the rocky gully floor.

Looking down at Blue Sky's spear and shield, the hill man smiled again.

If his purpose in the gully that night was to kill his visitor, he could've done it then without the slightest consequence to himself except the splattering of the intruder's blood on his own body. Blue Sky would've been as much trouble to kill as an innocent fawn.

The hill man instead laid down his own spear and shield next to Blue Sky's.

Blue Sky closed the remaining gap between them and embraced the hill man.

The hill man pressed his lips against Blue Sky's.

The encampment comrades had taught Blue Sky more than either they or he realized. What he'd seen them do in the forest together, he did with the hill man that night.

*****

One of the valley people's stories had it that when the river people first came up to their town, the visitors couldn't speak their hosts' language. So the court people and tellers taught them how to speak it. They did it by pointing at something, such as wheat or cattle, or doing something, perhaps eating bread or drinking wine, and saying what they called it. It was difficult for the river people at first, but gradually they learned enough words to understand what the valley people were saying and to make themselves understood as well.

Blue Sky never heard anybody tell that story and specify how their people and the river people had made their initial contact. Surely, the river people didn't just arrive in the town one day needing to be taught the valley people's language. Why hadn't the guards at the lower gorge turned them back or killed them? Why had anybody given a thought to the possibility of teaching intruders their language? What was their purpose?

Most of the tellers dealt with Blue Sky's questions by reminding him the events in the story took place a long time ago, and what he was asking about, which wasn't very important to begin with, had been forgotten, as trivial matters always were. A few tellers—including Fair Judge and those close to her—admitted they had no knowledge of a story in which the questions had been raised, much less answered, and that omission did seem unfortunate.

The significance of the story lay elsewhere, the majority of the tellers assured Blue Sky. The river people always gave one-tenth of their cargoes to the king, asking for nothing from him in return except his permission to come up the river to the town and trade the remainder of their goods to the people. The story said the reigning king promised he and his successors would always give the river people's tribute to the court people and tellers as their reward for teaching the river people the valley people's language.

What the court people and tellers didn't need of the king's tribute they were in turn free to trade to the farmers. The farmers didn't care who was on the other side of a trade. They only cared how much they had to give for what they were getting.

No matter why the king's tribute from the river people went to the court people and tellers, it was clearly done for the benefit of the farmers. Before the river people came, the farmers had to give the court people and tellers a portion of their crops and livestock. But they did it without getting anything in return except the hope that the court people and tellers would run the kingdom honestly and wisely. But that hadn't always been the case. After the river people came, the farmers only paid tribute, as did the tellers and court people, for the army.

That the river people relieved the farmers of the burden of supporting the court people and tellers was, without question, the most important part of the story.

Except for the lack of a proper beginning, the story of the river people and the solution to their language problem seemed right to Blue Sky. Knowing even a few of their hosts' words would've greatly assisted them in specifying, say, how many cartloads of wheat, barley, or lentils they wanted for how many jars of salt, bolts of linen, or items of pottery.

*****

Blue Sky therefore pointed at the hill man's spear and his own and pronounced his people's word for them.

The hill man looked at the spears.

Still pointing, Blue Sky repeated the word.

Amused, the hill man attempted to say the valley people's word for "spear" but missed.

Blue Sky pointed at many things—trees, bushes, stones, the sky, the stars—and said the words by which his people knew them.

Each time, the hill man seemed to try to say the same word, often came very close, but for some reason could almost never get it right.

He was laughing, too, each time Blue Sky named something and he failed to repeat it.

Blue Sky, who was far from laughter at that point, gave up.

The hill man laughed again.

Although Blue Sky was quite certain it hadn't taken the hill man long after their first embrace to figure out he was with a neophyte, he'd given Blue Sky no reason to believe his awkwardness mattered. Blue Sky, delighted to discover the hill man was anything but inept, had gladly let his new friend do all the leading in that night's dance.

Since they didn't speak the same language, though, there wasn't anything the hill man could've said about it anyway. Or so Blue Sky thought.

Still laughing, the hill man pointed at a male body part of Blue Sky's, and then at his own, and said a word. Blue Sky assumed he was calling it what the hill people called it.

Blue Sky tried to repeat the word.

The hill man seemed quite satisfied with Blue Sky's very first attempt.

They both repeated the word several times, laughing each time they said it.

It wasn't much different from the word Blue Sky's people used for the same body part.

Blue Sky pointed at his own ear.

The hill man pronounced a word. It was also close to the word Blue Sky's people used.

Blue Sky pointed at his nose.

Again, the hill people's word for it was remarkably similar to the valley people's.

That was when Blue Sky began to see there were things beyond their valley that his people didn't understand at all.

The hill man hadn't been trying to repeat the words Blue Sky was saying for spears, trees, stones, and stars. He was saying what his people called such things. He'd sounded as if he were coming close to speaking the words Blue Sky had uttered because the hill people's words and the valley people's were, in almost every case, strangely similar—even, occasionally, identical.

And the hill man already knew that. He knew this, too: the differences in their words followed a pattern. For example, whenever the valley people used a "sh" sound in a word, his people used a "ch" sound, and whenever Blue Sky's people used a "b," his used a "p."

The hill man had figured it out by eavesdropping. When he was in the bushes at the upper end of the gully during the previous summer and autumn, he could hear the men in the guard post talking. He gradually came to understand most of what they were saying.

He'd chosen to listen in on that particular guard post because he'd earlier determined it was where the valley people sent their apprentice tellers. He also wanted to make contact with Blue Sky's people. And he couldn't imagine he'd find a better place to do it.

Then, one autumn day, a new valley man called "Blue Sky" opted not to kill him—and confirmed the hill man's belief that the Blue Sky he'd spied upon would never do such a thing.

The hill man decided the strangely forlorn Blue Sky was the farmer he wanted to make contact with. During the winter, his desire to see Blue Sky again grew intense.

Then one spring evening, the hill man saw him kneeling on top of the boulder wall.

*****

After Blue Sky's first evening with the hill man, who was called Wandering Star, he sneaked down the gully to his campsite whenever he could. They'd achieve the main purpose of the visit, taking more and more time as they did so, and then they'd talk. Nonstop, they'd talk.

Whenever they were together, they were like children, looking for a new word to say. It reached the point where Blue Sky could often figure out, without being told, what the hill people's word for something was.

The hill man taught Blue Sky enough connecting and modifying words so they could understand each other in both languages, slipping in and out of them as they pleased, like clothes.

The main differences between their tongues were the phrases peculiar to each. The hill man still found it difficult to understand some of the valley people's. One night, after another hard rain fell and the brook rose, and they had to cross it in order not to be seen from the guard post, Blue Sky told the hill man he could easily jump over it. When he was done with his attempt, the hill man marveled that Blue Sky's people would use the expression "easily jump over" for "fall in and need the assistance of an enemy to get out again in order to keep from drowning."

Blue Sky also learned three nearly identical words in his and the hill man's languages were "prince," "tomorrow," and "execution."

*****

It stood to reason both peoples assumed they spoke very different languages. The only times they heard the other people speak were in their brief, clamorous mountain-pass encounters or in battles in their wars. Attempting to understand what the enemy warriors were screaming was the last thing on their minds—although, Blue Sky agreed with Wandering Star, it probably should've been the first.

Wandering Star was four years older than Blue Sky and a year older than Spring Rain and Many Numbers.

Both peoples' names for the sun, the moon, and all the significant stars, fixed or free to move about, were as consistently similar as all their other words.

So were the names of their gods and goddesses. Not only that, but each of them had accomplished the same remarkable deeds and taught mortals the same appropriate lessons. Who they were and what they'd said to humans, when they still spoke openly to them, were almost always indistinguishable.

There were a few differences. For instance, where the hill people's gods and goddesses blessed their people for their good behavior and obedience with a bountiful supply of wild animals, waterfowl, and fish in their hills and streams, the valley people's rewarded them with numerous cattle, sheep, and goats in their pastures and barns.

Wandering Star laughed. "It's nice of them to be so flexible on that point."

"Or maybe humans change the stories of the gods," Blue Sky offered, "for their own purposes."

They were sitting naked near Wandering Star's fire. Blue Sky was impressed that his hill man friend could do such a good job of shaving, looking at himself in a water bowl the way the valley people's ancestors did, before the river people brought them stone mirrors.

Wandering Star had glimpsed, as others of his people had, the containers the valley people—with the assistance of the hell gods they worshipped, the hill people assumed—got strangely docile, castrated male cattle to pull around. They could see that the containers rested on logs attached at either end to wooden boards carved and held together in forms as round as the sun and full moon. When the pulling beasts moved forward, the circular constructions rolled over the ground but somehow remained fixed in place relative to the container they supported.

Wandering Star had a great many inquiries about these contraptions and the animals pulling them. His people had no words in their language for "cart," "ox," "axle," or "wheel."

Wandering Star also surprised Blue Sky with the number of questions he asked about farming. Nothing Blue Sky told him regarding the planting of crops and the breeding of livestock failed to lead to more inquiries, whether in the same or a later conversation.

"Our tellers say your kings prohibit farming," Blue Sky said. "You can only eat and use what you find growing wild. You can't plant crops to harvest or raise animals to butcher."

Wandering Star nodded his head. "The penalty for any of that is death."

"Your people have stories where the gods told them the penalty for farming is death?"

This time Wandering Star vigorously shook his head.

"No god or goddess ever told my people they can't farm," he insisted. "Our kings and tellers say they can't."

"No stories from the gods? Just your kings' and tellers' say-so, and the penalty is death?"

"Our gods never prohibited farming. I made that argument to the tellers when I was one of them. I made it to the king. That's why the tellers expelled me from the tellerhood. That's why the king exiled me. That's why I live by myself. That's why I dreamed you'd come to see me."

His people's tellers had no farmers to advise on the planting of crops and breeding of livestock. They instead kept track of the seasons and the land they roamed to advise their people when and where to gather berries, roots, and grains and to hunt animals, fish, and birds.

Because Wandering Star was no longer a teller and therefore had no duties as a teller to perform—as well as no children, not even nieces and nephews, to feed, clothe, and shelter—he had time to travel extensively throughout his people's lands and remember what he saw.

As a result, he could find berries, roots, and nuts to gather, wild animals and waterfowl to kill, and nests to steal eggs from that his people's tellers in good standing knew nothing about. Despite his exile, his people would often come to him for guidance, and they were happy to share with him, then or later, whatever bounty he led them to.

His having been expelled from the tellerhood and exiled from his people hardly mattered to them, he told Blue Sky. His status seemed especially irrelevant when they were hungry.

*****

"Those men in the ravine last autumn were hunting," Blue Sky said.

"You could see that?" Wandering Star asked, putting another log on his fire.

"I saw the deer they were after. I couldn't see any reason why my people would wish to keep them from doing what they were doing. I wanted to see if they'd catch the deer."

"Did you tell your comrades that?"

"Yes."

"Did they agree with you?"

"No."

Wandering Star looked at Blue Sky. "What did they think those hill men were doing?"

"Attacking our guard post, our encampment. Testing us to see how vigilant and well trained we were."

"That's what your people think whenever they see hill men in the ravine?"

"Whenever they see armed hill men in the ravine. You know that's what they think."

"I know that's what they think whenever they see hill men armed for a hunt."

"How are my people supposed to know when those armed hill men are hunting and when they're attacking us? Unless one of us happens to see a deer jumping a brook—or the hunters' guide carelessly exposing himself?"

Wandering Star extended his arm around Blue Sky's shoulders.

"I'm grateful you didn't let your arrow go," he said.

As they often did when they were together, they spoke using the other's language, although Wandering Star sometimes had to supply a word for Blue Sky.

"What do your people think my people are doing?" Blue Sky asked.

"Being mean, unreasonable, brutal—not letting them come near your precious encampments even when they're only chasing a deer. They think your people do that because you hate them. Because your people think you're so much better than they are."

"But you know my people believe they're being attacked, and they're just defending themselves and their valley. You've figured that out by now."

"I figured that out some time ago. Yes, I did."

"But the hunters you're guiding don't believe you."

"No, they don't—no more than your comrades believe you. But your people do think they're superior to my people. My people are right about that."

Blue Sky looked down at the hills where Wandering Star's people lived.

"Your people are right about that," he agreed.

*****

The rain was beating on the roof of Wandering Star's tent, which was made of hides sewn together and draped over poles. It rose to a central peak like the wood and clay houses and huts the valley people built for the same purpose—to keep the elements out. Because the higher hides generously overlapped the lower, the tent kept its occupants dry during the heaviest downpours.

It was also as warm as the hut Blue Sky shared with Spring Rain, even for two men sleeping naked together during chilly spring nights in the mountains.

"You were warning those hunters not to get any closer to my people's guard post."

"That's right," Wandering Star agreed, laughing. "I was afraid you and that other man with you would slaughter them."

"More likely, your hunters would've slaughtered us."

"You were supposed to retreat. I heard your comrades yelling at you. But you were stubborn. You didn't move. I hadn't seen a farmer that brave before."

Blue Sky shook his head, remembering his folly that day. "I almost killed you."

"But you didn't."

"You had your back to me. If I'd let my arrow go, I'm certain I would've killed you."

"Why didn't you let your arrow go?"

As Blue Sky had sometimes done with Spring Rain, usually after consuming wine, he touched his hand to Wandering Star's face and caressed his lips.

"The man crawling in the bushes," he replied, "was damned pleasing to see."

"That's all that saved me? You would've killed me if you'd thought I was ugly?"

Wandering Star was making Blue Sky face the truth.

"No," Blue Sky replied. "I would've pitied you even more than I already did. I never could've brought myself to kill you."

"No matter what I looked like?"

"No matter what you looked like. But what you looked like did make me come down here to see you close up. I admit that."

*****

Toward the end of the previous autumn, Wandering Star had moved his tent, pitching it near one of his people's cold-weather encampments—and his mother.

The game his people didn't consume during the warm weather they smoked and dried for the winter. Again, despite the official constraints of his exile, the hunters he'd guided gave him his portions of their provisions when he showed up and asked for them, which was only when even he couldn't find game.

His father had been killed in the last war with the valley people. His mother then attempted to continue living with his father's family, as she was supposed to do. Blue Sky's people had the same law, but it was never enforced if the woman objected.

The relatives of Wandering Star's father's had a reputation for being difficult to get along with. They often spoke, in his mother's presence, of the hardship sharing their food, hides, and firewood with her and her bratty son was causing them.

She complained to the hill people's king, Lightning Spear, who let her leave them. Because her own family wouldn't take her back, and wasn't required to, she lived alone with Wandering Star after that. Despite having no family except each other, they'd survived.

The people Wandering Star wasn't supposed to have anything to do with included his own mother, even if that meant she starved to death from lack of food or froze in the winter without firewood or adequate shelter. Nevertheless, he did see her regularly, taking her game, hides, roots, and firewood. And he somehow got away with it.

*****

"Why do your people hunt so close to my people's guard posts?" Blue Sky asked. "If they're only hunting, and have no wish to fight us, why don't they stay farther away? Why do they take any chance on causing trouble with my people? They're always on the losing end of it."

As Wandering Star sometimes did when Blue Sky asked him questions, he laughed.

"You don't know," he said, 'how stupid those questions would sound to my people."

"I know many of my questions sound stupid. My own people have made that clear to me. If you find them as amusing as they do, though, I suppose that's reason enough for me to ask them. But I still like to hear the answers—however obvious they are to others brighter than me."

Wandering Star laughed again. "It's the animals we hunt. That's your answer."

Blue Sky shook his head. "I still don't understand. Why are animals the answer?"

"They're plentiful up here during the spring, summer, and autumn. They mostly stay on your side of the mountains because your people don't hunt them. But sometimes they come down on our side of the mountains. In this ravine, they do it to drink from the brook. You must be able to see them from your guard post."

"We often see them," Blue Sky said.

"And think nothing of them."

"And think nothing of them," Blue Sky agreed.

"Our people get hungry for them. They're sometimes willing to take the chance they'll cross into territory where your people don't want them to go. Several years ago, our king explicitly ordered our people not to fight with your people unless he tells them to. But when your people needlessly antagonize our hunters, they both get a fight no matter what Lightning Spear wants."

"Last summer my people killed two of your people here. Were they hunting?"

Wandering Star nodded his head. "Yes, they were."

"Were you guiding them?"

"Yes, I was. Your people goaded them into that fight. The hunters had no shields. They thought—I thought—that would let your people know they were hunting. But when they got within range of arrows from your guard post, your people fired on them anyway. The hunters retrieved their shields and charged up the ravine. I tried to talk them out of it, but they wouldn't listen to me. They were going to kill as many of your men as they could. Last autumn, you and your comrade didn't shoot any arrows at the hunters. That's why they left that buck in the thicket and went away. But the hunters last summer weren't so reasonable. They were hopelessly outnumbered from the start. Lightning Spear was angry. He said he had horrific dreams of your people celebrating the deaths of two of his people. He ordered the survivors of the skirmish to execute their leader for allowing it to happen. Each of them had to take a turn spearing him."

Meanwhile, Blue Sky's people had celebrated. Two hill men, supposedly warriors, were dead. The rest of them had run away. None of the valley people's guards were injured. The valley warriors, particularly those who'd sunk their spears in human flesh, were heroes.

"As if the hunting party hadn't suffered enough already," Wandering Star added, "they had to suffer even more because the king had bad dreams. I wasn't supposed to be there, but I was anyway. I watched the execution. The leader was foolish and impulsive, but he didn't deserve to die. I knew him and liked him. I begged the king to spare the man, but he told me to go away."

Blue Sky's people hadn't given any thought to the hill people's view of the encounter.

"I'd watched the fighting, too," Wandering Star continued. "From the bushes. All of it was senseless. What our hunters did. What your warriors did. What our king did. The leader's death was excruciating. Lightning Spear made certain it took all day for him to die. I was with the man most of the time. They wouldn't let me put him out of his misery. I begged to do it. Lightning Spear ordered me to leave—or I'd be the next to die."

And Blue Sky's people, as the hill people's king had assumed, were jubilant, sending profuse thanks up to the gods in heaven for saving them from their evil enemy one more time.

Chapter 10

Spring Rain guessed that Blue Sky's absences from their hut—mostly in the early evening, but a few times lasting all night—meant he'd broken his vow not to go with any man.

Blue Sky admitted he'd decided celibacy wasn't what he wanted.

But when he refused to reveal the identity of the man he was going with, Spring Rain wondered if he'd chosen to go with more than one man, as many of the tellers did.

It was morning. They were in the guard post. The brook below was sparkling in the sun.

Blue Sky refused to satisfy Spring Rain's curiosity on that point one way or the other.

Spring Rain laughed. "Are you still in love with the prince?" he asked.

"I'll always be in love with Morning Sun," Blue Sky replied. "And you."

Spring Rain was no longer laughing.

*****

When Many Numbers came to sunrise pass for the next full-moon holiday, the first of that spring, he couldn't wait to tell Blue Sky and Spring Rain the news from the other side of the forest.

"The kingdom is in turmoil," he said as soon as he reached their hut and set down his bags.

"Over a gully?" Blue Sky asked, handing him a cup of wine.

Many Numbers eagerly drank from it. "On my way back to the town, I stopped in the home village with Rose Leaf. I explained to your parents what you and Spring Rain showed me. They had no difficulty believing you could see a gully where others couldn't. All four of us went to the town the next morning. We saw Sturdy Limb. He refused to hear us. He told us only the king listens to the stories of a lunatic boy."

The "lunatic boy," sitting in the late afternoon sun with his heroes, laughed at that.

"I raised the matter in open court," Many Numbers continued. "I tried to convince Tall Oak the gully comes dangerously close to the apprentice tellers' guard post and encampment."

"What did the king say?" Spring Rain asked impatiently.

"He didn't pay much attention to what I said," Many Numbers replied. "He acted bored. He kept looking at Sturdy Limb and Law Keeper and rolling his eyes. He was deliberately rude—and making certain everybody could see it."

"What did he say?" Spring Rain insisted.

"When I finished, he merely looked at me and laughed," Many Numbers replied. "Then he turned to Green Field and asked him if his son had taken leave of his senses. The court people and tellers laughed at that. The great hall was packed by then. Tall Oak turned back to me and smiled the way he would with a person complaining his neighbors weren't being nice to him. He asked me if maybe Green Field's son had infected Spring Rain with his silliness simply by living in the same hut with him. Law Keeper laughed at that. Loudly, too. 'I predicted it!' he shouted. Then he suggested I might wish to have the people in question separated. The high tellers pretended that was a hilarious joke. I must say, though, Rainbow Evening made no effort to conceal her irritation at the remarks concerning the two of you. She didn't allow an exception for Tall Oak's either."

"Okay," Blue Sky said. "The king doesn't wish to see a gully where we see one. How does that send the kingdom into turmoil? I can't blame people for amusing themselves at my expense. I'm a farmer's simpleminded son who's never learned to keep his mouth shut. So what?"

"So what?" Many Numbers repeated. "You're Green Field and Gentle Brook's son. That's what. And nobody in the kingdom who thinks at all thinks you're simpleminded."

"Why is the kingdom in turmoil?" Blue Sky insisted.

"Your father rose to his feet," Many Numbers replied. "Like Rainbow Evening, he wasn't laughing. And suddenly, nobody else was. He told Tall Oak he was free to believe you'd taken leave of your senses. Everybody knows you have opinions of your own on a great many subjects. Everybody also knows you have no fear of voicing your opinions, even in the face of laughter."

"Tall Oak must've been pleased to hear those remarks," Blue Sky said.

"Hardly," Many Numbers disagreed. "Your father was just getting started. He said if you, Spring Rain, and I had carefully figured out there must be a hidden gully in a dangerous place, we should be taken seriously. It would be easy enough for Tall Oak to relax one law one time to prove us right or wrong."

Blue Sky was in full regret he'd ever mentioned the gully to anybody. He wished he were still free to deny it existed. Wandering Star had told him he was certain no other hill people knew about it.

"What did Tall Oak say to that?" Spring Rain asked, hesitantly this time, as if his desire to know might be fading.

"He didn't say anything," Many Numbers replied. "He merely shook his head wearily. It was very insulting. Rainbow Evening closed her eyes. The court people and tellers began to whisper among themselves. They'd never heard Tall Oak and Green Field take such clearly opposing sides of a matter before."

"And that sent the kingdom into turmoil?" Blue Sky asked.

Many Numbers shook his head. "Your father didn't stop there either."

"He didn't?" Blue Sky asked, failing to conceal the apprehension in his own voice.

"No," Many Numbers replied. "He also told Tall Oak any person who saw fit to laugh at and ignore what you, Spring Rain, and I had to say on such a serious subject could only be described as an arrogant fool."

Spring Rain looked at Blue Sky as one would a person perilously near the edge of a cliff.

"Can't you imagine how upset the people are?" Many Numbers asked. "The farmers—and even many of the court people and tellers—liked it that Tall Oak went to your father for advice. Now the two old hero friends are having a public falling-out."

"Two old hero friends calling one another fools in public," Blue Sky said, affecting a sneer. "I can't imagine that's ever happened before—not in our perfectly behaved kingdom."

Many Numbers shook his head again. "The king never called your father a fool. After your father made his 'arrogant fool' remark, Tall Oak simply sat there with the queen and remained silent. Everything seemed reversed. I wasn't the only one who saw it. Tall Oak looked like somebody Sturdy Limb's deputies had dragged into court to learn what his punishment would be. And your father looked like a king about to let the poor man know he'd soon be dead."

Blue Sky had heard the king and his father, in the heat of arguments, disparage one another's views as "foolish." Even, on occasion, as "senseless" or "inane." But they'd never done it in the presence of anyone other than their mates and children. It often seemed, too, the real purpose of their characterizations was to amuse, as if they were boys again growing up together.

"What happened then?" Spring Rain asked, almost whispering.

"Green Field announced he had nothing further to say and was going home," Many Numbers replied. "Nobody said a word for a long time after that. Everybody simply sat there watching as Gentle Brook and Rose Leaf got up and left the great hall with Green Field."

"He made no apology to the king and queen?" Spring Rain asked.

"None whatsoever."

"Did they say anything about Morning Sun and Rose Leaf?" Blue Sky asked.

"No, of course not," Many Numbers replied. "But that's the reason why the kingdom's in turmoil. The people very much want the prince to marry Rose Leaf in the autumn. They're saying every person who's physically able to show up for the wedding festivities will be there."

"So the people," Blue Sky asked, "don't think this is all about something so unimportant as a gully in the mountains—even if it exists?"

"No," Many Numbers replied. "They think it must be about Morning Sun and Rose Leaf. The high tellers say the king told Law Keeper he'll never allow them to live together and have children. But he wouldn't tell him why. And now your father and the king are openly feuding."

Spring Rain looked at Blue Sky. "Are Morning Sun and Rose Leaf brother and sister?"

"They can't be," Blue Sky replied. "My parents and the king and queen would've admitted that to them and me by now. They wouldn't have to let the people know. Morning Sun and Rose Leaf would understand. They'd be awfully unhappy. But they wouldn't go into the forest and hang themselves from a tree. They'd find other people to have children with."

Many Numbers quickly nodded his head. "That's what the court people and tellers say."

"Does Sturdy Limb know what the problem is?" Spring Rain asked.

"People say he doesn't," Many Numbers replied. "Tall Oak and Rainbow Evening flatly refuse to speak on the subject to anyone, beyond what the king said to Law Keeper. Sturdy Limb says he merely does what the king tells him to do. If the king doesn't want the prince having children with Rose Leaf, he'll make certain it doesn't happen."

"The season for treason approaches," Blue Sky remarked.

"I wish you wouldn't say that," Spring Rain said.

"But it does," Blue Sky countered. "If Tall Oak won't let the tellers perform a marriage ceremony, Morning Sun and Rose Leaf will have a child together anyway. They promise me they will. I assure you they will. Sturdy Limb can't stop them. Tall Oak has said he'll order any child of theirs killed. If he does, the tellers will have to declare he's no longer fit to be king. They'll never let him kill Morning Sun and Rose Leaf's child. The people will march on the town and stop it. The tellers will have to bless Morning Sun as the new king."

Spring Rain shook his head. "And if the people and the tellers let Tall Oak kill the child? Won't the child's parents also die? Having committed treason? And the three of us? Having helped them? And others? Don't our people execute traitors? Isn't that what Tall Oak promised?"

Blue Sky didn't hesitate. "If I lived in a kingdom with people who'd let their king kill an innocent child, I'd wish to be killed myself. And before, not after, they killed the child."

*****

Blue Sky might've been willing, at that point, to pretend Wandering Star's gully didn't exist, but his sunrise pass comrades weren't.

He and Spring Rain had sat with them in the guard post when the sun was in the right place, and its light let them see at least some of what Blue Sky saw.

Having been in the gully himself—although he couldn't let them know that—he was able to distinguish every top of a spindly tree growing in it from every scraggly bush on either side of it.

His comrades could see, more and more, what he saw.

Morning Sun and Solemn Promise came to their encampment and sat in the guard post themselves and began to see what Blue Sky saw.

They sent their comrades around the rim of the canyon to see for themselves.

During their visit over the first full-moon holiday of spring, Many Numbers and Rose Leaf had described for both encampments Tall Oak's refusal to take seriously Many Numbers' plea for an inspection of the clump of bushes to prove whether Blue Sky was right or not.

Most of the young women and tellers who'd come to sunrise pass for the full-moon holiday had been in court that day. They'd heard Many Numbers was going to confront the king about Blue Sky and Spring Rain's gully. They confirmed the truth of the story Many Numbers and Rose Leaf told, and they didn't leave out what Green Field had called his old friend the king.

The sunrise pass comrades were soon talking of little else but the gully. Groups of two or three discussing the matter became larger groups.

The court people's sons came to meet with the supervising and apprentice tellers, and they all viewed once again what they could make out of the gully from the apprentice tellers' guard post. Blue Sky no longer had to say a word. His comrades saw what he saw.

Both encampments soon agreed that leaving the matter as it was would be intolerable. If the gully existed, the kingdom was open to a surprise attack, and they would be the first to die.

And if the guards couldn't hold off the enemy at sunrise pass, the valley people would be fighting another war with the hill people that could be just as disastrous as the last one was.

For both peoples, Blue Sky saw fit to add.

*****

"You called my people thieves," Blue Sky said.

Wandering Star was standing in the spring-fed pond where the brook began. Grasping his spear with both hands, he had it aimed at the water. He'd promised to show Blue Sky how he caught fish.

The valley people didn't eat fish. River people did, cooking their catch over fires in the great tents they pitched below the bluff.

Spring Rain and Many Numbers had a friend among the river traders who prepared meals of fish for them, Rainbow Evening, and Fair Judge. They all said they enjoyed eating it.

"That day last autumn," Blue Sky began again. "You were calling my people thieves. I've figured it out. You were using your people's word for thief. You were telling the hunters to turn back. You were telling them the thieves were too close ahead."

"What was I supposed to call your people?"

"Your people don't call us valley people?"

Wandering Star laughed. "That's what you call yourselves. My people would never call your people that. I do it with you just to be polite. And I've come to like you, too."

On the other hand, his people did call themselves "hill people."

"Your people call us thieves?" Blue Sky asked.

"Of course we do."

"I don't see what's so amusing about that."

Wandering Star laughed again. "Thievery isn't amusing. But your ignorance is."

"I don't mind your laughing at that. I admit I'm ignorant. There seem to be too many things in this world I don't know enough about. But I hardly think my people are thieves."

Wandering Star stared at the water he waded in. "I thought you told me your people's tellers, like my people's, pass down the stories of your people from one generation to the next."

"They do. I told you they do."

"Don't they tell the story of how your people got their valley?"

The valley people's stories said only that their gods gave them their valley and promised them they'd keep it as long as they pleased their benefactors. And the valley people would do that by working hard and long with their crops in their fields, with their livestock in their barns and pastures, and with their comrades in their villages, training for the next war with their enemy.

The valley people's stories didn't tell them specifically how the gift of their valley was made—just as those tales failed to explain how the valley people first made contact with river people, or how the tellers knew what they claimed to know about the hill people.

"Your people stole the valley from my people," Wandering Star said.

He suddenly thrust his spear into the water, cutting into it cleanly, making no splash.

"Here we go," he said, withdrawing his spear from the water.

He'd impaled a fish as long as a grown man's forearm, thrusting his spear tip all the way through it. Now it was flopping about on the end of his weapon.

Wandering Star swung the spear tip around to within a finger's length of Blue Sky's nose.

Blue Sky stared into the unblinking eyes of the fish, which would soon see nothing.

"You don't know that?" Wandering Star asked, climbing out of the pond. "Your people don't know what your greedy, thieving, murdering ancestors did?"

"I've never heard anybody say my people stole the valley from your people."

"Your people don't know my people used to live in the valley? Your people don't know the valley used to be ours?"

"How did my people end up with it?"

"Your people came here from somewhere else. Most of the tellers think they came up the river from the south. Wherever they came from, they had their animals with them. They saw how fertile the valley was and decided in a glance they wanted it for themselves. They wanted the land to grow the crops they planted and feed the animals they kept."

"One of my people's stories has us wandering in the wilderness," Blue Sky said. "That's when the gods interceded on our behalf and gave us our valley."

Wandering Star pulled the fish off his spear.

"But your people already lived there?" Blue Sky asked. "Your people's story says that?"

"Your people attacked my people without warning, slaughtering most of them. The survivors fled over the mountains, many of them wounded, all of them starving."

He glanced toward the hills his people roamed and shook his head.

"Your people chased my people out of our valley," he continued. "To these barren, hopeless lands where we've lived and died in shame ever since. That's what your people did."

"This happened many years ago?"

"Several generations ago."

"And your people, unlike my people, haven't forgotten what happened."

"They'll never forget what happened."

In the swift water of the brook, Wandering Star washed the blood off his spear and hands.

"A long time ago," he said, "some king of yours must've prohibited the telling of the story. That would be the easiest thing to do—simply deny your ancestors did anything so horrific."

Blue Sky wished he could've proved his ancestors hadn't done that, but he couldn't.

"I've noticed in your people's stories," he said, "the gods gave them their land. The same as in my people's stories. My people assume the land in those stories is the valley. Is the land in your people's stories also the valley?"

"Of course it is. Plus all the hills outside the valley. All the hills we roam and the valley belong to us. None of it belongs to your people. That's what my people's stories say."

They walked along the brook to Wandering Star's tent. He was going to roast the fish over his fire. Blue Sky had accepted his dare to eat it with him.

"In my people's story," Blue Sky said, "the gods took the valley away from the people who were there previously because they'd disobeyed the gods' commands. The story doesn't say how those people incurred the wrath of the gods. It just says they did. Most of our tellers think it's because those people refused to farm and insisted on hunting instead. They say the gods wanted humans to use the valley for farming. Some of our tellers disagree. They say the gods would never punish anybody for that by taking their land away from them."

Wandering Star was wrapping the fish in leaves.

"Does your story say," he asked, "when the gods expelled those people from the valley?"

"No. My people assume it had to have been long before they gave it to us."

"Does the story say how your gods took the valley away from those previous people?"

"No, it doesn't. I've noticed that. It doesn't."

"Your people could've thought they heard their gods tell them to kill as many of those people as they could and chase the survivors into the hills. That's how your gods could've done it."

Wandering Star sat down on the log next to Blue Sky and put his arm around his shoulders.

"I suppose," Blue Sky said, shuddering, "that's how it could've been done."

In his people's stories, they'd sometimes brutally wiped out their enemies. And it was always because their gods had told them that's what they wanted them to do.

Wandering Star's people told the same stories, except in their versions they were the people rightfully exterminating their enemies— as they were in the last war for a brief while.

*****

The sunrise pass comrades continued their discussions. They sometimes left the prince, Solemn Promise, Spring Rain, and Blue Sky out of them.

Then those left out learned why they'd been left out.

Their comrades invited them to a meeting at Morning Sun's encampment.

Nobody, not even Noon Breeze, drank wine during that gathering. Nobody spoke of a revel either remembered or planned. Nobody told a joke or attempted a prank.

The sunrise pass comrades had decided Morning Sun, Blue Sky, Solemn Promise, and Spring Rain should go to see the king. What they were asking their four comrades to do was contrary to the laws of the kingdom. They had no right to leave their encampments except when it was their turn for full-moon leave, or if somebody agreed to swap leave with them.

Additionally, their comrades didn't want the four of them to wait until the next full moon. They wanted them to go as soon as they could.

There was an exception in the law. If an emergency arose, and the chief warrior and king needed to know about it, a messenger had to be sent to the town immediately.

It could be argued, though, a messenger, Many Numbers, had already been sent, and Tall Oak had already decided there was no gully and therefore no emergency.

The sunrise pass comrades countered that Many Numbers had gone to see the chief warrior and king on his own. He couldn't and didn't tell them all the warriors on sunrise pass had agreed there might very well be a gully where Blue Sky was convinced one existed.

It could also be argued there was no need to send four messengers when one would do.

The sunrise pass comrades insisted the matter was too important to be left on the shoulders of any one person, even if that person was the prince. Morning Sun's comrades needed to show the king they fully supported him.

They also argued it wasn't difficult to see who should go with the prince.

Solemn Promise wasn't merely the youngest son of the wealthiest family in the kingdom. He was one of the few court people the farmers respected. They knew he, unlike his father and mother and all his other siblings, favored his sister's mating with Autumn Wine's grandson, despite the status of the young wood-man's family as one of the least wealthy in the kingdom.

As for Spring Rain, many valley people traveled long distances to the bluff above the river. They came to see the river traders and their exotic wares, to see from the bluff-top their lovely valley and its protecting mountains, to see the town and its crowds of people dressed in linen, and certainly to see the court, the king, the queen, and the prince. But they came especially to see and hear Spring Rain. Some had gone so far as to say, after they'd heard him, that he proved the goddess of love was actually a god—as more than a few of the male tellers liked to argue.

As for Blue Sky, he'd discovered the gully and could recite all the evidence proving its existence. His comrades didn't need to mention he was also Green Field and Gentle Brook's son, the prince's best friend, Rose Leaf's brother, and the boy who'd grown up talking back to the king.

*****

Before the chosen comrades began their trek down the mountains to the town, Blue Sky had enough time to see Wandering Star and let him know where he was going and why.

Wandering Star once again told Blue Sky he was confident none of his people other than he realized they could use a hidden gully to mount a surprise attack on the valley people's encampments on sunrise pass. He cautioned, though, they might figure it out, as he had.

They agreed Blue Sky's people were fortunate none of the hill people had stumbled upon the situation before Wandering Star did.

Most of the valley people liked to think the gods were protecting them. Many Numbers and not a few others, though, believed they should always remember the gods sometimes weren't above surprising them. The last war with the hill people was an example of what the gods could stoop to. It might've been useful instruction for the mortals caught up in it. It might've also been little more than idle entertainment for the beings in heaven who'd let it happen.

Wandering Star promised Blue Sky he'd attempt to keep other hill people away from the gully, but he couldn't remain there guarding it constantly. He had to see his mother from time to time to ensure she had what she needed to get by in the unforgiving world they lived in.

*****

The four sunrise pass comrades emerged from the forest early in the morning.

Two of East Land's older grandsons, driving their family's livestock to their pasture for the day, saw them climbing over the wall.

"The prince," they whispered simultaneously, each with his eyes wide open like an owl's.

Nearing the prince and his comrades, the boys asked them why they'd left their encampments. Was the kingdom falling apart?

Morning Sun said they were on their way to see his father about the hidden gully near the apprentice tellers' guard post.

One of the boys immediately ran back to his village with the news.

East Land and the other members of his family came out to the main path to meet the prince and his party. They'd heard, as every other person in the valley had by then, all about Many Numbers' plea regarding the gully, the king's laughing dismissal of it as a product of Blue Sky's overworked imagination, and Green Field's angrily daring to call his old friend the king an "arrogant fool."

Observing the looks on the faces of East Land's family, and having heard the boys, Blue Sky concluded Many Numbers' assertion that the kingdom was in turmoil was based in fact.

As the older children did whenever there was news among the people needing to be told and retold, those in East Land's village were already running to neighboring villages to let them know the prince, Green Field's son, Spring Rain, and Solemn Promise had come down from sunrise pass and were on their way to see the king about the gully. Soon older children in those villages would run to more distant villages, from which more children would go out, until every village in the kingdom, as well as the town, had heard the news.

*****

By the time the four guards reached the point where the path from East Land's village merged with the path from the home village, they could see numerous groups of farmers ahead of and behind them on their way to the town.

If there was to be another confrontation in court, this one involving their beloved prince, they weren't about to miss it. The work of early spring would simply have to wait.

Many of them appeared eager to let the prince know that if he, Many Numbers, and the sunrise pass guards thought there might be a gully where Blue Sky said one was, it was a matter of grave concern to the entire kingdom. It was hardly something a person in full command of his reasoning powers would laugh about.

During the last full-moon holiday, Many Numbers told the sunrise pass warriors that the people were asking their favorite tellers to come to their villages. Fair Judge was walking from one end of the valley to the other and back again. The people wanted to hear the sad story of the king who'd lost his mind and forced the tellers to declare the prince the new king.

*****

Soon after the paths merged, Rose Leaf caught up with the four guards.

She'd started out from the home village as soon as she'd heard the news from a neighboring village's messenger boy, breathless but pleased he could forever after that day say he was the first to tell Rose Leaf, Green Field, and Gentle Brook.

Rose Leaf asked Solemn Promise and Spring Rain if she could speak privately with the prince and her brother.

"Of course," they said, having reason to suspect she wouldn't be talking about a gully.

"Many Numbers was right," Blue Sky said to Rose Leaf. "The kingdom is in turmoil. And all because our father called the king a fool."

"When everybody already knew what their king was," Morning Sun added, laughing.

Rose Leaf looked at Morning Sun sternly, as a mother would an especially naughty child. She was in no mood for humor.

"What are you doing?" she asked him.

Morning Sun looked at her and smiled. "Our comrades insisted we go to see the king."

"Warriors don't say no to their comrades," Blue Sky added, repeating a remark Noon Breeze often made use of.

Rose Leaf turned to her older brother as if he, too, were her child.

"I'm sure it was your idea," she said. "Having your comrades ask the prince and you to go to see the king. I'm your sister. I know how you are. You manipulate people."

Morning Sun laughed again. It hadn't taken much for Blue Sky to persuade him. After he agreed, Solemn Promise and even Spring Rain soon fell into line.

157

Morning Sun turned to Rose Leaf. "He got them to see there's a gully too near the apprentice tellers' guard post. That's all he had to do."

Rose Leaf shook her head. "The people know this is about more than a damned gully. Sturdy Limb knows. He says he's discovered there's a cabal in this kingdom willing to attempt treason. He's saying some of the would-be traitors are quite close to the king himself."

Morning Sun laughed once more. "This is remarkable. For the first time in his life, my uncle gets something right. I'll have to commend him for it."

"When will you do that?" Rose Leaf asked. "When he's got his executioner's spear aimed at your guts? Or when you're bleeding in the dirt, begging him to get it over with?"

The fading of the prince's smile was like the passing behind clouds of the heavenly body he was named for.

"We can't wait until a child of ours is facing my uncle's spear," he said. "We're having a wedding ceremony in the autumn. We've got to get matters settled before then."

When the prince turned to Blue Sky, though, the clouds were gone again.

"But today it's the gully," he said.

$$*****$$

"That's right," Many Numbers agreed. "Today it's the gully."

He, Spring Rain, and Blue Sky were whispering together while they waited with the crowd in the courtyard for the king and queen.

Far too many farmers from villages near the town had shown up for court to be held in the great central hall without excluding, and no doubt angering, most of them. What could the court people do? They announced that the king and queen would sit that day in the courtyard.

Despite the early spring chill, the sun was shining, and the people were protected by the surrounding buildings from the capricious morning breezes on the bluff top.

"And whatever else it might be," Spring Rain said, "it's treason."

Many Numbers looked at him and scowled.

"Would you prefer we call it something else?" he asked. "I've always thought that was the word we used whenever we described people seeking to overthrow their rulers, even their corrupt and inept rulers."

"Or a crazed ruler," Blue Sky said. "One who tries to tell us the prince and the woman he loves aren't free to marry—for some reason he won't reveal. If disputing that kind of ruling is treason, feel free to call me the chief traitor, the one who deserves to die the most agonizing death."

Chapter 11

Tall Oak and Rainbow Evening came through the main entrance to the courtyard, followed by Sturdy Limb and his high deputies and Law Keeper and his high tellers.

Morning Sun, Rose Leaf, Many Numbers, Solemn Promise, Spring Rain, and Blue Sky were standing in front of the dais the court people had hastily erected.

Immediately behind them stood their self-proclaimed "allies": younger tellers, friends of Many Numbers and Spring Rain; Valley Defender, his two brothers, and the older and younger brothers of Morning Sun's town companions on sunrise pass; Autumn Wine's grandsons and more than a few younger men and older boys from the nearby villages.

Rose Leaf wasn't the only woman in the group. Solemn Promise's sister was there, conspicuously standing next to Autumn Wine's older grandson. East Land's niece and the woman who lived with her in East Land's village were present, along with a number of other young women from the villages near the town.

Ordinarily, the only people who carried weapons in the town were the chief warrior and his deputies. But that day, every able-bodied male of age in the courtyard had brought his spear.

The young people standing with the prince and the woman he wished to marry made way for the king and queen and their party.

Tall Oak stared at Morning Sun as if he were encountering a stranger.

Somewhere beneath the king's notice, the boy prince the farmers were so fond of had become a man prince they adored. And if the man prince wanted a life and children with Rose Leaf—Green Field and Gentle Brook's daughter, no less—that was what the farmers wanted.

Tall Oak had ruled the kingdom from its reconstruction and recovery after the last war with the hill people to its present prosperity. Despite the occasional bumbling of his chief warrior and first teller—and not even the gods would wish to stay long in a dominion with no scandal at all—the valley people considered Tall Oak's reign the most successful the kingdom had enjoyed.

At least that was the case before he made known a decision that seemed to be irrational: the young woman most suitable for the prince in every way imaginable was the one the king said he couldn't have. And the king had compounded his error by steadfastly refusing to explain why the prince, the woman, and the people should accept such a bizarre ruling.

The king looked at Blue Sky the way he had the prince: as if he didn't know who the person in front of him was.

On more occasions than Blue Sky could count, he'd told the king that his chief warrior, first teller, and the people closest to them were using their positions to advance their own interests rather than Tall Oak's or, more importantly, the kingdom's.

Tall Oak would usually not respond to what Blue Sky said. When he did, it was only to mumble something to the effect that a kingdom had to be ruled in that manner, and people who believed it was wrong shouldn't delude themselves into thinking there was a better way to do it.

But he'd never heard Blue Sky make his argument with a spear in his hand.

Rainbow Evening chose to stop and embrace Morning Sun.

The prince handed his spear to Blue Sky and took his mother in his arms.

And when she let him go again, she had tears in her eyes.

She turned to Rose Leaf, Blue Sky, and the others who were standing with the prince.

"I'm so pleased to see you all today," she said. "When I look at you, I'm looking at the future of our people."

As was the custom, the onlookers closest to them repeated her words to those who were further away, who in turn repeated them to those who were still further away, until even those at the most distant fringe of the crowd got to hear what the queen had said.

Tall Oak was staring at Morning Sun again.

"Do you wish to join your mother and me on the dais?" he asked.

"No, sir," Morning Sun replied. "If you don't mind, I wish to remain with the people."

Their words went out to the crowd as Rainbow Evening's had.

Sturdy Limb, looking on, couldn't conceal his contempt for the queen's sentimental effusions, the king's abject request, and the prince's defiant reply.

His high deputies and Law Keeper and his high tellers did their best to mimic—and in some cases, outdo—the chief warrior's scornful countenance.

The people from the villages, on the other hand, couldn't hide their approval of what they'd seen and heard so far. They sent up a loud cheer.

As the king and queen mounted the dais and seated themselves in their chairs, Sturdy Limb and his high deputies and Law Keeper and his high tellers took their usual places on their benches on either side of the dais facing the crowd. The chief warrior and deputies sat to the right of the king, the tellers to the left.

The king said he had no announcements to make. He asked his brother for his.

As Sturdy Limb mounted the dais, the crowd audibly sighed and found places to sit in the new grass and clover. They were expecting another of the chief warrior's lengthy descriptions of the behavior he and his deputies would not, under any circumstances, tolerate in their kingdom.

At least when he got to the crimes of fornication and excessive drunkenness, some of the onlookers—in many cases the people generally considered the most likely to be charged with those offenses, if anybody ever were again—would get their chance to loudly agree the acts were intolerable. And any people committing them should consider themselves fortunate the present king, unlike his predecessors, had refused to order such people punished for their misdeeds.

That morning, though, Sturdy Limb chose to speak of one crime only: treason. As he did so, he fixed his gaze on Morning Sun and Blue Sky as if they were already on trial for the offense.

Unfortunately for the chief warrior, he soon found himself severely upstaged.

The farmers nearest the main entrance to the courtyard were rising to their feet and noisily greeting two late arrivals.

The entire crowd stood up to see who they were: Green Field and Gentle Brook.

Like a calf bawling for its mother in a violent storm, Sturdy Limb attempted to make himself heard above the tumult that followed. But he soon had to give up.

The newcomers, spotting Morning Sun, Rose Leaf, Blue Sky, and their allies in front of the dais, proceeded toward them.

The crowd, still letting them know, quite loudly in some cases, how welcome they were, opened a path for them.

Sturdy Limb, glaring at Green Field and Gentle Brook, got down from the dais and resumed his usual position with his high deputies.

Green Field and Gentle Brook embraced Morning Sun, Rose Leaf, and Blue Sky and took the hands of Many Numbers, Spring Rain, and Solemn Promise.

Too late for the chief warrior, the crowd resumed its respectful silence.

The king asked, as he always did, if anybody present had a plea for him to hear.

Since nobody else in that huge crowd chose to speak, Blue Sky rose and began his: "There's a gully too near the apprentice tellers' guard post on sunrise pass. A gully where hill warriors can hide and not be seen by our people's guards."

As those words went out to the crowd, Sturdy Limb got to his feet and waved his spear in Blue Sky's direction.

Morning Sun stood up. As did Rose Leaf, Many Numbers, Spring Rain, and Solemn Promise. As did the young tellers, court companions, and farmers surrounding them.

As did the high deputies and tellers. As did all the people except the king and the queen.

"The king has already heard your plea," Sturdy Limb announced, bellowing now like a bull denied a cow in heat. "He chose to believe, as any sensible person would, the gully exists only in your imagination. I forbid you to say another word on that subject. The time of the king is too precious for your nonsense—no matter who your father and mother happen to be."

Blue Sky waited for the repeaters to finish their work before he replied.

"Nobody's time is too precious for such an obvious threat to the kingdom," he said. "Not even the king's—no matter who he happens, at this moment, to be."

Sturdy Limb pointed his spear in Blue Sky's direction, as did Law Keeper and the high deputies and tellers.

"Hold your tongue!" Sturdy Limb screamed. "If you don't, I'll order my men to remove you! If you put up any resistance, I'll have you confined in a cage! You'll only come out of it for your trial for treason! I'm the chief warrior in this kingdom, and you'll do in this court, as well as in your encampment, what I tell you to do!"

Hearing that, most of the crowd groaned.

"The hill people can sneak into our kingdom and attack us," Blue Sky said. "Is that something a sensible chief warrior considers nonsense? Or is it very wrong to assume this kingdom has a sensible chief warrior?"

As his words went out to the crowd, Sturdy Limb and his high deputies approached him.

The prince gestured to the court companions, young tellers, and sons and daughters of farmers surrounding him and his allies to part just enough to let the chief warrior and his minions walk between them single file.

Morning Sun, visibly tightening his grip on his spear, positioned himself between his uncle and Blue Sky.

"Don't you or any of your people," he said to Sturdy Limb, "lay a hand on this man. If you do, you'll be in a fight with me. He's my comrade. And I'm telling you he can say in this court, to this king and this queen, my father and my mother, anything he pleases."

Some of the court companions, not unlike Morning Sun, were facing their uncles. A few, including Valley Defender, were daring their own fathers to fight them. In the skirmish on sunrise pass the previous summer, the first hill man to die did so with Valley Defender's spear in his belly.

"Step aside!" Sturdy Limb ordered his nephew.

Morning Sun remained motionless. "You can't say that to me," he said to his uncle. "I'm the prince in this kingdom. You're only the chief warrior. I don't step aside for you. And my comrades don't shut their mouths for you."

The crowd, getting what it had come for, greeted those remarks with approving hurrahs.

"Disperse!" Sturdy Limb ordered, waving his spear at the prince and Blue Sky and those standing with them. "Leave the courtyard at once! Otherwise I have cages for you all!"

Nobody moved.

Tall Oak and Rainbow Evening stared at the confrontation unfolding beneath them. This wasn't supposed to happen in their court. Many valley people might question, in private, the judgment of the chief warrior, but never in public in front of the king. That by itself could be treason. On the other hand, the chief warrior, as he'd so often done, was asking for trouble.

A voice in the crowd loudly promised that anybody who dared fight the prince would die.

Rainbow Evening rose from her chair, and the crowd chose silence again.

"Chief warrior," she said, "you and your men may not touch my son. As he informed you, he's the prince in this kingdom. He's a man now as well. He doesn't answer to you. He answers only to the king, myself, and the people."

As soon as the farmers heard what Rainbow Evening said, they thundered their approval.

The queen continued. "If the prince wishes to have his friend Blue Sky make a plea in this court, you may not interfere with him. You and your men will lower your spears, take your usual places, and remain silent while he has his say."

Many in the crowd other than the usual repeaters chose to echo Rainbow Evening's last statement. And not to the further reaches of the crowd but back to the people to whom it was originally directed.

Few people in the kingdom could've failed to know Rainbow Evening detested the king's brother. Still, even she had never directly confronted the man in public.

Tall Oak sat hunched in his chair on the dais, appearing much older than Green Field, his boyhood friend. Green Field worked every day of his life. Tall Oak was a waited-upon king.

Green Field decided which of his family's livestock they should butcher and eat. Tall Oak sent humans to their graves.

"Sturdy Limb," the king said to his brother, "call your men off."

Sturdy Limb and his men, even including Law Keeper and his, were no match for Morning Sun's mostly younger, stronger, faster, and more agile spear-bearing supporters.

And any blow landed on the prince or an ally standing with him could've brought down on the miscalculating assailants the entire crowd, could've inflamed the armed onlookers to the point where fatally wounding people they'd long since come to despise could seem, one cloudless spring morning, a perfectly appropriate thing to accomplish.

By the time Tall Oak chose to ask Sturdy Limb to call his men off, the chief warrior, somewhere behind his disdainful sneer, was no doubt grateful his brother had made that choice.

*****

The king, his chief warrior, and the crowd in the courtyard got to hear in meticulous detail why it was highly likely there was a gully on sunrise pass posing a danger to the kingdom. They heard it not only from Blue Sky but also from Spring Rain, Many Numbers, Solemn Promise, Rose Leaf, and the prince.

At the end of the arguments of the prince and his allies in the courtyard, Tall Oak didn't ask if anybody had anything to say in opposition.

Instead, he turned to his brother, who rose from his bench.

"The chief warrior will go to sunrise pass," the king said. "While he's there, he'll see for himself what our warriors see. He'll determine what needs to be done to keep the hill people from using the gully, if it exists, to endanger the kingdom. He'll then take whatever steps are necessary to accomplish that."

At that point, Tall Oak turned to Morning Sun.

"I thank you for attending court today," he said. "And I hereby pardon you and your three comrades for being absent from your posts without permission."

Sturdy Limb's scowl deepened. He'd gone around telling people he had four empty cages he was hoping to fill that day with deserters.

After Tall Oak made his remarks, even after they went out to the farthest edges of the crowd, even after the courtyard became strangely silent again, he continued to stare at Morning Sun without speaking, as if perhaps he didn't dare try.

Morning Sun held his father's eyes, giving him the same beguiling grin he'd given the children he and Blue Sky had met on the path coming back from the creek, the same look of placid amusement he'd displayed to the crowd demanding he and Early Harvest run their race again even though he knew he'd won it.

Finally, the king spoke: "Your mother and I have missed you more than you'll ever know."

Many in the crowd later insisted Tall Oak had tears in his eyes when he said that.

Blue Sky let the people set forth their own arguments for what they thought they'd seen. He, standing next to the prince with the best view of them all, knew they weren't making it up.

*****

Many Numbers and Blue Sky had both noted in their remarks that Rose Leaf had made her observations from the apprentice tellers' guard post during her full-moon visits to sunrise pass to be with the prince.

In private later, Spring Rain accused them of not bearing to think someone might leave the courtyard that day without fully understanding where the kingdom was headed.

Blue Sky and Many Numbers readily admitted Spring Rain was right.

Many Numbers offered his explanation: "When the people need to rise up, somebody has to be willing and able to let them know in unmistakable terms the time for it has arrived."

"And the two of you," Spring Rain said, "have appointed yourselves to that position."

"That's exactly what we've done," Blue Sky said.

"And we've volunteered you for it, too," Many Numbers added, his arm around Spring Rain's midsection. "We need a person with your acute sense of responsibility to help us."

Blue Sky stared at the sweet severity of Spring Rain's pouting lips and could only wonder if they'd feel as delightful as Wandering Star's did where they mattered the most.

*****

That afternoon, the home village hosted a feast.

Some of those invited as guests—the young farmers, tellers, and court companions who'd stood with the prince in the courtyard—came and did the work. If preparing food, serving wine, and making music on such an occasion by such people could be considered work.

Those in the courtyard that day who wished to show their gratitude to the guests for what they'd done were also invited. Few among the second group, and none of those who lived outside the town, declined the invitation.

Morning Sun and Rose Leaf greeted them all by name and thanked them, as the king had the prince, for their attendance at court that morning.

Soon after the sun went down that evening, the feasting, drinking, and dancing came to an end, and the guests left. There was work to be done in the fields the next day.

Green Field and Gentle Brook told Morning Sun, Rose Leaf, and Blue Sky they wished to speak with them. The night being chilly, they sat on the benches at the table in the house the way they'd always done when the prince came to visit: Green Field and Gentle Brook on one side, and Rose Leaf and Blue Sky on the other with the prince between them.

"We want you to know we've changed our minds," Green Field began. "Morning Sun, we believe your father should allow you and Rose Leaf to marry in the autumn."

"We'd believe that," Gentle Brook added, joy and tears coexisting in her eyes like right and wrong in the human world, "even if you didn't have most of the people on your side."

"And with the people on their side," Blue Sky noted, "it's pointless for Tall Oak to continue to oppose their marriage."

"Let's hope it doesn't come to that," his mother said.

"We saw Tall Oak and Rainbow Evening after court," Green Field added. "We also told them we've changed our minds."

"Did they agree with you?" Morning Sun asked.

"Your mother said she understood why we've changed our minds," Gentle Brook replied.

"Your father doesn't agree with us," Green Field said. "Or the people. He seems to be digging in his heels. He says the people want a lot of things they can't have."

"His reason for not agreeing with you or the people?" Blue Sky asked. "Can you finally tell us what that is?"

"We can't," Green Field replied. "We've told you before we can't do that."

"You don't want to know the reason," Gentle Brook said, taking Blue Sky's hand. "Believe me, you don't."

Even as Blue Sky gratefully held his mother's hand in his own, he shook his head.

"There's nothing I don't want to know," he insisted. "There's nothing humans shouldn't want to know. And I don't give a damn what the gods say about that either."

Morning Sun, laughing, put his arm around Blue Sky.

"You'd better be careful," he said. "I can save you from my uncle Sturdy Limb, but I don't know if I can save you from the gods."

"Let me worry about the gods," Blue Sky said.

"In any event," Green Field said, "we gave our word to Tall Oak long ago. We promised we'd never speak to anyone of the matter you're asking about."

Gentle Brook nodded her head. "We only want now what Morning Sun and Rose Leaf want. We hope Tall Oak will let it happen. It'll be best for the kingdom. And then we can all forget there ever might've been a good reason to keep it from happening."

"But I'll always want to know what the reason was," Blue Sky said.

"I'm sure you will," Gentle Brook agreed. "You're my son."

Morning Sun slept with Rose Leaf in her bed that night. It was the first time the prince paid a visit to the home village when he didn't sleep with Blue Sky in his bed.

At dawn the next morning, the prince, Spring Rain, Solemn Promise, and Blue Sky, having been pardoned by the king for their insubordination, began their return to sunrise pass.

*****

Wandering Star was apparently as glad to see Blue Sky again as his farmer friend was to see him. They spent Blue Sky's first evening back at sunrise pass in Wandering Star's tent.

When the time came for talk, Wandering Star had a great many questions for Blue Sky about the confrontation in his people's courtyard.

"I don't understand your people," he said at one point. "They expect their king to care what they think?"

"Of course they do. Tall Oak's father was a kind, reasonable, and generous human and king. Everybody agreed he was. But he also blundered as badly as a ruler can. My people don't want their king putting them through anything like that again."

"His retreat. In your last war with my people."

"His stupid and cowardly retreat. In that last damned war your people's king started."

"Your people think they can help their king avoid making that kind of mistake?"

"What else can they think? The gods didn't help. Tall Oak's father should've listened to the rebels—including his son and my father. They would've saved him from himself."

*****

When the next full moon came, Morning Sun, Spring Rain, and Blue Sky greeted Rose Leaf and Many Numbers in the clearing where the five of them had built the most talked-about hut in the kingdom. The three hosts had prepared an evening meal for their guests: roast beef, baked bread, and a cheese sauce with early onions, tubers, and leaves Blue Sky had found in the forest, the kind Wandering Star used in his cooking.

Since Blue Sky couldn't tell the others how he'd learned about the plants, he said he'd guessed they'd like them because they were similar to those their people grew.

Morning Sun had once again grumbled that the common people in the kingdom knew how to cook food and make wine and beer, but their prince didn't. So here he was, having to be told what to do by an orphan boy and a farmer boy. How right was that?

As soon as their guests arrived and finished embracing them, the three sunrise pass comrades could wait no longer for the latest news from the valley.

"We were expecting to see my uncle and his men up here by now," the prince said.

"I doubt you'll see him anytime soon," Many Numbers responded. "He says he and his people are simply too busy to be climbing mountains. They have more important things to deal with than an imaginary gully. Summer is fast approaching, and too many silly disputes among our quarrelsome farmers need to be attended to. He says they wouldn't cause him and his people so damned much trouble if Tall Oak had the guts to order more of them executed."

Sturdy Limb liked to complain that the tellers only had to decide who was right and who wrong. That was the easy part. His people had the more difficult job: enforcing those decisions.

On the other hand, Law Keeper and his high tellers were quick to note that enforcing decisions was a lot more fun than making them. The chief warrior and his minions got to beat people, take their property, lock them up, and kill them. And the deputies could taunt them all the while they did it. That was no small pleasure for people who'd been sworn to uphold the laws.

"My uncle's defying my father?" Morning Sun asked.

"Oh, no," Many Numbers replied, taking the cup of wine the prince offered him. "He's saying your father didn't specify how soon he had to make his journey to sunrise pass. He says he's certain he'll be up here before autumn is gone—unless snow comes early this year."

"Who runs this kingdom?" the prince asked, spitting out his words. "My father, the benevolent king—or my uncle, the brutal chief warrior? And for whose benefit? The people's? Or the chief warrior's?"

None of the other people present chose to reply to those questions.

"That isn't the most important thing we came to tell you," Many Numbers said.

"I didn't think it would be," Blue Sky said.

"The people know," Many Numbers continued, "Green Field and Gentle Brook have changed their minds about the desirability of a certain wedding celebration this autumn."

"Did somebody pass that information to the people?" Blue Sky asked.

Many Numbers looked at Blue Sky and laughed. "Somebody must've. Some gossip who couldn't keep his mouth shut. I suppose we'll always wonder who that person was."

Morning Sun also laughed. "I'd want the person to know anyway how grateful I am."

Many Numbers laughed again. "And I imagine the person in question would be pleased to hear that. Especially from the prince."

"And what do you suppose," Rose Leaf asked, "the farmers are saying about Green Field and Gentle Brook's change of heart?"

"Let me guess," Spring Rain offered. "If Green Field and Gentle Brook see nothing wrong with the prince and their daughter mating and having children together, then the king can't possibly have any good reason to prohibit it."

Rose Leaf took hold of Spring Rain's shirt, pulled him toward her, and gave him more than a brief and perfunctory kiss on his lips.

Many Numbers glanced at Morning Sun and Blue Sky and ever-so-slightly smirked.

"Good guess," Rose Leaf said, letting Spring Rain go.

"The farmers are saying something else," Many Numbers said. "They're saying they want the matter settled now. They won't wait until autumn to find out whether their king will attempt to forbid a wedding ceremony he can't possibly forbid. Not if Green Field and Gentle Brook want it."

"The same king," Spring Rain saw fit to say, "who lets his chief warrior and first teller and their cronies mistreat the people."

"We won't let the people wait beyond the first full moon of summer," Morning Sun said.

Which would be the second full moon after the present one.

Morning Sun and Blue Sky had decided that was when they'd go to the town again, after letting everybody in the kingdom know what they intended to do.

They'd raise the issue in open court and dare the king to tell the people the prince and Rose Leaf couldn't marry. And if Tall Oak did dare to do that, they'd further dare him to reveal his reason for such a strange and hurtful decision. And if the king didn't dare to do that, they'd finally dare him to insist he was still the king—and hear the people laugh as he said it.

Chapter 12

Blue Sky was secretly glad Sturdy Limb and his people hadn't come up to sunrise pass to resolve the gully issue. Until they did, Blue Sky could see Wandering Star any time he wished.

Whenever Wandering Star left to visit his mother, Blue Sky would become increasingly restless waiting for him to return. He'd offer to sit in the guard post in place of a grateful comrade. He didn't want to miss the first campfire smoke Wandering Star would send up beyond the thicket at the bottom of the ravine to let Blue Sky know he was back.

When Wandering Star was away and Blue Sky noticed other campfires close by on the eastern side of the mountains, he'd go down to Wandering Star's tent, where he'd be able to see any hill people heading toward the pass and its vulnerable gully. He sometimes slept in the tent all night, certain he'd be roused if hill people came near it.

They might succeed in killing him, but not before his screams would alert his comrades.

*****

When Rose Leaf and Many Numbers arrived in the clearing for the next full-moon holiday, the third and last of that spring, they scarcely had time to embrace their three hosts and accept their cups of wine before they began telling the latest news.

The people in the villages from one end of the kingdom to the other were alarmed. They'd heard Sturdy Limb had vowed to have his men put Morning Sun and Blue Sky in his cages if they came near the town again without his permission. And the only reason the prince and Blue Sky would go to the court to see the king would be to hear the chief warrior and first teller present arguments that they were traitors leading a rebellion and should receive the only punishment suitable for the crime of treason: execution.

Sturdy Limb would also argue that treason required him to prolong their deaths—ideally from dawn to sunset on a long, hot summer day—no matter how much they might beg for mercy.

"They'll both smell of death," the chief warrior had promised, "long before they're dead."

After the people witnessed the agonizing deaths of those two and their allies—as they'd certainly wish to do, all the while drinking the king's and the tellers' wine and beer—they wouldn't soon again think it either wise or amusing to side with traitors.

Not a few of the farmers had just as adamantly sworn that no such proceedings would take place in their kingdom.

They agreed with Fair Judge: the prince, Rose Leaf, Blue Sky, and their allies were free to attend court and say anything they pleased. If what they said seemed wrong or fanciful, the chief warrior and first teller were also free to point that out, however entertainingly those officials might stumble as they attempted to do so.

The chief warrior insisted, though, the prince and Green Field's obnoxious son weren't paying a visit to the town to engage in some idle debate about an invisible gully. This time they were coming to overthrow the king—to commit treason. They had no right to talk about that.

The great fear in the kingdom was that fighting would break out, with the court people and tellers on one side and the farmers on the other.

Rose Leaf had remarked on the matter to her companions during their trek to sunrise pass for that full-moon holiday: "The court people and tellers would be fools to start a battle they can't hope to win."

All her traveling companions were either tellers or daughters of court people.

In the clearing that evening, though, she wondered if Morning Sun and Blue Sky were miscalculating. If Sturdy Limb and Law Keeper charged them with treason, and the king explicitly ordered the people not to interfere, would the people defy their king?

Morning Sun and Blue Sky refused to believe their people wouldn't.

They took turns insisting, though, if the people did stand by and do nothing while Sturdy Limb and his men executed them, they'd be better off dead anyway.

Hearing those arguments, Rose Leaf and Spring Rain threw their arms around one another.

Many Numbers and Rose Leaf had news from the upper valley as well. Early Harvest had let it be known he was also paying a visit to the town during the next full-moon holiday.

"That other farmer boy," Morning Sun murmured.

"Your rival," Blue Sky said.

"He intends to speak to the king in open court," Rose Leaf said.

"What's he going to say to the king?" Blue Sky asked. "He agrees with him you aren't a suitable wife for the prince?"

Rose Leaf laughed. "Not Early Harvest. He says he wants to ask the king why Morning Sun and I can't marry. And if Tall Oak can't give the people a damned good reason, Early Harvest is going to ask him to abdicate and let Morning Sun become his successor."

"Early Harvest is bringing a number of his cousins with him," Many Numbers added. "They'll all have their spears in hand. They'll all be prepared to use them, too. Early Harvest has openly promised he'll personally kill Sturdy Limb if that becomes necessary."

After Rose Leaf had returned to the valley following her last full-moon visit to sunrise pass, Autumn Wine and her grandsons questioned her about the planned confrontation. As a result of the discussion, the older grandson decided to go to the upper valley and see Early Harvest in his encampment. During Early Harvest's visits to the home village, he and the grandson, both desiring a woman they feared they couldn't have, frequently drank together late into the night.

More than once, Morning Sun had let it be known that he couldn't imagine why Solemn Promise's family would object to his sister's marriage to Autumn Wine's older grandson.

"Does Early Harvest have permission to leave his post?" Blue Sky asked.

"He says he doesn't care if he has permission or not," Rose Leaf said. "The prince, Solemn Promise, Spring Rain, and you got away with leaving your posts without permission. So why can't he? He's not about to be told he can't do what the prince and his comrades do."

"He won't be alone," Many Numbers added. "The farmers are saying they'll be there with Early Harvest. We've heard that from one village after the other. All of them promise they'll send a contingent of able-bodied warriors, even if it's the time of the year when those warriors should be in their fields."

"And my fool of an uncle?" Morning Sun asked. "What's he saying about Early Harvest and the farmers coming to see the king?"

Many Numbers grimaced. "He tells people he'll have cages ready for them all—the men leaving their posts without permission, as well as any farmers who might want to cause trouble by siding with them. And if it turns out he doesn't have enough cages, he'll put the whole lot of them in the courtyard and secure the gates. He might not have enough food for so many prisoners, but he won't lose any sleep over that. Nor should the king, facing all-out treason. If traitors starve, they starve. They'd have to be killed anyway. It'll mean less work for him and his deputies. They'll just dig a hole and throw the bodies in."

Blue Sky turned to the prince. "We'll starve in the courtyard with Early Harvest and the farmers. We'll be heroes forever in our people's stories."

Spring Rain looked at Blue Sky and shook his head. "What if the farmers desert you? That way nobody will starve, but you and the prince will still die. Remember what happened in the last war? Didn't the warriors in the rear ranks decide at the last moment to side with the king? Then didn't the middle ranks and most of those in the front ranks retreat with them? Didn't they leave your father and Tall Oak and their few loyal friends to face the enemy alone?"

Many Numbers threw his arm around Spring Rain's shoulders and shook him.

"Our fathers did as they were told and retreated," he said. "After our mothers died, our fathers hoped the hill people would kill them and put two cowards out of their misery. They got their wish, too."

*****

Even in the mountains, the days became more like summer than spring.

Messengers from neighboring encampments paid visits. They came to say they also wanted to send men to the town to stand with the prince during the next full-moon holiday.

Word eventually came around the valley from all the encampments: not one wished to be left out. Each of them promised to send men without permission to leave their posts. They'd all be equally guilty. Sturdy Limb couldn't possibly execute such a huge number of warriors, even if Tall Oak were foolish enough to order it done.

And more sunrise pass comrades wished to go to see the king this time. If Early Harvest and men from all the other encampments were going, Noon Breeze argued, the two sunrise pass encampments should show up in force.

He selected himself for one of the positions in the apprentice tellers' contingent.

The goddess of doubt, though, still had Spring Rain in her grip. He told Morning Sun and Blue Sky that during the recent feast in the home village, he and Green Field had a discussion concerning the last war.

Blue Sky had seen them talking together for an inordinate length of time, like lovers.

Spring Rain learned that Green Field and Tall Oak had spoken with a great many warriors during the night before the second day of the opening battle on sunrise pass.

Not one warrior failed to assure Tall Oak and Green Field that they and their comrades would never obey the king's order to retreat to the town.

Even Sturdy Limb, who was among the first to retreat, had given them his vow.

*****

Wandering Star and Blue Sky were near the peak of a mountain on the valley people's side of sunrise pass. Blue Sky had found a way to get there from the gully without being observed from either the guard post or the encampment.

Like high-flying birds, they could take in the entire lower valley, eastern mountains to western, lower gorge to upper, in the light of an early summer afternoon.

Blue Sky had confirmed he'd be leaving the next day to go to his people's town.

"And commit treason," Wandering Star said, "for your sister and your prince."

"Treason it will be," Blue Sky agreed, "for my sister and my prince."

Wandering Star stared at the valley for a long time as if he were gazing upon another person's lover he deeply, obsessively wished to have for himself.

"You really believe what you told me?" Blue Sky asked. "You really think your people would be better off raising crops and livestock the way my people do?"

"I see what I see," Wandering Star replied. "Your people send all your new men up to the mountains for a year just to keep my people away. So many of them. So well-supplied."

Wandering Star had seen most of the valley people's encampments, getting himself as close to them as he could. He'd figured out on his own how they kept them manned.

"The valley seems large to you," he continued, "but it's practically nothing compared to the lands my people roam. From the valley, though, your people still get the food and other things they need to keep all those men in the mountains for a year. My people could never do that."

Until Blue Sky began discussing the matter with Wandering Star, he'd never considered his people's valley insignificant in regard to anything else. But what Wandering Star said had to be true. Seen from the mountaintops, his people's hills appeared to go on forever, like the sky.

"It must be the farming," Wandering Star said. "I told our tellers and our king that's why we lost the valley to your people—and every war we've fought over it since. They didn't want to hear what I said. I told them your people have animals pulling things around for you. They bring your supplies up the mountains. That's how you do it. The animals do the work for you. Your people somehow get those castrated bulls to do what you want them to do. Why can't my people do that? And plant things, too, and know where they'll be when the time comes to harvest them."

The hill people's first teller had attempted to persuade their king, Lightning Spear, to execute Wandering Star for saying what he'd said about the farmers and farming.

His people's tellers had their own explanation for why they'd lost the valley to the thieves: their people were lazy and selfish and didn't offer enough of what they gathered and killed to the gods. Since the tellers took the offerings to the gods and used them as they saw fit, it was no surprise the gods always wanted more. The tellers claimed the paucity of their people's offerings angered the gods so greatly they'd refused to interfere when the farmers came to take the valley. For the same reason, the gods had refused to help the hill people get their valley back.

In the valley people's kingdom, only the king made offerings to the gods—which, as in the hill people's kingdom, went to the tellers—but only out of the tribute he received from the river people. The farmers told stories of wicked tellers who'd insisted upon greater and greater offerings to appease the gods. One of the good kings of that time had sided with the farmers and put strict limits on what the tellers could ask of them. Later, after the river people came with their tribute, the tellers as well as the court people could no longer levy any tax on the farmers.

Blue Sky turned and looked at his hill-man friend. "Have you ever dreamed," he asked, "of your people rising up and overthrowing your tellers and king?"

"Every day of my life," Wandering Star replied.

He got to his feet and looked from one end of the valley to the other.

"Every day of every year," he said. "Every day of every year since that last war with your people. I wasn't very old at the time, but I can remember it. I saw the bodies of a lot of warriors your people killed. Your people had slit most of their throats. My people were grateful for that."

There was a strong breeze from the south that afternoon. The farmers—small children and many of the otherwise indolent included—would be working in the fields long past sunset.

Suddenly, like an angry god, there being nothing but sky beyond him, Wandering Star looked down and glowered at his farmer companion.

"My people's princess would be about your age," he said. "You've never mentioned her. Where does she live among your people? What do you call her?"

"Your people's princess?" Blue Sky asked.

"Lightning Spear's daughter. His only child. She's my people's princess. Your people probably wouldn't refer to her as a princess."

Wandering Star looked at the valley as if he were an eagle seeking prey.

"Can't you imagine how ashamed my people are?" he asked. "Your people have had our valley for so many years now. And since that last war, you've had our princess, too."

"Your princess?" Blue Sky asked again.

The eagle peered down at him as if it were fast descending upon a field mouse.

"You don't know anything about her?" Wandering Star demanded.

"Your people's princess?"

"Your people don't know she lives among them?"

"Your princess?"

"She'd be your age now, maybe a season or two younger."

Blue Sky rose to his feet. "I've never heard your princess is living with my people."

"She's either living with your people, or she's dead. She must be dead. She was just an infant, but that didn't stop your prince and his comrade. They took her and killed her."

Blue Sky stared at Wandering Star. It didn't seem possible those last remarks could've come from his mouth.

"Our prince and his comrade?" Blue Sky's voice trembled. "They took your princess?"

"That's something else you don't know? That's something else your people don't know?"

"When did they take her?"

"During the war, of course. Why don't you know this? Why don't your people know?"

Blue Sky looked down at his people's valley as if it were as new to him as it was to his hill-man friend.

"My people captured your prince and his comrade in the war," he heard Wandering Star say. "You know that, don't you?"

"I know that. My people know that."

"My people drank your people's beverage and took a liking to it. They drank so much of it they fell into a delirium. All of them. Even the king and the queen. Even the warriors. Your people's prince and his comrade escaped and took our princess with them. My people haven't seen her since. And you say your people don't know anything about her? My people have always assumed your prince and his comrade killed our princess. Many of our tellers say your people sacrifice children to the gods. I've never believed them, but maybe they're right."

Tall Oak had worried that Blue Sky wouldn't produce heirs for his parents—as if Blue Sky didn't have a sister and his parents a daughter.

"She was a baby," Wandering Star continued. "I saw her myself. She was our princess."

Blue Sky put his arm around Wandering Star's shoulders, as much for his own consolation as for his hill-man friend's.

"But why wouldn't your people know she was sacrificed?" Wandering Star asked. "Why wouldn't you know about it?"

Blue Sky let his tears fall. "My people don't sacrifice children," he said. "And they didn't kill your people's princess."

*****

Blue Sky informed his comrades he'd start down the mountain that evening by himself. Those from both encampments assigned to accompany the prince were leaving in the morning.

Blue Sky said he wished to speak with his father, mother, and sister before the full-moon confrontation with the king.

A number of his comrades said they wouldn't want to be alone deep in the forest at night.

Blue Sky reminded them he'd climbed the mountains with no companion during a snowstorm the previous winter, in nights as dark as death. And he'd lived to tell them about it.

Noon Breeze laughed. "But what if you run into that savage hill man you saw in the ravine last autumn? What if he's come up the gully and sneaked into the forest, and our guards didn't see him? What if he's in there right now waiting for you to come by on the path so he can kill you?"

"That man would never attempt to kill me," Blue Sky scoffed. "I'm quite certain he'd want to keep me alive. You should've seen him in the bushes. It was obvious he wanted to go with me."

Those wildly imaginative remarks got the loud round of jeers and laughter they deserved.

Spring Rain had never discussed with their encampment comrades Blue Sky's occasional all-night absences from their hut. Despite Blue Sky's many denials, Spring Rain was convinced he was going with one of their comrades. He said he couldn't understand why the person and Blue Sky were concealing their affair, but if that was the way they wanted it, he'd go along with it.

He wondered if maybe Blue Sky was going with another person who already had a lover.

Which was precisely what Blue Sky had been hoping all winter would happen.

On the other hand, Noon Breeze and their other encampment comrades had long since assumed Spring Rain and Blue Sky had become clandestine lovers. The reason for their secrecy was obvious: Many Numbers.

Noon Breeze said he was happy to see Blue Sky start out ahead of everybody else. He'd already talked Spring Rain into sharing a tent with him. And without Many Numbers and Blue Sky around, Noon Breeze wondered aloud, who could say what might happen in that tent?

Blue Sky was glad his comrades were in a mood for banter. It helped him conceal from them his discovery that their world wasn't at all what they'd been led to believe it was.

"Promise me one thing," Spring Rain demanded privately, in a prolonged farewell embrace just before Blue Sky left. "Promise me you won't cause any trouble before we get down there."

Blue Sky kissed the lips of the second man he'd fallen in love with but couldn't have.

"I won't make any promise I might not be able to keep," he said. "Sometimes a kingdom needs trouble. Or needs to know what trouble it's already in—so it can get itself out of it."

"And you're the one the gods have sent to our people to deal with that trouble?"

"If I believed the gods existed, yes. I'd have to think that's precisely what they've done."

*****

Blue Sky found his father in their field of grass and clover, gathering the first hay of the season. It was still morning, but the dew had dried. Green Field's stallion and the stallion's favorite mare were pulling the cart.

Green Field and Rose Leaf had cut the hay two days before. Since then, it had lain in the sun and dried. Now Green Field was raking it into piles and tossing them into the cart.

Blue Sky left his weapons and other belongings on the path and began crossing the field.

Green Field looked up from his work and stared at his son, squinting his eyes in the intense early summer light. Blue Sky was born on such a day.

Green Field and Gentle Brook had assumed Blue Sky would arrive in the town the next morning with the prince, for the confrontation with the king they were insisting upon.

Although Green Field and Gentle Brook hadn't spoken of the matter publicly, they'd told Rose Leaf they hoped she, Morning Sun, and Blue Sky would ask their allies and the people not to force Tall Oak's hand. If they chose to wait, Green Field and Gentle Brook promised they'd make every attempt, between then and autumn, to change the minds of the king and queen.

Of the five people who knew about Green Field and Gentle Brook's plea, only Spring Rain had spoken in favor of it. Morning Sun, Rose Leaf, Many Numbers, and Blue Sky had opposed it.

Blue Sky had argued that Rose Leaf and Morning Sun weren't livestock whose mating desires their human caretakers could choose either to encourage or thwart. Besides, the people, egged on by those same five people, wanted the matter decided then, not in the autumn.

"I met a hill man," Blue Sky said to his father in the hay field. "I went beyond the guard post. I made contact with him in the gully Sturdy Limb tells us doesn't exist."

"You met a hill man?" Green Field asked, frowning as if his son had told him winter followed spring. "Beyond the guard post? Didn't he try to kill you?"

The neighbors working in their fields weren't close enough to hear what Green Field and Blue Sky said, but they were paying attention.

"He had no wish to kill me," Blue Sky replied. "He's the one I saw last autumn—when Spring Rain and I supposedly held off attacking hill warriors all by ourselves. He's the one who was warning the hunters not to get any closer to our guard post. I could've shot him with my arrow and killed him. But I refused to do it. I decided I'd rather be his friend. Now I am."

Green Field shook his head. "A friend of a hill man? You can speak with him?"

"You were right about that. Their language is similar to ours. Surprisingly similar."

Green Field laid down his rake and let the horses go.

"The hill man taught me his language," Blue Sky said. "He'd already taught himself ours. He did it listening to our men in the guard post."

The horses walked away with the cart. They knew where to find the basin of water Green Field had set out for them beside the path.

"He let me know," Blue Sky said, "what Tall Oak doesn't want our people to know. Rose Leaf isn't my sister. She was born a hill child. You and Tall Oak brought her to the valley with you when you escaped from the hill people."

Green Field, his eyes fixed on his son's, remained silent for a long time.

When he was finally able to do so, he spoke softly: "I'm glad you found out the truth."

The neighbors were sneaking glances at a hero with his grown son, both of them in tears.

"There were some things the hill man couldn't tell me," Blue Sky said.

"What else do you want to know?" Green Field asked. "Whatever it is, I'll tell you."

"Why did you and Tall Oak take Rose Leaf with you? Why didn't you just run away by yourselves? Why did you take a hill child with you? Did you know she was their princess?"

Green Field looked in the direction of sunrise pass as if he were gazing into hell itself.

"When they first took us to their king," he replied, "the queen was holding a baby girl in her arms. We knew the girl must be their princess. We didn't think the queen would be sitting with the king holding any child but their own. You've heard what happened. The hill people began drinking our wine and got drunk. The king and queen themselves were drunk. When we freed ourselves, the girl wasn't far from us. Nobody was watching out for her. The blood had gotten her attention."

"The blood spraying from the throats of the warriors who'd been guarding you? The warriors you killed?"

"Yes. We picked her up and took her with us."

"Why did you do that?"

Green Field drew his breath as if he were facing an opponent with a spear.

"We were going to kill her," he replied.

"You were going to kill a child, an innocent child?"

Green Field looked at Blue Sky for a long time again before he attempted to answer that.

"We wanted to get back at their king," he said, "for what he'd done."

"You thought his starting the war justified killing his infant daughter?"

For yet another extended period of time, Green Field stood silent in the morning breeze.

"It was more than that," he finally replied.

Blue Sky felt as if he'd stepped off a high ledge, not knowing where or how he might land.

"Did the hill man say," Green Field asked, "if Rose Leaf has any brothers or sisters?"

"He told me she's their king's only child."

"We thought that would be the case. We assumed we were taking their king's only child."

"Why did you assume that?"

"She was the only child with him and the queen. They both looked as if they weren't far past coming of age. We decided the girl must've been their only living child. And we knew the king wouldn't have any more."

"How did you know that? How did you know he wouldn't have more children?"

"He'd suffered a terrible injury in the fighting. One of our warriors, aiming for his belly, had thrust his spear too low. The king made us look at him. His manhood was gone."

Green Field glanced at sunrise pass again as if he were somehow under its spell.

"The king gave his warriors some orders," Green Field continued. "I thought I could understand what he was saying. Even though he was going to have Tall Oak and me executed the next day, they were to immediately do to us what our people had done to him. Then the enemy prince and his comrade would know what it was like before they died."

Blue Sky looked at sunrise pass himself. Was this the way the gods punished humans who, god-like, loudly demanded to know the truth?

He'd gone too far. He'd laughed at his people's laws. He'd mocked the gods. He'd only answered to himself. He'd gone well past where he was supposed to go.

He should've been content remembering his people's stories, working in the fields, roasting beef, drinking wine, dancing to the music, and looking for another man to live with for the rest of his life. He should've left all his countless questions unasked, unanswered.

After the last war with the hill people, Green Field and Gentle Brook, as well as Tall Oak and Rainbow Evening, had no children born to them, dead or alive. Blue Sky had never seen his father without clothes on. Other fathers swam naked with their sons. Green Field didn't. Morning Sun had also never seen his father without his clothes on. Nor did they swim naked together. Morning Sun and Blue Sky had often remarked on the strange modesty of their fathers.

When a man was working or training in warm weather, people observing him could sometimes glimpse what they weren't supposed to see behind his loincloth, especially if they deliberately stared at him the way Noon Breeze did, carefully choosing the angle of their vision.

Green Field and Tall Oak, though, never wore their loincloths that loosely.

"What did the hill warriors do?" Blue Sky asked, his voice quavering.

The neighbors had stopped their work, alarmed by the tears neither Green Field nor Blue Sky made any attempt to conceal.

"What our warrior had done to their king," Green Field replied, "their warriors did to Tall Oak and me. It took ten of them to hold each of us down."

As their neighbors watched, Blue Sky took his father in his arms.

"No," he whispered. "No. No. No. No."

Father and son clung to one another.

"Why would the gods let such a thing happen?" Blue Sky asked. "To you and Tall Oak? Why are we supposed to believe they protect humans who obey their laws? They can't possibly exist. All the things we've ever heard about them are lies."

Blue Sky freed his father from his embrace.

"But you didn't kill Rose Leaf," he said.

"We couldn't bring ourselves to do it. Even if her father was the hill people's king. She was an innocent child. We couldn't do it. We looked at her and realized we could never do it."

Tears slid down the faces of both the father and the son as freely as brooks ran down the slopes of the mountains.

"We had to take her with us," Green Field said. "We didn't dare take her back to her people. We couldn't abandon her. She would've died. Hungry wolves or bears would've eaten her. We brought her to the valley with us. As soon as your mother saw her, she wanted to keep her."

Blue Sky knew his mother would've wanted to keep Rose Leaf the moment their eyes met.

"Then and there," Green Field said, "Rose Leaf became my daughter and your sister. We're more like the prince than he knows. We never asked to be the people we turned out to be in this story."

Despite the hill people in their dreams, Gentle Brook once told Blue Sky, she was certain they were as capable of reasoning and caring as the valley people were. Now Blue Sky could see why she'd said that: she was raising a hill child as her daughter.

And that was the one thing his mother could never tell Blue Sky.

"Your mother hid in the forest from our own people," Green Field said. "With you, the prince, and Rose Leaf. Only Rainbow Evening brought her food and hides. The old men and boys were guarding the livestock. Your mother and Rainbow Evening suckled all three of you. When the war was over, we told the people your mother had given birth to Rose Leaf in the forest. They had no reason to believe she didn't have a child growing inside her when the war began."

Having already jumped off the ledge, Blue Sky could only plunge further into the abyss.

"Why did you do that?" he asked. "Why did you pass the hill people's princess off as your daughter? Why didn't you just tell our people who she was? Why weren't you truthful?"

"You don't understand how it was then. We'd fought a horrifying war with the hill people. If we'd told our people that Rose Leaf was the hill people's princess, they would've killed her. They would've taken her from us and killed her. Too many of our people had died in that war."

"They would've killed her," Blue Sky spat, knowing his father was right. "They would've killed an innocent child."

Blue Sky also knew he'd grievously erred.

"Forgive me," he begged his father. "No wonder you and Tall Oak didn't want the people to know. I should've respected your wishes. I should've listened to you. You had every right to keep what happened a secret. I was wrong to insist you tell me."

"But now you know anyway," Green Field said. "And I'm glad you know. And Rose Leaf will know, too. She'll finally find out who she is. She'll know why Tall Oak thinks he can't let her give birth to Morning Sun's children. She has to know that. So does Morning Sun. I'm glad you found out the truth. I'm glad you're my son. I'm glad you lived to come of age."

Blue Sky knew something else: he could never hope to be the person his father was.

"I'll tell Rose Leaf everything," Green Field said. "I'll tell her how glad I am she's alive. I'll tell her how glad I am Tall Oak and I brought her home with us. I'll tell her how glad I am she and Morning Sun fell in love and want to have children together."

Blue Sky looked at his father as one would a god who'd chosen to pay a visit to the meaningless world humans lived in—and often, inconceivably, fought to their death in.

"You and Tall Oak must've been bleeding," Blue Sky said. "Every step of the way must've been an agony for you. You must've taken turns carrying an infant child. You must've squeezed juice from wild fruit to feed her. You must've washed her in mountain brooks."

One hopeless winter night in their horse barn Blue Sky had dared to insult this man.

"You saved her life," Blue Sky said. "You brought her home to live in the forest with Morning Sun and me and our mothers. You were maimed, but you continued to fight. Day after day, you killed enemy warriors coming up the bluff. You won the war for our people."

Blue Sky, who'd grown taller than his father, wrapped his arms around him again.

And he also knew, even if the gods existed and had all the many powers they claimed to have, it still would've been pointless to ask them to stop his and his father's tears.

Chapter 13

When Blue Sky and his father were once again able to do so, they finished filling the cart with grass and clover and led the horses pulling it to their village. After stacking the hay in the mow below the rafters in the cattle barn, they joined Gentle Brook in the house for the noon meal.

Green Field and Gentle Brook sat on their side of the table, Blue Sky on the side Rose Leaf, the prince, and he had long ago claimed as their own, their backs to the wall, their faces to the fire.

Gentle Brook had seen her husband and son in the field with their arms around each other. Knowing the story Green Field had told Blue Sky, she wished to hear her son's: how he'd crawled down the wash to the gully unseen. How he'd met a hill man there named Wandering Star.

Imagining, as he had at the time, he was in great danger, she often grimaced.

Blue Sky told her also how the hill man came to reveal to him the truth about Rose Leaf, whose father was, as Green Field and Tall Oak had assumed, the hill people's king. Known as Lightning Spear, he was still their king.

Gentle Brook shook her head.

"Rose Leaf is my daughter," she insisted. "She's your father's daughter. She's your sister. We can't let the people know she's the hill people's princess. Not if she's going to marry Morning Sun. Our people will never let that happen. We can't tell them."

She was pleading with Blue Sky.

Green Field, Rainbow Evening, and she had readily gone along with Tall Oak's request that they not tell Blue Sky the truth. They were as afraid as Tall Oak was he'd tell the people.

"The prince, Rose Leaf, and you have the people with you now," she added. "But if they find out who she is, they'll desert you. You and Morning Sun will be traitors in their eyes. Sturdy Limb will finally have the people on his side. He'll gladly kill the two of you and Rose Leaf. And Many Numbers, Spring Rain, Solemn Promise, Early Harvest—who knows how many others?"

*****

Green Field, Gentle Brook, and Blue Sky spent most of that afternoon gathering hay, bringing it home, and stacking it in the mows below the barn rafters. Their livestock would consume it in the winter in the warmth of their barns when snow and ice covered their pasture—and the wild counterparts of those animals in the forest suffered.

Blue Sky had to force himself to concentrate on his work. Whenever he let his mind wander, he thought of his father and mother and what they, Tall Oak, and Rainbow Evening had gone through in silence, keeping their secret. A secret their children, who'd grown up believing themselves free to question anything they chose, could no longer let them keep.

And the tears, like the seasons, inevitably came again.

His mother and father would look at him and say nothing.

He didn't dare ask himself if he could ever be as brave as they'd been.

The three of them stopped their work, though, as soon as they saw Rose Leaf coming along the path from a neighboring village. She'd spent most of the day there cutting down clover and grass for old and ailing people. They'd now have to hope they'd be as fortunate as Rose Leaf's family was and no rain would fall for the next two days while the hay dried in their fields.

Rose Leaf looked up from the path ahead of her and saw the three people she still innocently believed were her mother, father, and brother. As the late afternoon sun lit her face, her frown reconfigured itself into a smile like a hard, coiled bud becoming a blossom.

Blue Sky hadn't yet divulged to Morning Sun, Spring Rain, or anybody else what he'd learned from Wandering Star. He'd wished to confront his father and mother first and find out why they and the king and queen had done what they'd done.

He was glad he'd kept his mouth shut. His mother and father and Morning Sun's mother and father had suffered, in silence, a loss in the last war as great as any Rose Leaf and Morning Sun would endure if they weren't permitted to live together and have children.

Blue Sky and his parents quickly crossed the field and met Rose Leaf on the path.

"It's time you knew the truth," Gentle Brook said, embracing her.

To Blue Sky, the falsehood that Rose Leaf was his sister seemed far more like the truth than the truth itself—that she was the daughter of a king who went by the name of Lightning Spear and had ordered the mutilation of Green Field and Tall Oak.

"The truth?" Rose Leaf asked. "The reason the king says Morning Sun and I can't marry?"

"That," Gentle Brook replied, "and much more."

"Please always remember one thing," Green Field said to Rose Leaf. "I love you."

"As do I," Blue Sky said.

Rose Leaf turned back to Gentle Brook. "Please tell me the truth. Whatever it is."

"Here?" Gentle Brook asked, glancing at the neighbors in their fields. "Now?"

"Here," Rose Leaf replied. "Now. What better place for the truth than a field of clover?"

As before, their neighbors were observing them without being close enough to hear them.

"You aren't my daughter," Gentle Brook said, biting her lip, tears forming in the corners of her eyes. "You aren't Green Field's daughter."

Blue Sky placed his arm around Rose Leaf's shoulders.

"I never bore you," Gentle Brook continued, getting the words out as best she could.

Rose Leaf shuddered. "Don't say such a thing."

"I must say it," Gentle Brook said. "I have no choice. It's the truth."

Rose Leaf stared at the woman she'd always believed was her mother.

"You're not my mother?" she asked. "You never carried me in your body?"

"No," Gentle Brook replied, her eyes filling with tears.

Rose Leaf turned to Green Field. "You're not my father?" she asked.

"No," Green Field replied.

Rose Leaf looked at Blue Sky. "You're not my brother?"

"I'll always be your brother," Blue Sky replied. "Even if we don't have the same parents."

Rose Leaf turned to Green Field again. "This is why Tall Oak won't permit me to have Morning Sun's children?"

Green Field, Gentle Brook, and Blue Sky stood silent.

"Whose daughter am I?" Rose Leaf asked.

Green Field chose to reply: "You're the daughter of the hill people's king."

"His name is Lightning Spear," Blue Sky said.

Rose Leaf trembled again.

"Your mother is their queen," Blue Sky continued. "Her name is Thistle Dew."

Rose Leaf stared at the person she'd grown up with believing was her brother.

"I met a hill man," he said. "I can understand his people's language. He can understand ours. His name is Wandering Star. He remembers seeing you when you were a baby. He was five years old. You're the hill people's princess. Any son you have will be the heir to their kingship. The king and queen, your father and mother, have no other children."

Softly, slowly, taking turns speaking, divulging fact after ineluctable fact that day on the path between their hay and lentil fields, Green Field and Gentle Brook told Rose Leaf how she'd come to live with them and why they and Tall Oak and Rainbow Evening had kept the matter a secret: to forestall any harm coming to her.

"Our people would've killed you," Gentle Brook said. "Too many people had died in the war. We had no choice."

Hearing what the hill people's warriors did to Green Field and Tall Oak, Rose Leaf wept.

"And you're telling me," she asked, "the person who ordered them to do that is my father?"

"In a war, people do terrible things," Green Field replied.

"The gods seem unable to stop them," Blue Sky chose to add.

"Now the choice is yours," Green Field said to Rose Leaf. "As it should be. You'll always be the hill people's princess. Our people will always be our people. Do you want them to continue believing you're our daughter and sister? Or do you want them to know who you really are?"

Green Field glanced at Gentle Brook and Blue Sky.

"We're prepared to let the secret go on," he continued, "if that's what you want. We're prepared not to reveal any of this to any other person. We'll go to our graves with the secret. We're prepared to give you our oath. I give you mine now."

"I give you mine," Gentle Brook said.

"And I give you mine," Blue Sky said.

"You'll be safer that way," Gentle Brook added. "We'll still be mother and daughter."

"The war wasn't that long ago," Green Field added. "You can't imagine how our people suffered in it. The hill people killed and injured too many of us. Our older people who survived it might not talk about it much anymore, but I can assure you they'll never forget it. So many of the people they spent their childhoods with were killed or maimed in that war. If they were to suddenly find out who you are, who can say what they'd do?"

"You think they'd want me killed?" Rose Leaf asked.

Gentle Brook closed her eyes at the thought of it.

"I'd hope they'd never do that," Green Field replied. "They might insist, though, you leave the valley and go live with the hill people."

Gentle Brook closed her eyes again.

"What about Morning Sun?" Rose Leaf asked Green Field.

"You'll have to decide for yourself," he replied, "whether he should know."

"That's not my question," Rose Leaf said. "I've already decided that. He must know."

"You wonder," Gentle Brook said, "if he'll still wish to have children with you."

"That's for him to decide," Rose Leaf said.

"He will," Blue Sky said. "I know he will. Whoever you are, he loves you."

"But if the people find out who I am," Rose Leaf asked Green Field, "will they let their prince have children with me?"

Green Field shook his head. "No, they'll never do that. That's why Tall Oak and Rainbow Evening don't want you and Morning Sun to marry. They fear the people might someday find out who you are. Nobody can predict what they'd do if they realized the mother of a future king of the valley people was the hill people's princess."

"Don't think of letting the people know," Gentle Brook said to Rose Leaf. "Morning Sun can only father your children if you remain our daughter in the eyes of the people. Tall Oak and Rainbow Evening will just have to live with the fear of being found out. So will we."

Rose Leaf turned to Blue Sky.

"Do you agree with what they're saying?"

Blue Sky looked at his mother and father. "May I speak freely?" he asked.

"You always do," Green Field said.

"I won't attempt to stop you," Gentle Brook added.

Blue Sky turned to Rose Leaf. "No, I don't agree. I don't think our people are that stupid. They can learn. The hill people are no different from us. Look at yourself. Everybody thought you and I were sister and brother. And why not? It's easy for me to understand what a hill man is saying. His people and our people have the same gods. The only difference between the hill people and ourselves is how we harvest the earth. And that's not a real difference. The only thing about it that matters is that our way is more productive than theirs. And I believe our people are capable of seeing that's all that matters. So are the hill people."

"So what would you have Rose Leaf do?" Green Field asked.

"I'd have her do whatever she chooses to do," Blue Sky replied.

"Still," Green Field insisted, "what would you do if you were Rose Leaf?"

"I'd tell the people the truth," Blue Sky answered. "Every last detail. I'd leave nothing out. Nothing at all."

Gentle Brook shook her head. She'd hidden in the forest with him, the prince, and Rose Leaf, the three of them infants, unable to fend for themselves. They'd survived childhood.

"This hill man, Wandering Star," Green Field said to Blue Sky, taking Gentle Brook's hand. "You said he told you his people believe our ancestors stole this valley from them."

"Maybe our ancestors did," Blue Sky said. "Many years ago. It sounds possible to me. Maybe even probable. After all, we're here, and they're not. But what difference should that make now? Why couldn't we let them hunt all the deer they want in our forests? And fish in the river? You've seen the fish. They eat them. Spring Rain and Many Numbers eat them. I've eaten them. And why couldn't we teach the hill people how to farm?"

Green Field stared at the mountains to the east.

"Maybe we could," he replied. "Maybe we could."

Then he looked at the too-fearless youth his son had become.

"If," he added, "unlike your kindly hill-man friend, they didn't kill us first."

*****

Farmers from as far away as the upper valley stayed in the home village that night. The villagers left their livestock in their pastures so those visitors who couldn't fit inside the houses could at least sleep in the barns.

Rose Leaf said the village where she'd worked that day was just as crowded as theirs.

The farmers from the upper valley assured them Early Harvest and his cousins would arrive in the morning. His party was considerably larger than anybody had thought it would be. And, the upper-valley farmers added, Early Harvest had wanted Rose Leaf for himself.

Once, after somebody mentioned Full Harvest, Gentle Brook and Blue Sky found themselves looking at one another.

Blue Sky had never asked her about him. Now he had no need to.

This was where the devastation of the last war had left them: Tall Oak had the kingdom. Rainbow Evening had Fair Judge and her own point of view. Green Field had his life as a farmer and the overwhelming admiration of the people. Gentle Brook had Green Field, Full Harvest, and four children: Blue Sky, Rose Leaf, Morning Sun, and Early Harvest. Only one of them was in fact hers, but all of them she loved equally.

Blue Sky thought it was fortunate his family were busy seeing to the needs of visitors. It took their minds off the possible calamity waiting for them the next day if they told the people the truth—or the endless lying they'd commit themselves to if they didn't tell the people the truth.

*****

Blue Sky did find the time, though, to take part in a somewhat inebriated conversation in the orchard, where Rose Leaf had staged her drama. He was drinking wine and beer with Autumn Wine's older grandson and the men he'd shared his encampment year with. They were celebrating the fact that all of them were present and accounted for—and ready, willing, and able to do whatever the prince asked them to do.

For their amusement, each of them described how, when the fighting began the next day, he'd be the one who killed Sturdy Limb, as a deliriously joyful crowd cheered him on.

When they were done, Blue Sky dismissed all their claims with a laugh.

"If anybody kills Sturdy Limb tomorrow," he said, "I'll be the one who does it. Think how it'll happen. The chief warrior has promised he'll personally restrain his nephew, the prince. When he attempts to do so, I'll be standing next to the prince. And nobody will expect him to kill his own uncle. That wouldn't be right at all.

Somebody will have to do it for him. And I sure as hell will kill the man before any of you, or anybody else, gets close enough to him to strike a fatal blow."

Those remarks drew the snickers and sneers Blue Sky had expected and wanted. If he were to fail in the next day's fighting, for whatever reason, he'd still want them to succeed.

"Some people are saying," one of the comrades chose to inform him, "when Morning Sun becomes king, you'll run the kingdom. You and the two orphan boys."

Blue Sky scowled at the man who made those remarks, which didn't describe the kingdom Blue Sky had in mind when Morning Sun became the king.

"Many Numbers, Spring Rain, and I will be glad to give Morning Sun our advice," he said. "As will Rose Leaf, Solemn Promise, and Fair Judge. As will Early Harvest. As will you. And the prince might very well decide, as he can, you make a lot more sense than I do."

"That would be a shame," the man said, his remark as surprising to Blue Sky as the taste of Wandering Star's fish. "I was hoping the people I heard were right. I don't know anything about running a kingdom. Why would a king want my advice?"

"Drinking and fornicating," Autumn Wine's grandson chose to let Blue Sky know, "are more fun than advising a king or running a kingdom."

He'd left out roasting beef and dancing, but Blue Sky wasn't about to quibble.

*****

Morning Sun intended to see Tall Oak and Rainbow Evening alone before they sat in court the next day. He was more than willing to dare Sturdy Limb to attempt to stop him.

He'd specifically thanked Spring Rain for alerting him to the possibility that their present self-proclaimed allies might see fit not to keep their promises. He could imagine doing that himself, especially if he wondered if the person he was following was actually worth risking his life for. But he'd decided it wouldn't do him any good to worry about it.

"Who were the heroes in the last war with the hill people?" he asked. "And who weren't? Why do so many of our people despise Sturdy Limb? Why do so many love Green Field?"

Morning Sun was going to tell his father and mother he and Rose Leaf would have a wedding ceremony in the autumn whether Tall Oak allowed it or not.

Rose Leaf would be at his side. Sturdy Limb would have no reason to stop her from paying a visit to the royal family. If he knew the truth about her, though, he'd have a sworn duty to order her killed as soon as any of his people caught sight of her. Rose Leaf was a hill person where she wasn't allowed to be: in the valley the gods had promised the farmers.

*****

"What if the king still says no?" Green Field asked.

He, Gentle Brook, and Blue Sky were in the village orchard in the light of the full moon. Their guests had taken to their skins and hides for a good night's sleep before their confrontation with the king they respectfully disagreed with and the chief warrior they loathed.

"You'll see in court tomorrow," Blue Sky replied. "Morning Sun will tell the people he and Rose Leaf will be married in the autumn. He'll be surrounded by encampment comrades and farmers. He'll do what he did before. He'll dare Sturdy Limb to stop him."

Green Field and Gentle Brook looked at one another, both of them shuddering.

They'd fallen into a trap of their own creating. They'd encouraged Blue Sky, the hero's son, to question everything, even as they knew there was one answer he must never hear.

Blue Sky continued: if Tall Oak ordered the tellers not to bless the marriage of the prince and Rose Leaf, Morning Sun would ask the people to recognize him as their king in place of his father, who'd clearly proved himself incapable of remaining the king a moment longer.

Morning Sun would then order the tellers to prepare to conduct the autumn ceremony. In the meantime, he'd sit in court, making final decisions on every matter that came before him. Ten plus two people—Rose Leaf, Green Field, Gentle Brook, Rainbow Evening, Fair Judge, Many Numbers, Spring Rain, Solemn Promise, Full Harvest, Early Harvest, Valley Defender, and Blue Sky—would advise him, each with an equal voice.

If the chief warrior and first teller and their people chose not to bow to the wishes of the people and obey Morning Sun, he'd gladly replace each and every one of them.

Gentle Brook looked at Blue Sky. "You told him what to say. You've always done that. You did that when you and he were boys. I heard you do it."

His mother's words stung Blue Sky like angry bees.

"I give the prince my advice," he insisted. "Morning Sun chooses for himself whether to go along with it or not."

"But now when you do it, you're men," Gentle Brook said, ignoring her son's posturing. "What you do counts. You aren't boys anymore. You can get yourselves killed. Sturdy Limb tells people the most satisfying execution he'll ever carry out will be yours."

Blue Sky had heard whispers to that effect himself.

Green Field gave him a pleading look, the same look he'd given him when Blue Sky was a boy and did something wrong. Green Field had almost never raised his voice to him. Nor had he struck him—although he often admitted he'd been tempted to. He'd instead persuaded his son to modify his behavior by convincing him that what he was doing was a disappointment to his father.

"Do you wish," Green Field asked his son in the orchard, "to force your mother, Rose Leaf, and me to watch Sturdy Limb and his men kill you?"

"If that's what it takes," Blue Sky replied, the words spilling out of his mouth like wheat from a toppled cart. "You'll have to be brave. At least you'll know I knew what I was doing—dying for something far more important than myself. Both of you, you'll have to be brave. I'm not afraid of dying tomorrow. Sometimes, some people have to be willing to die. My father was, the last time our people rebelled against their king. I have to be true to my father. I'm his son. I'm required to ask any questions I wish—and take the answers wherever they lead me."

By the time he'd finished those remarks, his parents were visibly horrified, forcing him to embrace them. And promise them, too, he wouldn't speak or act quite so recklessly the next day.

*****

Rose Leaf, Blue Sky, and Many Numbers met Morning Sun, Spring Rain, Solemn Promise, Noon Breeze, and their sunrise pass comrades as they emerged from the forest in the twilight before dawn.

On the path to East Land's village, Rose Leaf walked and spoke with Morning Sun alone.

When the prince turned and looked at Blue Sky, shaking his head as he did so, Blue Sky suspected Rose Leaf had gotten to the part of the story where he'd thrown caution to the wind as if it were chaff, went into the gully, and met a hill man.

When Morning Sun suddenly looked as if an unseen god had reached down from heaven and given him a powerful blow to his head, Blue Sky assumed Rose Leaf was telling him what Lightning Spear had ordered his warriors to do to Tall Oak and Green Field.

And when Morning Sun put his arm around her shoulders, drew her close to him, and kissed her, Blue Sky gathered she'd disclosed her father wasn't Green Field, the valley people's hero, but Lightning Spear, the hill people's wicked king.

The day's most important question, though, wasn't whether the prince should be told. Rose Leaf's decision to tell him herself was, Blue Sky thought, indisputably the right one.

The crucial issue was whether the people should be told. More specifically, would the people remain on the side of the prince if they knew Rose Leaf wasn't the daughter of Green Field and Gentle Brook but was in fact the daughter of a cruel king? A king who'd caused the needless deaths of so many of their people and the senseless destruction of their property, crops, and livestock—to say nothing of their many people who'd spent the rest of their lives maimed?

The younger men and older boys from East Land's village were waiting for them on the path to the town. So were the men and boys from elsewhere who'd been their guests the previous night. So were East Land's niece, her mate, and a number of other younger women. So was East Land himself. And every able-bodied man carried a spear.

It was the same for all the villages between the forest and the river: far more people than the rebels had anticipated were on their way to the town for the confrontation with the king.

"The chief warrior won't be putting anybody in his cages this day," they promised.

"Not unless he and his deputies," someone else would add, "are eager to die this day."

*****

In court the previous day, East Land had bluntly told his comrade in the last war, now the king, the people wouldn't accept his refusal to approve Morning Sun and Rose Leaf's marriage unless he offered some kind of explanation for such an extraordinary ruling.

"It seems," he went on to say, "the people love their prince more than his father does."

Sturdy Limb loudly ordered East Land to say nothing further and sit down.

But all the farmers who spoke after that ended their remarks with the same comment.

*****

At the main fork in the path, the people from the home village and their guests were waiting to join the procession. Green Field, Gentle Brook, Autumn Wine, and her grandsons were among them. The sun was breaking over the eastern mountains.

Green Field, though, was the only able-bodied man who wasn't carrying a spear.

As Morning Sun and Rose Leaf had done since they reached East Land's village, they walked among the newcomers, greeting every person along the way. They smiled, even laughed occasionally in response to the many clever remarks the people had for them, mostly regarding the chief warrior.

As they approached Green Field and Gentle Brook, though, the seriousness of the occasion visibly weighed on them both.

As if to compensate, the prince handed Blue Sky his spear.

Reaching Green Field, Morning Sun embraced him.

Those who were close to them, as Blue Sky was, could tell the prince had tears in his eyes.

A long time had gone by since Blue Sky last saw the prince weeping in public.

"I'm sorry," Morning Sun whispered in Green Field's ear.

Blue Sky knew what the prince was saying only because he was near enough in the dawn light to read his lips.

"You and my father," Morning Sun said, his voice breaking.

Morning Sun embraced Green Field again.

"I'm very sorry," he whispered.

He embraced Gentle Brook as well, letting his tears fall.

The other people nearby—Spring Rain, Many Numbers, Solemn Promise, Noon Breeze, and Autumn Wine among others— were clearly shocked to see the prince in such a state.

As the closest onlookers whispered the news of the prince's unusual display of emotion to those farther away, the people became so quiet they could hear the birds singing sunrise songs.

The gods were supposedly telling the valley people they cared what happened to them and would always protect them.

Morning Sun wiped his face with his sleeve, stepped back from Green Field and Gentle Brook, and took Rose Leaf's hand.

"I wish to live with your daughter, Rose Leaf," he said, speaking loudly and distinctly, making certain nobody could fail to understand what he was saying. "I wish to have children with her. I wish to be her mate, husband, and friend until the end of my life."

People up and down the path repeated his words for those who couldn't hear him.

Green Field spoke first: "Gentle Brook and I understand Rose Leaf wishes to live with you and bear your children. I believe she's chosen wisely."

After Morning Sun lifted his face from his sleeve once again, he looked at Gentle Brook.

"I can only hope your marriage to my daughter," she said, as if she were in song, "pleases the gods and our people as much as it does me."

As Morning Sun's, Green Field's, and Gentle Brook's remarks went out to the crowd, the initial murmurs of approval became a roar.

Morning Sun and Rose Leaf, both having dried their tears, waved to the people, acknowledging their consent as well as that of the two people who were holding themselves out to be the father and mother of the person the prince would have for his wife.

As the noise of the crowd subsided, Morning Sun faced those two people again.

"When we arrive at the court," he said, "Rose Leaf and I intend to see my father and mother in their room. We'll ask them for their permission to have a wedding ceremony in the autumn."

The crowd enjoyed those remarks. Before the end of the day, Tall Oak would either change his mind, explain specifically why he wouldn't change his mind, or watch the people recognize Morning Sun as their king and help him oust any officials who refused to obey him.

The people might also have to kill those who physically resisted. Nobody could name an armed man approaching the town who hadn't promised he'd do that if it became necessary. Word of the promises had reached the officials in question, too.

"Will you come with us when we visit my father and mother?" Morning Sun asked Green Field and Gentle Brook.

"Yes," Green Field replied.

"Yes," Gentle Brook repeated.

Morning Sun looked at Blue Sky, letting a smile break through the clouds.

"And you, farmer boy," he said, giving the onlookers a welcome opportunity to snicker. "Will you come with us?"

Blue Sky, knowing what the crowd wanted, laughed with them, suppressing his tears.

"Yes, prince boy," he replied. "For you and Rose Leaf and our people, I will."

*****

Early Harvest and his many cousins, including those like Good Harvest who might've been his brothers, were waiting for the crowd at the bridge below the bluff. They'd come down the river on rafts. Full Harvest was with them.

"Sturdy Limb won't dare try anything now," one of the younger tellers close to Many Numbers and Spring Rain said.

After everybody who wished to do so had greeted their upper-valley allies, they crossed the bridge and passed the river people standing in front of their tents and the goods they had for trade. Speaking to one another in their own language, they appeared to have been taken unawares, even frightened perhaps, by the astonishing number of able-bodied men brandishing spears.

Many in the crowd spoke to the river people, assuring them they meant them no harm.

Many Numbers and Spring Rain, who could speak their language, stopped to explain to them what was happening.

From any second-floor window on the east side of the court, Sturdy Limb could look down and see the people climbing the twisting path from the river to the top of the bluff. He could see their spears as well. He could also see his deputies and allies were hopelessly outnumbered.

Law Keeper was undoubtedly among those most alarmed to see the mob coming to impose its will on the kingdom. The people had heard by then all they wanted to hear about what that man had tried to do to the two orphan boys they loved.

When Autumn Wine's older grandson and his comrades were describing, the evening before, how they'd kill the chief warrior, each of them invariably assigned to his best friend the lesser but still necessary task of putting to death the first teller.

As they climbed the path to the town, Blue Sky fell into a conversation with Good Harvest and the other upper-valley cousins he hadn't seen since the full-moon holiday the previous summer when the people had insisted Early Harvest and Morning Sun run a second race.

Green Field and Gentle Brook walked on either side of Full Harvest, whispering to him, one after the other, making certain nobody else could hear what they were saying.

Full Harvest glanced in the direction of Morning Sun and Rose Leaf.

Then he turned and stared at Blue Sky, who was laughing at a facetious remark Good Harvest had made, saying the two of them should convince Rose Leaf to drop the prince in favor of Early Harvest. After that, everybody in the kingdom would be friends again, and they could go home and work in their fields.

"We have any number of beautiful women in the upper valley," another cousin, who happened to be a teller, offered. "One of them might be glad to have Morning Sun for a husband."

"True," another cousin interjected, "but he'd have to compete with us for her."

The teller cousin laughed. "But don't forget, he's the prince, and you're not."

Full Harvest was looking at Blue Sky as if the hero's son were a malicious intruder who'd suddenly thrown open the door to his house in the middle of the darkest night.

That was when Blue Sky realized Full Harvest was the fifth person in the kingdom, along with Green Field, Gentle Brook, Tall Oak, and Rainbow Evening, who'd always known the truth.

Now, thanks to Blue Sky's trespass—thumbing his nose at their people's laws and their gods on sunrise pass—Full Harvest was one of eight who knew. And he'd just found that out.

Chapter 14

The six people climbing the bluff that day who knew the truth felt its weight as if they bore outsized baskets of grain, one on each shoulder. Their allies, though—even those who'd reached Autumn Wine's remarkable age—danced up the path in their innocence as if they were butterflies.

Blue Sky had insisted upon the truth like a farmer demanding the return of a stolen cow—as if he owned it. Now he feared all he'd get for his high-minded effort would be the imprisonment of his sister, his boyhood friend, and himself inside the secret with the five people already there.

The secret, feeding on the dreary, daily lies it required for its sustenance, would live on.

As the crowd reached the top of the bluff and surged into the town, the court people and tellers kept their distance.

They ordinarily liked to make their presence vividly known, especially during a full-moon holiday. The farmers believed that was their way of emphasizing how close they were to the king and his highest officials—and how the farmers were actually strangers in their own kingdom.

The town people weren't wearing linen that full-moon holiday. If fighting began, the combatants would do it in hides. Not even the court people and tellers trained for warfare in linen.

When Morning Sun first saw them cowering in the side pathways, he greeted them by their names, as the old friends they mostly were. His allies quickly followed his lead.

The court people and tellers nervously returned the greetings of their numerous visitors, many of them bearing spears.

When the prince reached the main entrance to the court, he turned and faced the crowd. He said he was certain only a few people would need to escort him, Rose Leaf, and her family to his father and mother's room. He invited everybody else to wait in the courtyard, where the king and queen were to sit that day.

Those entering the court with the prince and Rose Leaf's family included Solemn Promise, Fair Judge, Full Harvest, Many Numbers, Spring Rain, the other comrades from the sunrise pass encampments, and Early Harvest and his cousins.

The prince had chosen for his guards the last people Sturdy Limb would wish to start a fight with. If any of them were harmed or killed, the chief warrior and his deputies would face an enraged crowd—and very likely the agony of death at spear point.

*****

Blue Sky and Early Harvest led the guards into the great central hall. They could see at a glance that the chief warrior and first teller had ordered their people not to stand in the way of the prince. They lined the walls, holding onto their spears as if they were saplings rooted in the ground and not instruments for the killing of humans by the removal of guts from bellies.

When Sturdy Limb had publicly promised to cage the prince, Blue Sky, and their allies, or lock them up in the courtyard without food or water, he'd assumed the threat alone would be enough to keep the rebels from going forward.

Now he could see for himself the farmers he often referred to as "simpletons" weren't repeating the mistake—choosing conformity over rebellion—he and so many others had made in the last war with the hill people.

The prince and his allies greeted the deputies and high tellers as they had the town people in the walkways. And they got the same uneasy responses for their efforts.

After Morning Sun handed his spear to Solemn Promise, and Blue Sky his to Spring Rain, they mounted the stairs with Rose Leaf, Green Field, and Gentle Brook.

Sturdy Limb's two men standing guard outside the entrance to the king and queen's room made no attempt to stop them. Instead, the guards greeted the guests as courteously as they always had when Green Field and Gentle Brook's family paid a visit to the royal family.

But they couldn't conceal their apprehension as to how that day might end.

*****

Tall Oak and Rainbow Evening were waiting for their visitors and wordlessly rose from their chairs when they entered the room.

The king and the queen were the only people wearing linen that day, which was so pleasant the court people had long since taken the shutters and hides away from their windows.

Morning Sun embraced his parents, first his mother and then his father.

Again, he made no attempt to hide his tears.

"I'm sorry," he said to his father.

"Sorry?" Tall Oak asked, apparently puzzled as much by his son's weeping as his remark.

"For what happened to you and Green Field in the war," Morning Sun replied. "For what the hill people's king did to you and Green Field in the war."

Tall Oak and Rainbow Evening stared at the prince.

"I'm also sorry," Rose Leaf said, embracing the king, "for what the person who was my birth father did to you."

"As I am," Blue Sky said, embracing Tall Oak in turn.

"And I'm grateful, too," Rose Leaf added. "I'm grateful you and my father Green Field didn't leave me behind. I'm grateful you brought me back with you to the valley. I'm grateful Gentle Brook is my mother and Blue Sky my brother. I'm grateful I live in a kingdom where you're the king and Rainbow Evening is the queen."

"We're all grateful," Morning Sun said to Rose Leaf, "you live with us."

For a long time, seven people said nothing further, as if they were purposefully listening to the crowd in the courtyard below, its fear-defying laughter coming through the windows like a song those in the king and queen's room could listen to but never again sing themselves.

Wiping his sleeve across his face, Tall Oak looked at Green Field and Gentle Brook.

"You told them?" he asked.

"No," Blue Sky replied for his father and mother. "They didn't tell us. They did as you asked them to do. I found out on my own what happened."

Tall Oak and Rainbow Evening looked at the man who used to be the boy who enjoyed making outrageous remarks in their presence. They were, after all, the king and the queen.

"I found it out from a hill man on sunrise pass," he explained.

Tall Oak and Rainbow Evening continued looking at Blue Sky as if he'd reached the point where his remarks were too bizarre to fit into the world they lived in.

Blue Sky told them what he'd done, freely admitting he'd committed treason when he'd made contact with a hill man—and not bothering to conceal how far the contact went.

"You can speak with a hill man?" Rainbow Evening asked.

"Our languages are much more similar than the tellers say they are," Blue Sky replied. "My hill-man friend learned on his own how to speak ours. He taught me how to speak theirs."

Rainbow Evening looked at Green Field. "You were right about that."

In private, the queen often questioned many of their people's accepted beliefs, some of them regarding the hill people. But Blue Sky hadn't been able to persuade her that their people could be convinced their beliefs regarding their enemies lacked proof as well as logic. Like Fair Judge and the tellers close to her, she thought most of their people didn't wish to be bothered with arguments of that sort.

Perhaps, Rainbow Evening allowed herself to wonder aloud on more than one occasion, they were simply too pleasure-loving—and maybe, as her brother-in-law the chief warrior would agree, not all that bright to begin with.

Morning Sun liked telling her they could easily forgive people for failings such as those.

The people in the courtyard were laughing at remarks loud, crude, and clever while the leaders of a rebellion—the prince and the family of the woman he wished to have children with—were supposedly handing down their terms to the king and queen: Tall Oak could either agree to the marriage or attend a ceremony that same day in which the tellers, with the high tellers at spear-point if need be, found him incompetent and declared the prince to be the new king.

But the seven individuals upstairs, all of them knowing the truth now, were looking at one another with tears in their eyes.

Rainbow Evening embraced Rose Leaf. "I'm glad you know the truth," she said. "I'm glad you know I suckled you in the forest with the prince and Blue Sky. You've always been as much my daughter as you were Gentle Brook and Green Field's. And I regret my part in what we did. I regret all those years we said you and Morning Sun couldn't marry."

"It didn't do us any good anyway," Gentle Brook said. "We would've been better off saying nothing about it."

"I still would've fallen in love with Rose Leaf," Morning Sun agreed. "It doesn't matter to me who her father is. I wish to have children with her."

For some reason, the crowd outside had grown quiet.

Rainbow Evening looked at Morning Sun.

"And I believe you should," she said.

Morning Sun turned to his father. "I'm asking for your permission to marry Rose Leaf in the autumn."

Tall Oak turned to Blue Sky. "Have you told anybody else who Rose Leaf is?"

"No," Blue Sky replied.

Tall Oak glanced at Rose Leaf.

"Does her father live?" he asked.

"He does," Blue Sky said. "He's still their king."

"Her mother?"

"Yes."

"Does Rose Leaf have brothers or sisters?"

"No."

Tall Oak looked at Green Field. "You were right about that, too," he said.

After glancing at Blue Sky, Tall Oak turned to the prince.

"What will you do if the people find out Rose Leaf is the hill people's princess?" he asked.

"Rose Leaf and I intend to tell the people who she is. We want them to know she's the hill people's princess. We want to stop the lying now."

Gentle Brook put her arm around Rainbow Evening's waist. Both of them were trembling.

"We also want the people to know," Morning Sun added, "how Rose Leaf got here."

Tall Oak turned to Blue Sky. "I imagine that's what you want, too."

"Yes, it is," Blue Sky agreed.

"Did your father and mother tell you why we kept Rose Leaf's identity a secret?"

"Yes. To protect her from the people. Originally, you were no doubt wise to do that."

"But not so wise today?"

"Unnecessarily cautious."

"You think we should tell the people the whole truth?"

"Yes."

"Yes," Morning Sun agreed. "The whole truth. Everything."

"What if the people who love you now turn against you?" Tall Oak asked. "What if they don't want a future king whose mother or grandmother was the hill people's princess?"

"I'll grant them their wish," Morning Sun replied. "I'll give up my right to succeed you—as long as Rose Leaf can remain in the valley and be my mate for the rest of my life."

In his youth, Tall Oak hadn't looked forward to becoming king any more than Green Field could imagine himself as chief warrior. They'd have to order, and carry out, the killing of humans.

"Rose Leaf and I will farm," Morning Sun continued. "I know some kindly villagers I'll ask to show me how it's done. Valley Defender will someday be king. He won't like that, but too bad for him, that's the way it'll be. I never asked to be the prince in this kingdom. I never gave my consent to that. And we won't need his."

"I don't wish to be a princess or a queen," Rose Leaf added. "I only want to live with Morning Sun and have children with him. It doesn't matter to me who he is. He could be the least successful farmer in the valley. I'd still want to live with him for the rest of my life. Such a person would be happier anyway than a prince or a king."

The courtyard crowd was laughing at and loudly repeating a remark Good Harvest had tossed in the court people's direction. Everybody knew, he'd assured them, the only interest they had in farming was to find out how to go with livestock—how to please the animals so much they'd welcome subsequent trysts.

A common joke told among the town people began with a recitation of the well-known fact that male farmers didn't worry a lot about how often they shaved, bathed, and changed their clothing. But who could blame them? With compliant cows, ewes, and nannies no more than a barn door away, they didn't need other people to go with and expose to their beastly odor.

Rainbow Evening shook her head. "Won't the people also force Tall Oak to abdicate? He and I, their king and queen, have lied to them for many years now, passing off the hill people's princess as Green Field and Gentle Brook's daughter. Why shouldn't we be punished for that?"

"That assumes," Blue Sky replied, "the people would rather have Sturdy Limb for their king than Tall Oak."

The seven people in the king and queen's room knew that if Sturdy Limb became king, he'd order the execution of them all. And Rose Leaf's presence in the valley would be the only excuse he'd need to do it. The execution order would surely include others, too.

"We have to leave our fate to the people," Blue Sky continued. "We have to assume they'll never ask Tall Oak to abdicate. He's been as good a king for them as they could possibly expect a king to be. That's my opinion, but I'm certain it's one the people share."

Tall Oak looked at Blue Sky as if those remarks surprised him.

Blue Sky turned to the king. "The farmers don't want Sturdy Limb for their king. Nor do most of the court people and high tellers. I know he's your brother, but I'd be far less than honest if I didn't tell you the people despise him, in many cases even more than I do."

"But not," Rainbow Evening said, "more than I do."

Tall Oak turned to Green Field. "What do you say?" he asked. "What's your opinion? What would you do if you were me?"

"Like my son," Green Field replied, "the gods seem to be insisting we take a chance. As they did when the hill people attacked us on sunrise pass. We've got to take a chance the people can see what we see this time. I'd give Morning Sun and Rose Leaf permission to marry. I'd also tell the people the truth. If they don't want Morning Sun for their next king, I'd be disappointed. I can only hope Blue Sky is right, and the people would never ask you to abdicate and let Sturdy Limb become their king. I hope instead they'd want Valley Defender to be your successor. If he surrounded himself with individuals like Solemn Promise and Many Numbers, the kingdom might continue to prosper."

Blue Sky looked at Tall Oak. "I'd beg the gods on my knees to let you outlive your brother. Once you did that, the kingdom could rest easy again."

"The farmers," Gentle Brook said, "will all be down on their knees with you."

Tall Oak looked at Gentle Brook. "Will you tell me what you think we should do?"

The four men present were aware the three women present could run the kingdom as well as they could. The only difference for their people was this: the women could neither kill other humans, nor die themselves, in battle. But the men could and did. Therefore the men had to rule, whether they wished to or not.

"Like Green Field," Gentle Brook replied, "I'd be deeply disappointed if Morning Sun isn't our next king."

The prince she'd suckled in the forest with Rose Leaf and Blue Sky extended his arm around her shoulders.

"But if that wasn't to be," she continued, "if that wasn't what the people wanted, I'd gladly teach him what I know about farming. He's a hard worker, and he's certainly strong enough. He could live in our village. So could his and Rose Leaf's children. I'd welcome them all. We'd build a house for them. The gods wouldn't be as happy in their heaven as I'd be in our village."

By the time she finished those remarks, seven people were once again wiping away tears.

Rainbow Evening, turning to Blue Sky, chose to break the silence.

"I'm not glad you risked your life meeting a hill man," she said. "Your mother and father love you. We all do. Your death would've horrified us. But I'm glad you found out the truth."

She turned to Morning Sun and Rose Leaf.

"If I were the king," she continued, "I'd let you marry and have all the children you wanted. And if you told me you wished for the people to know the truth, I'd make certain they heard it. After that, I'd let the people have whatever kingdom they desired. If they decided Sturdy Limb should be their king, so be it. A people that foolish would deserve him. But if they chose to wait for Valley Defender, I'd be the first to congratulate them on their wisdom."

Tall Oak also turned to Rose Leaf and Morning Sun.

"You have my permission to marry in the autumn. And we'll tell the people the truth. We'll do it today."

He turned to Blue Sky.

"While so many of our people, for some reason, are here."

Now it would be the seven of them against the world.

That could violate one of their people's elemental rules of warfare: wise leaders never began a battle against an enemy whose numbers exceeded their own.

*****

Green Field sat in the chair the prince ordinarily occupied on the dais with Tall Oak and Rainbow Evening.

Sturdy Limb and his deputies and Law Keeper and his high tellers were in their usual places on their benches.

The people had seated themselves in the tall grass, which was growing in the courtyard so abundantly then it hid the spears lying next to the men who'd brought them. Early Harvest, Full Harvest, Gentle Brook, Rose Leaf, Morning Sun, Blue Sky, Spring Rain, Many Numbers, Fair Judge, Valley Defender, and Solemn Promise were in the first row, in that order.

The river traders, having no customers to exchange goods with, had also come up the bluff to the courtyard to attend the proceeding.

After Tall Oak informed the crowd that Green Field would tell them a story they hadn't previously heard but needed to know, the trepidation of the people was as visible on their faces as it would've been if the sun that cloudless day had suddenly gone dark, without a hint from the gods to the tellers beforehand.

Green Field didn't leave out the beginning: his and Tall Oak's capture by the hill people as a result of their refusal to heed Tall Oak's father's order to retreat to the bluff.

East Land loudly interjected at that point: "We could've stopped the hill people's army at sunrise pass! Green Field and Tall Oak were right! Many lives would've been saved!"

"They were damned right!" another farmer yelled.

Other farmers added their own "Damned right!" and "Many, many lives!" to the clamor.

The older court people and tellers, though, taking their cues from Sturdy Limb, remained silent and expressionless. They had obeyed the king and retreated.

"I believe there are times," Green Field said, "when the people are right to defy their king. But those times are rare, as they should be. Otherwise, why would the people ever need to obey the person placed, by the gods and his birth, in their charge?"

After he and the prince had gotten themselves separated from their comrades, Green Field continued, confirming the usual version of the story, their captors easily could've killed them. The hill warriors had to have figured out what the valley warriors were yelling, and they realized one of the two warriors they'd surrounded was the prince. While he was a prisoner of the hill people, Green Field came to believe he could understand some of the things they were saying.

"Now I've learned," he said, "what I guessed then is in fact the case. The hill people's language is remarkably similar to our own."

The crowd, not knowing how he could've learned that conjecture was true, murmured.

Green Field bravely led his audience through the events of the evening of his and Tall Oak's captivity, simply setting forth the facts. The hill people's king ordered his warriors to take the manhood of the captives as revenge for a valley warrior's taking his in battle.

"The hill warriors held us down," Green Field said, "and did as they were told."

"No!" someone in the crowd screamed.

"No!" others repeated, screaming the word from one end of the courtyard to the other.

And yet it had to be true. Neither Rainbow Evening nor Gentle Brook had carried a child after the war. And they'd both apparently become, with their partner's consent, another person's intimate friend. Even though one might question why the gods, who supposedly favored the valley people, would allow the hill people's king to do what he did to the valley people's prince and his comrade, it all fit together too well.

The explosion of shouts soon gave way to something else.

East Land rose to his feet. "Damn the hill people!" he bellowed. "Damn their king! May the gods help us kill every last one of them!"

Any number of other people, almost all of them men who'd fought in the last war, also rose to their feet and loudly repeated East Land's remarks, adding to them as much of their own vitriol as they could muster on such short notice.

Morning Sun took Rose Leaf in his arms. Full Harvest took Gentle Brook's hand. Rainbow Evening, on the dais, closed her eyes.

After observing those people, Spring Rain turned to Blue Sky, who assumed his own dread was as conspicuous as lightning in the night.

Green Field, though, patiently waited for his comrades in the war to have their say before he returned to his story.

He described the hill people's quick descent into drunkenness after imbibing the farmers' wine, and his and Tall Oak's ridding themselves of their bindings. But he chose not to explain specifically how they'd accomplished their freedom. The omission confirmed to the crowd that he'd somehow removed his bindings and then freed the prince.

At that point in his story, Green Field's face was strangely contorted.

The valley people had seen it previously, almost always when older people attempted to explain what happened to them in the war. They often couldn't continue, and the people around them learned not to insist on hearing those stories to their end.

Green Field, though, continued. He'd reached the heart of the matter: the hapless infant, no doubt the hill people's princess—another fact recently confirmed, he added—left alone, with no sober hill people nearby to protect her.

Spring Rain looked at Rose Leaf, took Blue Sky's hand, and wept.

"What could we do?" Green Field pleaded, not bothering to wipe his own eyes. "We realized we couldn't kill an innocent child no matter who her father was or what he'd done. We couldn't take her back to her people. We couldn't abandon her to the wolves. We had to bring her home with us."

The people in the court yard, murmuring again, could see now, as Spring Rain already had, where Green Field was taking them—and their kingdom.

The crowd walked over the mountains with Green Field and Tall Oak, bleeding from their wounds, carrying the hill people's princess—who'd done nothing to start the war, and who could've been, from her appearance and behavior, any other girl child born in the valley.

The people were still with them during their reunion in the forest with their horrified wives.

They were with Gentle Brook, too, deciding she had to keep the baby as if she'd given birth to her.

Green Field stared down at Rose Leaf, Morning Sun, and Blue Sky.

"What came next," he said, "was my fault, and my fault alone: shameful years of silence and deception. I imposed them on the only other people who knew who Rose Leaf was. I realize now my doing so was very wrong. I apologize to all of you for what I did."

The great hero who'd saved the life of the present king was placing the full blame for those "shameful years" on his own broad shoulders, attempting once again to save Tall Oak—and the kingdom.

"I foolishly thought our people might kill Rose Leaf," Green Field continued. "I thought they might kill her simply for being the hill people's princess, the daughter of the king who'd caused us such a great number of deaths and injuries and such a vast amount of destruction. Our people's understandable need for vengeance, I wrongly feared, might lead them to kill a child."

Green Field was pausing after every remark he made, letting each of them sink in, letting those hearing his story make any comment in rebuttal they might wish to make.

But nobody was choosing to do that.

"I was a young man then," Green Field continued. "I thought I knew a lot of things, but I didn't know our people. I didn't understand they'd never kill a child, not even a hill child, not even a child whose father was the hill people's king."

Although nobody chose to interrupt Green Field, Spring Rain leaned toward Blue Sky.

"You'll never know how much I envy you," he whispered in his hut-mate's ear.

"What are you talking about?" Blue Sky asked, whispering himself.

"That man, Green Field, is your father," Spring Rain replied.

"Our people never would've killed a child," Blue Sky's father continued. "I should've insisted they know the truth. They would've shrugged their shoulders and said, 'So be it. The hill people's princess lives with us. We'll have to make certain she feels welcome in our valley. We'll treat her as we would any other infant child who lives among us.'"

Spring Rain whispered in Blue Sky's ear again: "He knows they would've killed her."

Whether the valley people once would've killed Rose Leaf or not, most of the women and children present, and many of the men, East Land included, were in tears.

Spring Rain was no doubt right. But now the people could more readily see how evil the killing of a person they and the prince had fallen in love with would've been.

"I concealed the truth from the people, from you," Green Field said. "I was wrong. I apologize. I beg for your forgiveness."

Green Field was creating a new truth to take the place of the old. He was describing the valley people not as they'd been, or even as they'd become, but as they ought to be.

"Whoever else Rose Leaf is," Green Field added, "she is and will always be my and Gentle Brook's daughter, and we'll always love her."

Glancing at Blue Sky, Green Field briefly appended to his story an explanation of how he'd recently learned some of his suppositions regarding the hill people and their language were correct, and why he'd come to understand all the valley people should know the truth.

"My son went to see for himself if there was in fact a hidden gully in the ravine. He could've been killed. Instead, he found the gully. He found a friendly hill man, too. And he found the truth. I apologize to him, and to all of you, for making him do what he had to do to learn it."

Green Field sat down, the repeaters finished their work, and the silence in the courtyard became as shocking as the cries for killing every last hill person.

Like dancers wishing the musicians could play on forever, the people listening to Green Field that day suddenly missed his voice and his story. And his was a tale they'd never imagined themselves in, a dance they'd never expected to dance.

Tall Oak embraced Green Field, letting his own tears fall on his old friend's shirt.

Many of the men who'd fought in the last war wept easily, even in public. The valley people's stories made the point: after a warrior killed other humans in battle, or saw his comrades die in one, he sometimes couldn't help himself no matter how hard he tried—he wept openly.

Tall Oak stood up, facing the people he'd feared to entrust with the truth.

"The war with the hill people was a long time ago," he began. "Their princess has become one of us. I'm therefore ordering that Rose Leaf may freely live in our valley, that no person may harm her in any way for being a hill person, and that all our people will continue to accept her as one of our own."

Nobody in the crowd chose to question whether that decision was right and just.

"Furthermore," Tall Oak continued, "Rainbow Evening and I wish for you to know that we've gladly assented to the marriage of the prince, Morning Sun, and Rose Leaf. As Rose Leaf's parents in this kingdom, Green Field and Gentle Brook have assented as well. We're therefore asking all our people to join us this autumn for the celebration of the ceremony the tellers will perform blessing the marriage."

As the repeaters carried out their task, Tall Oak took his seat again.

And after everybody got to hear what he'd said, the renewed silence of the people in the courtyard was, like death, the only thing that mattered. The people ordinarily greeted the announcement of the marriage of the king's immediate heir with cheers and jubilation.

In this case, though, they'd be celebrating the marriage of the prince not to a daughter of farmers, as they'd assumed she was, but the daughter of the hill people's monstrous king, who might someday be the grandfather of the valley people's king.

On the other hand, how could the people oppose Tall Oak and Morning Sun? They were all that stood in the way of Sturdy Limb's becoming their king.

Still, the people remained silent.

Morning Sun kissed Rose Leaf and began rising to his feet. The time to give up his position in the line to succeed his father had arrived.

Blue Sky, though, grabbed Morning Sun's shirt and pulled him back to the ground.

Early Harvest was also rising to his feet, facing the crowd.

"Imagine," he began, "what the hill people's king did to Tall Oak and Green Field. Imagine as well, seeking rightful revenge, they took that king's only child but soon discovered they couldn't possibly harm her. They had to bring her with them to our valley. Who of us could argue they were wrong to do that?"

After pausing for the repeaters and allowing more than sufficient time for anyone present to attempt an answer to his question, Early Harvest continued, staring at Rose Leaf.

"Our prince, growing up, fell in love with Rose Leaf. So did I."

Like many others that day, Early Harvest was paying no attention to his tears.

"None of us knew she was a hill person," he resumed. "We all thought she was the daughter of farmers we loved and admired. We could find no reason not to love her as much as we loved them. She may have been born a hill person, but she was also born a human. And that's all she needs to be to live with us. That's all she needs to be to marry our prince. For myself, I'm deeply sorry Rose Leaf chose Morning Sun over me. But since she's chosen him, and he's chosen her, I say they must have each other. As far as I'm concerned, Rose Leaf is still the daughter of Green Field and Gentle Brook, and our people should welcome her marriage to the prince."

Good Harvest rose and placed his arm around his cousin's shoulders.

The valley people could see, many fully confronting it for the first time, the truth behind the truth: hill people were as human as they were.

After Early Harvest and his cousin sat down, Full Harvest, his face creased as much as Green Field's from his own remembrance of the horrific past, rose and turned to the crowd.

"Our king and Green Field had no choice but to bring an innocent child to our valley. Now that innocent child and our prince wish to live and have children together. If we honorably disagree with one another on certain things, we do agree on this: nobody but the two of them can have a say in the matter."

As Green Field, Tall Oak, and Early Harvest had done, he paused, giving ample opportunity for the airing of any opinion to the contrary.

Hearing none, he boomed his conclusion: "I stand with the king."

Early Harvest, Good Harvest, and the other upper-valley cousins, having risen as Full Harvest spoke, declared as one: "I stand with the king."

Autumn Wine and her two grandsons rose. East Land and his family rose. Their neighbors rose. Neighbors of those neighbors rose.

Farther out, like a field of grain near harvest resuming an upright position after the passing of a vigorous breeze, all the farmers present rose.

And each of them, after rising, loudly affirmed: "I stand with the king."

Many Numbers, Spring Rain, Fair Judge, the younger tellers, the women tellers, Noon Breeze, and his apprentice-teller comrades stood up, declaring: "I stand with the king."

Valley Defender, his brothers, Solemn Promise, and the court companions rose to their feet, loudly letting their position be known: "I stand with the king."

Sturdy Limb was no fool. As long as his brother remained the king, he remained the chief warrior. And what else could he hope for? The prince and his friends, especially Green Field's son, would take his position from him and laugh as they did it.

Sturdy Limb rose, declaring: "The war was long ago. I stand with my brother the king."

His deputies, their families, Law Keeper, his high tellers, their associates, and all their current mates rose.

"I stand with the king," they affirmed, in unison, as a chorus would.

Even the river people, the valley people's guests, rose to their feet, and all of them loudly repeated the same five words in the language of their hosts: "I stand with the king."

Only seven people were left.

Morning Sun, Rose Leaf, Gentle Brook, and Blue Sky rose.

On the dais, Tall Oak, Rainbow Evening, and Green Field rose.

Morning Sun, the valley people's prince, and Rose Leaf, the hill people's princess, turned to the crowd.

"I'll never forget the kindness of every person in our kingdom," Morning Sun said. "I therefore promise you I'll always do everything I can to keep this kingdom safe."

"As will I," Rose Leaf said. "I might've been born elsewhere to parents I'll never know, but I'll always be a farmers' daughter who fell in love with your prince. I'm deeply grateful you'll let me marry and have children with him. But I'm most grateful Green Field and Gentle Brook and Tall Oak and Rainbow Evening let me live my life in this valley with you."

*****

The people, cheering, asked the gods to bless the marriage of Morning Sun and Rose Leaf, and they loudly promised to attend the wedding ceremony and festivities come autumn again.

Tall Oak spoke the last words from the dais that morning, looking at his son, his many allies, and all the farmers beyond them: "Nobody attending court this day will suffer any penalty for doing so, no matter what laws they might've transgressed in coming here. I pardon you all."

*****

Holiday drinking, dancing, singing, and feasting followed in the courtyard—all as a gift from the king.

"You fell in love with the hill man you saw in the bushes," Spring Rain said to Blue Sky as soon as he could speak with him alone. "That's where you were when you were gone all night."

"Since I couldn't have Morning Sun or you," Blue Sky agreed. "Would you like to meet my hill-man friend?"

Blue Sky had honestly replied to Tall Oak when he said he'd told no other person who Rose Leaf was. But one other person did know who she was.

Wandering Star had seen, in the apprentice tellers' guard post, the young woman who was supposed to be Blue Sky's sister. He thought she remarkably resembled his own people's king and queen. Then Blue Sky told him the farmers' king was unreasonably refusing to let their prince marry her, even though she was the daughter of a great hero, Blue Sky's father.

By the time Wandering Star spoke with Blue Sky high on a mountain, he realized Rose Leaf was his people's missing princess. But he didn't want to come right out and say the valley people's king and queen, as well as Blue Sky's own father and mother, were liars and participants in the abduction of an innocent infant child.

After Blue Sky learned the truth, he insisted Wandering Star go down to the valley with him. Wandering Star had initially refused. But Blue Sky knew his hill friend would eventually give in. The man badly wanted to see, up close, how farmers lived.

Blue Sky sneaked him in from the forest and hid him in the woods on the bluff.

And everything they did on the valley people's side of the mountains was as delightfully illicit as it had been on sunrise pass. In both of their peoples' stories, going with an enemy was a hideous kind of treason requiring an execution as prolonged as the executioners could make it. More than anybody else, Blue Sky needed the king's pardon.

Wanting his people to see and speak with his forbidden friend, Blue Sky asked Tall Oak, who was sitting at his table drinking wine, for his permission to bring the hill man into the courtyard.

Sturdy Limb chose to wax sarcastic. Bringing a hill person into the valley, he said, used to be treason, pure and simple. But since treason was now freely permitted in the kingdom, what difference would it make if Green Field's son brought a hill man into the courtyard?

Many Numbers noted that Blue Sky had done nothing more than what Tall Oak and Green Field had when they brought Rose Leaf home with them. In neither case was the hill person hostile or armed.

Law Keeper ignored the orphan boy he detested even more than he did Green Field's son.

"You went beyond the guard post to meet this hill man," he said, wagging his finger at Blue Sky. "That was treason right there. Why would you do such a thing?"

Blue Sky couldn't help himself.

"You of all people can understand why I did it," he said, not without sneering. "I saw a hill man in the bushes. And I very much liked what I saw. I went with him one night I'll never forget. Many times since then I've gone with him again. I've enjoyed going with him so much I confess I've fallen in love with him."

Blue Sky could see Law Keeper did understand, even as he attempted to appear perplexed.

"Is that what you'd call treason?" Blue Sky asked. "Would you have us believe you wouldn't give in to that kind of temptation? Even if the hill man turned out to be as pleasing to your eyes as the valley man who calls himself Spring Rain?"

The prince, Early Harvest and his cousins, Valley Defender and his brothers, the two orphan boys, and the younger court people, tellers, and apprentice tellers laughed, taking no small delight in the first teller's discomfort, even as his high tellers smirked behind his back.

Rainbow Evening, Green Field, and Gentle Brook responded without laughing, but also without concealing their amusement at the first teller's expense.

They said they'd like to meet the hill man.

Fair Judge said she wished to learn the hill people's language. Spring Rain and Many Numbers readily agreed it could be as interesting to speak and hear as the river people's was.

Rose Leaf said she especially wanted to meet the hill man. He was her kinsman, after all. He could tell her who she was—and what her fate would've been if Green Field and Tall Oak hadn't brought her to the valley.

"Your sister's as much of a hero as you are," Spring Rain whispered to Blue Sky.

"I'm not a hero," Blue Sky whispered back. "I merely happened upon the truth."

Tall Oak assented to Blue Sky's request.

*****

Blue Sky brought Wandering Star into the courtyard and introduced him to the king, the queen, the prince, Green Field, Gentle Brook, and Rose Leaf.

As Blue Sky did so, the people turned and stared at the hill man. They were surprised to see him shaven and hear him speak their language fluently. He'd even cut his hair as short as Blue Sky's.

When Blue Sky introduced him to Fair Judge, she asked him why he wasn't hostile toward the valley people if he believed they'd stolen the valley from his people.

"There's no reason for hostility," Wandering Star replied. "My people can learn from your people. You have the harvest of the earth at your fingertips. In your barns and your granaries. My people often roam their hills all day and still go to sleep hungry. Blue Sky showed me your crops in your fields and your livestock in your pastures, and I confess: if I could, I'd gladly choose your way of life."

The people repeated his remarks for those who weren't close enough to hear them.

"Now I've been told," he continued, "you'll let your prince marry my people's princess. I confess again: my people are wrong about many things concerning your people. Most of all, they shouldn't consider your people their enemy. The time for that, if there ever was one, has passed."

While the people repeated those remarks in the usual fashion, Wandering Star turned and stared at Tall Oak and Green Field.

"The farmers' prince and his comrade," he said. "I saw you the day you were captured."

That revelation startled Blue Sky as much as it did Tall Oak, Green Field, and the people.

"I was only five years old," Wandering Star continued. "But I'll never forget what I saw. The king, Lightning Spear, made us watch. He made everybody watch what his warriors did to you. Even the children. He made us watch."

For a long time after those disclosures went out, the crowd stood silent again.

Rose Leaf took Wandering Star's hand.

Only Green Field found words to say: "I saw the children. You were among them?"

"Yes, I was," Wandering Star replied. "And I'm sorry for what my people's king and warriors did to you. There was no excuse for it. It was evil. I'm very sorry it happened."

Tall Oak and then Green Field embraced Wandering Star.

None of them was above letting his tears fall freely.

After the repeaters finished their work, and while Rose Leaf, Morning Sun, Rainbow Evening, Gentle Brook, Fair Judge, Spring Rain, Many Numbers, Full Harvest, Early Harvest, Valley Defender, Solemn Promise, and countless others embraced Blue Sky's hill-man friend, the people could hear the summer breeze, light as it was that day, in the treetops high above the courtyard.

That was all they could hear.

Character List

Autumn Wine: Green Field and Gentle Brook's elderly neighbor. Her two grandsons, orphaned in the last war with the hill people, live with her.

Blue Sky: Green Field and Gentle Brook's son and Rose Leaf's brother. He's also the best friend of the prince, Morning Sun.

Early Harvest: Morning Sun's chief rival in the coming-of-age games as well as in their pursuit of Rose Leaf's consent to be their mate.

East Land: an outspoken farmer who fought alongside Green Field, Tall Oak, and Full Harvest in the last war with the hill people.

Fair Judge: a special friend of the queen, Rainbow Evening, and the teller who's in charge of the education of the prince, Morning Sun, as well as the orphanage where Spring Rain and Many Numbers grew up. The people insist upon calling her Fair Judge.

Full Harvest: Early Harvest's father, who fought alongside Green Field and Tall Oak in the last war with the hill people. He's now a wealthy upper-valley farmer and the apparent father of a large number of children born to women whose mates, his brothers, died in the war.

Gentle Brook: wife of Green Field, mother of Blue Sky and Rose Leaf, and cousin of the queen, Rainbow Evening. She and Full Harvest dance together as if they're lovers.

Good Harvest: said to be a cousin of his best friend, Early Harvest, but more likely his half-brother.

Green Field: Gentle Brook's mate and Blue Sky and Rose Leaf's father. He's a farmer-hero who saved the life of his best friend, Tall Oak, then a prince, in the last war with the hill people.

Law Keeper: the kingdom's first teller and Sturdy Limb's submissive ally. The farmers openly laugh at his awkward attempts to impress them with his authority.

Lightning Spear: the hill people's king.

Many Numbers: a young teller who lives with his mate, Spring Rain, in an ivy-covered house. He believes he has good reasons to wish to see the downfall of Law Keeper and Sturdy Limb.

Morning Sun: the prince, the only living child of Tall Oak and Rainbow Evening. He's also Blue Sky and Rose Leaf's best childhood friend. Perhaps as a result of that, he tends to side with the farmers against his father's officials.

Noon Breeze: a no-apologies pleasure-loving son of poor farmers who becomes an unlikely friend of Blue Sky's in the apprentice tellers' encampment.

Rainbow Evening: the queen and Gentle Brook's cousin. She despises Sturdy Limb and Law Keeper and spends a good deal of her time with Fair Judge.

Rose Leaf: Green Field and Gentle Brook's daughter and Blue Sky's sister. Morning Sun, Early Harvest, Valley Defender, and many other young men wish to be her mate. The king, queen, and her parents have warned her she can't choose Morning Sun.

Solemn Promise: a son of a wealthy court family and a friend of the prince, Morning Sun.

Spring Rain: Many Numbers' mate, a young teller the people favor for his singing in ceremonies, patience in hearing their arguments, and pleasing looks. As a supervising teller, he shares a hut with Blue Sky in the apprentice teller's encampment.

Sturdy Limb: Tall Oak's brother and chief warrior. Most of the farmers would be pleased to see him dead, with no chance of his ever becoming their king.

Tall Oak: the king, Rainbow Evening's mate, and Morning Sun's father. He appointed his brother, Sturdy Limb, to be chief warrior after Green Field turned down the position.

Thistle Dew: the hill people's queen.

Valley Defender: the oldest of Sturdy Limb's three sons and Morning Sun's first cousin. He also wishes to be Rose Leaf's mate.

Wandering Star: a hill man who becomes Blue Sky's friend. They're both aware they commit treason every moment they're together.

www.ingramcontent.com/pod-product-compliance
Lightning Source LLC
Chambersburg PA
CBHW061141170626
46809CB00003B/939